CHRISSIE WARREN:
Pirate Hunter

By JOHN BAUR

Cover art and illustrations by Katherine J. Bishop

Sue —

Smooth Sailing!

Love, John

John Baur

This book is a work of fiction. Any references to historical events or persons are used fictitiously. All other names, descriptions, characters and events are products of the author's imagination. Any resemblance to actual places, events or persons, living or dead, is entirely coincidental.

First Edition

ISBN: 978-0-692-45904-1

John Baur can be reached online at his blog, Baurlife.com, or by email at chumbucket@talklikeapirate.com. He is represented by Eddie Schneider of the JABberwocky Literary Agency. All inquiries regarding rights to this or other literary works by the author should be addressed to Schneider at JABberwocky Literary Agency, Inc., 49 W 45th St., 12N, New York, NY 10036-4603. He can be reached by phone at 917-388-3010.

Katherine J. Bishop can be reached online through her website: www.behance.net/katbishop

Published in the U.S.A

*To Tori: You are my heartbeat and my grand adventure.
This book is yours; it would not exist without you.*

CHRISSIE WARREN:
Pirate Hunter

Chapter 1

Happy Birthday

Hampton, Virginia Colony
September 22, 1717

Chrissie blew gently on the tin flute, watching the tears running down her father's face as he sang the popular ballad of lost love.

And when death takes his due, Eileen aroon!
What should her lover do? Eileen aroon!
Fly o'er the bounding main
Never to love again,
Eileen aroon!

He paused, laughing, holding up a hand in protest while wiping the tears from his eyes with the other.

"Stop Chrissie, stop!" he said, laughing. "You know I can't sing that all the way through without bawlin' like a baby. Me, a man who's sailed around the world and crossed the line six times, and I can't make it through a simple song. You don't want to spend your birthday watching your father blubber!"

Chrissie threw her arms around him.

"I thought you sounded fine, papa," she said.

Then he pulled back and looked at her, a smile lighting his face.

"*You* played beautifully," he said, then turned to her uncle, Joe O'Riley, and added, "It was a gift well given."

"Well, she's been using mine so much I thought it was time she had one of her own," Joe said. "Now we can play some duets together, 'eh Chrissie?"

Chrissie nodded and looked around the room at the small gathering. Beside her father, there was her uncle Joe and Mrs. Garrity, the housekeeper who had raised Chrissie since the day the girl's mother died giving birth to her. Her father, a merchant sailor, came and went; Joe and Mrs. Garrity had been the two constants in her life.

"Well," Mrs. Garrity said with a smile, "are we ready for pudding?"

Everyone murmured in anticipation as Mrs. Garrity went to the kitchen. There was a hiss of steam, then the housekeeper emerged carrying a platter with a small steamed pudding, as perfect and round as a cannon ball.

"A masterpiece, Mrs. G!" Dan crowed. "I've dined with maharajas and eastern potentates – S'true, every word!" he added as the party smiled, "but I've never, in all me life of rovin', ever seen a finer pudding, and that's a fact!"

Mrs. Garrity beamed with pleasure, but before she could start serving a knock at the door interrupted her.

"Who could that be at this hour?" Mrs. Garrity grumbled as she crossed the room. She opened the door a crack and Chrissie could hear a voice from outside, though she couldn't make out the words. Mrs.

Garrity opened the door wider and gestured for the interloper to come in.

"You'll find him at the table," she told the man who stepped into the room.

He pulled off his cap and lowered his head as he stepped toward the table. He couldn't have been anything but a sailor. He was short and wiry, his face bronzed, and his clothes and hair, though tidy, were faded from sun and salt. The few steps he took from doorway to table revealed a rolling gait that spoke of more time spent on a ship's deck than on land.

"Pardon the intrusion, Dan – ma'am, – everyone," he said. "But I've been asked to make the rounds and they only gave me the list an hour ago."

"Silas!" said Dan, flustered. "Silas David, this is my family – Mrs. Garrity, the housekeeper, you've met. Joe O'Riley, my late wife's brother, and this is my daughter, Mary Christine Warren. It's her birthday today, her thirteenth. She's become a lady! Pull up a chair!"

"I can't, but many happy returns of the day miss," he said, nodding in Chrissie's direction. "I've two more calls to make. Just came by to offer Captain William's compliments, Dan, and he wanted me to tell you we sail in three days."

Chrissie stifled a groan. She'd known it was coming, but that didn't make it any easier.

"Well," Dan said to cover the uneasy silence. "At least you'll have time to help us eat this delightful pudding, won't you?"

The sailor gave Chrissie a glance, his eyebrow raised in frank appraisal, and she shrank from his gaze. Chrissie had noticed lately that boys her age in town tended to stare at her like big, dumb cows. But in David's brief glance Chrissie felt something of the wolf licking his chops. Neither Dan nor Joe seemed to notice, but Mrs. Garrity gave a snort and pursed her lips in disapproval.

3

"Mr. David," the housekeeper said, briefly pulling the newcomer's glance away from Chrissie. "What is this ship you mention?"

"Oh, *Gladys B.* Dan's to be ship's carpenter and we sail in three days. She's a beauty, Mrs. ... I'm sorry, I didn't catch your name?" His eyes slipped back to Chrissie while he addressed the older woman.

"Garrity," she snapped.

"Yes, yes, My pardon. Anyway, she's a beauty," he said with his eyes now fully on Chrissie.

"Not now, Silas," Dan said.

"Well, yes, but the captain said ..."

"I understand and you can tell him I got the message."

Dan glanced sheepishly at his daughter, who simply stared at him, one eyebrow raised. He turned back to the sailor.

"Well, then, Silas, could you at least join us in a toast?"

He agreed, and soon four mugs of punch were raised, with Chrissie uncomfortably the center of attention.

"Chrissie, in thirteen years you've grown into a lovely young woman," said her father, facing her across the table. "While I can't claim credit for your upbringing, no father could be prouder of his daughter than I am of you. Ladies and gents, I give you Mary Christine Warren!"

"Mary Christine Warren," the others said, raising their glasses and drinking. David drank with the rest, draining his tankard, which he set back down with a thump.

"And now, Dan, I really must go," he said, aware he was the cause of the tension in the room but unsure quite why. "Miss Warren, I'm afraid I have other stops to make. Perhaps when we return in the spring I'll be able to call on you. Until then, the best wishes of the day to you."

She nodded, averting her eyes as her father showed the man to the door.

They ate the pudding in silence, then Joe helped Mrs. Garrity clear the table and the two went off to the kitchen. Dan stared down at the table in front of him.

"So Pa," Chrissie said. "Where are you going this time, and when will you be back?"

Dan looked sheepish.

"I'm sorry. I wanted to tell you tomorrow morning, after your birthday."

"I thought you were going to stay," she said.

"I have stayed. I've been ashore four months this time, Chrissie. That's a long time for me to stay anywhere. I have to make a living, darlin'. I'm a sailor. It's what I do."

Chrissie knew that. Her whole life had been punctuated by her father coming and going, starting even before she had been born.

"Don't get me wrong, Pa," she said. "I love Uncle Joe, he's raised me since I was a babe. Him and Mrs. Garrity, they're family, right enough. But you're my pa, and you're gone more than you're ever home. Don't you love me?"

"Never doubt that, Chrissie," he said, his voice catching in his throat. "You're all I have in the world, and that's treasure enough for any man. But Hampton has never been my home. It was your mother's home, and when I came ashore the first time, it was just another port I'd be sailing away from and maybe never see again. Who knew I'd come down the gangplank and get struck by lightning at the sight of her."

Chrissie knew the story; she loved to hear how Kathleen O'Riley and Dan Warren had fallen in love at first sight. Within a week they had "an understanding." Three weeks after that they'd been married. Three months after that Dan had sailed away, telling his bride he'd be back.

When he returned, racing down the gangplank to find her, he had

5

been shocked to learn that he was both a widower and a father.

"That's a sailor's life, girl," he said. "I'm a poorer man for it, but it's all I know. But you know that wherever I go, the winds will always blow me back to you."

"They'd better," she said, "or I'll come looking for you."

"Ah, Chrissie, I believe you would," he laughed. "I believe you could do anything. But never you fear. I'll come home to you. Count on it."

Chapter 2

Farewell and a Meeting

September 25, 1717

Chrissie tried to squeeze all she could out of every moment with her father, but all too soon she was standing at the end of the gangway with him. Dan dropped his sea bag beside the gangplank and turned to her.

"Time's a'wastin', darlin'. I have to get aboard, and you'd best head home before Mrs. Garrity wonders what happened to you."

"Can't I stay with you a little longer?" she begged. "I'll run straight home so she'll never know I'm late."

"Ah, Chrissie," he said. "You know the docks aren't a proper place for a young lady. And if you don't know it, Mrs. G. certainly does, and won't want you dilly-dallyin' about with a broken down old sailor like me."

Chrissie laughed at the thought of her strapping father, who was only in his early 30s, as a "broken down old sailor."

The pier was alive with sailors coming and going, some calling out to old friends, others rushing off on last minute errands.

"Time to go," Dan said. He held her out at arms length and said, "Let me have a look at you."

She looked into his eyes – so much like the ones that looked out of the mirror at her – as he drank her in for a full minute. Then he lowered his arms and sighed.

"The prettiest girl in the colonies. I can't wait to get home to see how much more beautiful you've become."

"Why not stay and see for yourself?" she asked.

"We've talked this through. I'm a sailor, and it's time to sail."

He held her in a long embrace, then chucked her under the chin and smiled.

"Don't you worry," he said. "Seven months from now, maybe sooner, not more than eight, I'll charge down that gangplank. You take care of your Uncle Joe while I'm gone, and don't let Mrs. Garrity steal the silver."

"Pa, we don't have any silver," she laughed, thinking of the tin utensils they used.

"Ah! She's pinched it already, has she! I'll have words with that woman when I get back, see if I don't," he said.

"Just get back, Pa. That'll be good enough for me."

She watched as he hoisted his sea bag over his shoulder, turned and marched up the gangway with a stride that suggested he owned the world. At the top, he saluted the man on deck and stepped aboard. Dropping his bag he looked back out at the pier, raising an arm and waving vigorously.

"So long Chrissie!" he shouted. "I'll see you in the spring!"

With that, he disappeared into the ship. She watched for a few minutes before accepting that – yes, he was gone. And it was time for her to go, too. She began winding her way along the familiar path from the waterfront to her home.

Chrissie turned up an alley that ran alongside the Dolphin, a tavern popular with sailors. The alley was littered and smelled bad, but it was the most direct route home. Picking her way past the discarded crates and old barrels, she didn't notice anything until she heard a burst of laughter ahead, followed by the sound of voices talking low, then another laugh.

Chrissie crept forward.

Suddenly, one of the voices snapped out angrily, and another cried out in surprise or pain.

Peeking around a crate, Chrissie saw three men, one sprawled on the ground. Another, a big man, had his back to her. Though he seemed to be the largest of the three, he was backing away cautiously from the third.

"How many times do I have to tell you?" hissed the third man, who was hidden by the big one. "We move when I say we do, and not before. That means we wait until we're in the Caribbean to take the ship. Ya see?"

"Aye," the fallen man said.

The third man, the one who seemed to be in charge, extended his hand, a smile breaking across his face almost instantly.

"Splendid," he said. "Now make sure the others understand. No man moves before I say. Anyone even talks about our plans – I'll lay stripes on his back meself!"

He pulled the first man to his feet and stepped back, giving Chrissie her first glimpse of them. The man who'd been knocked down was short and skinny, with thin, sandy hair. The big man was built like an ox, with a thick, bushy beard, coal black eyes and hair that ran in a long black braid down his back.

But there was something about the third man that held her eye. He was of medium height and build, with long dark hair tied in a pigtail and eyes that burned darkly out of a face that would have been handsome except for the leer that seemed to be a permanent feature. Unlike his comrades, who were dressed in common sailors' slops, the man in charge wore a blue broadcloth coat over a white shirt and yellow waistcoat, and his head was covered with a tricorn hat with a long, orange feather.

"Then we understand each other?" he asked the two.

"Right Davy," the smaller man said sullenly, his hand on his cheek where he'd been struck.

"Right who?" the man said, his voice cracking like a whip.

"I mean, aye Mr. Leech," the smaller man said, cringing.

"That's more like it," the one called Davy said. "You can't forget and slip. Until I give the order, I'm Mr. Leech, and we're not brothers. We've never met."

The two men bobbed their heads, murmuring agreement.

"Good. Then get aboard with ye, you're running late. I'll be there shortly. It wouldn't do for us to show up at the same time and have people noticing us together," Leech said.

They turned to go, and that's when they spotted Chrissie. She froze, then turned – too late – to run. They were on her before she could retreat half a dozen strides, crowding her against the rough planking of the tavern wall.

The big man's eyes blazed with anger, and the small one's ran up and down her body with a cool look that made Chrissie's skin crawl. But it was the middle man, Mr. Leech, who took command and turned her blood cold with a look.

"Well missy," he said with a leer. "And what are you doing creeping through alleys and listening in on somethin' that's none of your business?"

Chapter 3

Trouble in the Alley

The face that stared at Chrissie was untouched by human warmth, the eyes cold as a lizard's. He smiled, but the smile was only a muscular twitch that pulled back the corners of his mouth, without any humor in it. Menace radiated from him like heat from the sun.

The smaller man stuck his face in, asking, "Spyin' on us? Why?" His rancid breath hit her with physical force, and she pressed back harder to the wall.

"Spying? No, I ... I'm waiting for my father. He'll be here any second."

"Then why were you listening to us?" Leech asked.

"I wasn't ... I didn't ... I was stretching my legs. I didn't even see you."

He leaned in towards Chrissie, pinning her with his stare.

Like a rabbit mesmerized by a snake, Chrissie was frozen. The man leaned towards her, blocking her in. His other hand reached out to her face, and she flinched as the nail of his outstretched finger traced the curve of her chin.

"These two men are shipmates of mine – good lads, practically choir boys. But some men don't like being spied on. A person who heard something she shouldn't might get more than her legs stretched, even if it's a very pretty girl like you."

The man grinned, an even viler expression than the simple smile had been. The smaller man gave a low chuckle, and turned to Leech.

"Can I have her?" he asked, wiping his lips with the back of his dirty sleeve. "She won't speak to no one when I'm done wif her."

"There's no time," Leech said. His eyes flicked up and down the alley as his hand stole to his coat pocket. Her eyes followed the movement and saw him start to withdraw a short, thin knife.

The back door of the tavern banged opened and an older woman leaned out and tossed a bucket of greasy water into the alleyway. She glanced up and shouted, "'Ere now! None o' that or I'll call the constable!"

Leech's head jerked toward the sound of the voice, but he kept one hand firmly on Chrissie's shoulder. That was all she needed to keep him at the right distance. Chrissie's knee shot up and connected with him in the way Uncle Joe had taught her, solidly between his legs. Leech let out a gasp and staggered back, tumbling into the larger man.

Chrissie ducked as the smaller man reached for her, turning away from his clutching hand and running the other way, past the startled barmaid and out into the crowded street a block up from the waterfront.

Heart pounding, she plunged into the crowd, weaving and ducking as fast as she could. At the corner she risked a look back. The smaller man had just made it to the head of the alley and was looking about, but hadn't seen her. She forced herself to slow down as she turned right and walked uphill. She wanted to keep running, but knew she'd stand out more on the crowded street if she was the only running figure.

Halfway up the block she stepped back into a doorway and peeked down the street. The three men were nowhere to be seen. She leaned back against the doorframe and let out a long, shuddering breath, hands and knees trembling.

A sound behind her made her spin in alarm, her hands raised in defense. The door had opened and a voice said, "Excuse me, miss. Are you alright?"

The man behind her had a fringe of white hair and a clean-shaven face that looked in surprise over the top of spectacles. She finally recognized him as one of Hampton's shopkeepers.

Chrissie tried to speak, but her head spun and her breath came in short gasps. The man held out a hand to steady her.

"What is it?" he asked.

"We've got to stop the ship!" she gasped.

"You're Joe Riley's girl, aren't you? He's your uncle? And Muriel Garrity is ... your housekeeper?" he asked.

She nodded.

The man turned to a young girl peering nervously from behind the counter and said something to her, but Chrissie couldn't tell what he was saying. The girl ran for the door, then the man turned back to Chrissie.

"I've sent for your uncle. Now, tell me what happened," he said. "You're in a state."

Chrissie didn't want to have to go over the story. She caught her breath, then started to rise.

"I'm fine; I have to go," she said.

"Can't you tell me what the problem is."

"I have to go find my pa."

"Well, let's wait for your uncle, how's that? I'm sure he'll be here in no time."

She wouldn't listen as the man – Mr. Evans, that was his name, she remembered – pressed her to wait. But when she tried to get to her feet, she suddenly found her legs were like rubber. She sank back in the chair.

Don't be silly, she argued with herself. *You don't have time for this. Those men are up to something bad, and it might be Pa's ship.*

Mr. Evans passed her a mug of water and she drank it down quickly. Then she took three deep breaths, shook her head and stood.

"Now, you just sit," Mr. Evans said. "Your uncle or Mrs. Garrity will be here any minute. Let's just wait for them."

"Can't!" she blurted as she raced for the door. "Have to find Pa!"

She was back on the street, taking the longer way around to avoid the alley and anyone who might still be lurking there. Turning the corner on the waterfront, she pelted toward where *Gladys B.* was docked.

But the ship was no longer tied up. It was moving slowly away from the pier, and as the tide built, it caught the current and began picking up speed.

Even as she watched, she could see sailors scurrying up the ratlines, sails blooming on the yards, snapping open with a crack as they caught the breeze. Chrissie stared and was rewarded by a glimpse of her father on the deck talking to someone. There was no mistaking the crown of golden hair over his broad frame. Then the ship began to turn and she could see who he was talking to.

A chill ran though her. Even at that distance she could see the man was wearing a blue coat, with a touch of yellow at the waist, and a black tricorn with a long, orange feather.

Chapter 4

No News

No one would listen to her.

Chrissie tried to explain to anyone on the pier that the ship had to be stopped, turned around, or at least that an armed group needed to go out to it. But a working waterfront is a busy place and no one had time to listen to what they thought was an hysterical girl. Even when Joe found her an hour later, he was hard to convince.

"Are you sure you heard 'em right?" he asked, to Chrissie's annoyance. She repeated the conversation, emphasizing the phrase, "We'll take the ship in the Caribbean." Joe was silent, mulling it over.

"Lot of men wear blue coats," Joe mused. "Mighta been someone completely different. Did you see clear whether it was this same fella?"

"No," Chrissie had to admit. "I didn't see his face. But he was the same height and size. He was dressed the same. He had the same feather!" She was shouting now. "It was him, I know it was."

"But you said they were going to the Caribbean. Dan's ship is heading to England before it goes down to the islands. Two other ships left here today, and there's another three getting ready to sail in the next few days. Some, of 'em must be headin' south," Joe said. "And *Gladys B.* is past the cape by now; we'd never catch her to send a message."

He thought for a moment, then finally looked up.

"Tell you what, me and some of the boys will ask around at the taverns tonight, see if anybody has heard anything about this man and his friends."

"Joe, he's dangerous," Chrissie protested, but her uncle held up a hand to calm her.

"I know he's dangerous," he said firmly. "I can be dangerous too, especially when someone threatens my family. And I won't be alone. I'll take a couple of lads from the boats. We can handle ourselves."

Chrissie had never seen that look in Joe's eyes, never seen him so serious. She knew her uncle could be a tough man in the right circumstances, and that there weren't any slackers and softies among the local fishing crews. But she didn't think Joe understood. This wasn't some dockside rowdy. This was evil.

"We'll pass word among the sailors shipping out in the next few days to be on the lookout, and to leave word on Nevis for when Dan's ship docks there. But right now let's get you home. Mrs. Garrity will be worried sick."

Despite her protests, Joe walked Chrissie home. Mrs. Garrity fussed over her for an hour before Chrissie agreed to go to bed just to get her to stop. As she lay under the covers she found herself reliving the attack in the alley over and over, until all she could see were the man's black eyes burning at her in the dark of her room.

She woke in the morning after a troubled sleep, hoping to talk to Joe about what he'd found last night. But he'd already gone back out, and

Mrs. Garrity wouldn't hear of Chrissie leaving that day until they knew more.

"Maybe today would be a good day for us to work on something besides fishing," Mrs. Garrity said hopefully. "Let's sit down with the sewing and ..."

"Sewing? How can I sew when there's a ... a ... when that man is out there somewhere?"

"And haven't I said it's times like these that keeping your hands busy can keep your mind from worrying something to death when there's nothing you can do about it?"

"But I can!"

"No you cannot," Mrs. Garrity said. Then, softening, she put a hand on Chrissie's shoulder and said, "I know you're worried about your father and about your uncle. But they're good men, and they can take care of themselves."

"But what if those men from yesterday find out who I am, and come looking for me?"

"Well, that means they're not on your father's ship, doesn't it?"

Chrissie hadn't thought about it that way. Suddenly she grinned.

"Well, then let's hope they're coming for me," she said. "I beat 'em once, and I can beat 'em again."

"They'll have to get past me first," Mrs. Garrity said, with a steely look in her eye. "And I'm not as easy as I look. I'm even tougher with a needle in my hand. Let's sit down and I'll show you a thing or two."

Chrissie groaned as she let Mrs. Garrity lead her to the window seat. She tried to concentrate, tried to follow the older woman's instructions, but her mind kept wandering back to the alley and the blue coat she'd seen on the ship.

Four hours later, Mrs. Garrity clucked her tongue as she examined the sewing Chrissie had been doing.

"Is this supposed to be a seam?" she asked.

"It's straight enough!" the girl protested.

"Aye, straight enough, but how do you expect it to stay together if you're putting in stitches like that?"

"That's the same stitch I use mending Joe's sails," Chrissie said.

"Is this a sail?"

"No, it's a blouse," Chrissie mumbled.

"A blouse? Really? And who'd wear such a thing?"

"I would," Chrissie shot back.

"Not if I have any say so. You'd shame your poor uncle and meself, going out in a thing like that. Now come here and let's see if we can set this aright."

Mrs. Garrity deftly removed the stitching Chrissie had labored over, then began re-sewing the two pieces of fabric.

"Now keep the stitches nice and tight and close together. And then ... Chrissie? Chrissie!"

Chrissie had heard a sound from outside and ran to the window. Moments later the door opened and Joe walked in. Chrissie ran to him, but before she could ask what had happened he was shaking his head.

"No, there's no sign of any such man in town," Joe said as he hung his cap on the peg by the door. "Me and the fellas combed the waterfront, stopped at every inn and dive and sporting house, but no one knew anything about the man. A couple of people said they'd remembered seeing someone who looked like that, but given that they'd been drinking for the better part of a week that might not mean so much. And they never said they spoke to the man or his friends, just that they might have seen him."

"So what does that mean?"

"We'll keep asking around for a while, but it looks like our boy ran out of town. What that means, I don't know. But it looks like they won't be coming here to find you, sweetheart, and that's been my biggest worry."

"Yeah, but what about Pa?"

"We don't know. But he's a good man on a good ship and he can take care of himself. You'll see; he'll come off that pier singing and swaggering this spring, just like he said. So you can relax and stop worrying."

But she didn't stop worrying, as fall came, then winter. Fishing on the bay with her uncle, working around the house with Mrs. Garrity, walking through an ice-coated Hampton as winter winds blew in off the Atlantic, thoughts of her father nagged constantly at the back of her mind. Spring finally came, thin grass breaking through the crusts of snow, and Chrissie's worry grew as *Gladys B.* failed to arrive in March, then April, then May.

On a warm afternoon in early June, Chrissie and Joe were returning from a successful day on the bay, their hold stocked with fish. As they steered toward the dock, Chrissie noted a newcomer tied up at the main pier. It wasn't *Gladys.* This was a smaller, older ship, weather stained a drab gray, and Chrissie could make out the name *Montclair* in fading paint on the stern. Still, if they'd come up from the south they might have heard something.

As she and Joe finished unloading the day's catch, Chrissie could see the crowd growing along the waterfront. An excited buzz was building as she elbowed her way closer to the pier.

"Pirates, I say! Just like in Charleston last month," a man shouted.

Voices babbled, but Chrissie couldn't make out individual words. Joe's hand on her shoulder pulled her back.

"Get back to the house. I'll find out what's going on," he said.

"No," she said. "You're not sending me away."

Chrissie shrugged off Joe's hand and plunged into the crowd.

She made it close to the front, where she could see two sailors holding court at the foot of the pier. Chrissie turned to one of the men in the mob and grabbed his arm.

"What is it? Who are they?" she asked.

"Pirates!" he said.

"They're pirates?"

"No, they're from *Montclair*, just got in this morning from St. Kitts. They say they saw pirates."

"No, ya fool," one of the two sailors said with contempt. "We didn't see no pirates. But there's two lads aboard who did. We picked 'em up after they'd been marooned by pirates."

Chrissie went cold at the words, but she shouted out, "What are their names? What was their ship?

"Taylor and Watkins," the man said. "Seemed like good men, but they're broken. There wasn't much in the way of food or water on their little island where we found 'em, and they were there more'n two months."

"What ship were they on?" Chrissie repeated.

"Didn't I say? *Gladys* somethin' or other."

Chapter 5

Pirates!

"Pirates," Joe reported when he got home.

He'd found Chrissie in the crowd and managed to get her home before returning to the waterfront to find out as much as he could. When he got back late that night he found Chrissie sitting up in the front room waiting for him.

"Chrissie! You ought to have been asleep hours ago," he said.

"And you should have been home hours ago," she retorted, not backing down.

"Well, it took a while to hear all there was to hear and piece it together."

"And I'm not going to bed without hearing the story."

He stared at her for a moment, then shrugged and motioned her to a chair.

"Sit, it'll take some telling," he said.

Once he'd settled in the other chair he sighed and said, "It was your father's ship true enough, *Gladys B.* There was a mutiny, the gang took the ship two nights out of Nevis."

Before Chrissie could break in, he held up a hand.

"We don't know much of what happened," he said. "Those two fellas went overboard early in the fight. We don't know what happened to your pa. But what we do know ain't good. The mutineers killed the captain and ..." he paused and looked away for a moment, drawing a long breath before he continued. "And they probably killed most of the crew that wouldn't join 'em. At least that's what those two fellas told the captain of *Montclair*. He tried to keep it quiet, of course. No captain wants his crew thinkin' about a mutiny. But every man aboard knew the whole story before the next watch change."

"How did they know?" Chrissie asked. "The two men that got rescued, I mean."

"Well they were there, weren't they? One of the men, Sam Watkins, was on watch that night. I know him, he's not given to tall tales. He said when they came for him he gave a warning shout and went over the side. The other fella – Taylor – was below. He said he saw the mate coming out of the captain's cabin covered in blood. He ran and tried to sound the alarm, but it was too late. So he swam for it, too. They both ended up on the same little island. Must not have been much food there – both of 'em are half the size they used to be, and they were lucky they were spotted. A storm happened to drive *Montclair* east of its course or they'd never have found the fellas."

"But what does that mean? Where's Pa?" Chrissie demanded.

"There's somethin' else," Joe said, casting a guilty look at his niece. "The mate who led the mutiny?"

"What about him?"

"It was Davy Leech."

"I knew it!" Chrissie shouted, jumping to her feet.

"The men I talked to don't know much about him," Joe continued.

"He apparently sailed with some of the privateers a few years ago. From what little I heard, he's got a bad reputation even among that lot. Then about the time peace broke out it was like he disappeared. Not much word about him for three years. How he ended up in Hampton no one could say. But he's back in the Caribbean and apparently ready to make up for lost time."

"But what about Pa?"

"No one knows," Joe said sadly. "There's no rulebook on how these things happen, but if the loyal crew fought the mutineers – and you know your pa would never mutiny – it probably went hard on 'em."

"But they don't always kill everyone, do they? I've heard ..."

"Aye, we've all heard the stories. There was Blackbeard and his crew down in Charleston just last month and they say he acted like a real gentleman – except of course he was holding hostages and shut down the port 'til they paid him his ransom. These pirates are getting bolder, and that's a fact. Sometimes they offer the crew a chance to join them – but Dan Warren wouldn't go on the account, we know that. A stubborn man, your father can be. Those what don't join they usually set adrift or ..." Joe's voice tailed off.

"Sometimes they keep men they need, right?" Chrissie asked. "They force them to join if they've got a skill they need."

"Aye, navigators, doctors..."

"And carpenters, like Pa!" Chrissie had said.

"Well, yes," Joe said. "But that doesn't help much. Not every jury believes a man who says he was forced. Last year in Boston there was two men claimed they was forced. Even the pirates they were caught with admitted they'd forced 'em. They still got strung up along with the rest."

"But Pa promised he'd be back. He's either been marooned or forced, and we've got to ..."

"We've got to wait, and hope and pray that he's all right and comes home," Joe said. "We'll send out word with any ships heading south and ask 'em to be on the lookout for him. But there's not much else we can do."

"We can go down there and ..."

"And what?" Joe shook his head. "Chrissie, your father expects me to look after you, and I can't do that if I'm off chasing rumors in the Caribbean. If he gets home, he's gonna want to know you've been taken care of."

"When," Chrissie said firmly.

"What?"

"You said 'if he comes home.' It's when. Because he *is* coming home. He promised."

"Of course he is," Joe quickly conceded. "And we'll be here, waiting for him. Do you understand?"

"I do," she said, glad that her uncle hadn't asked if she agreed.

Chapter 6

Making Plans

Chrissie started planning. Each day that she walked to the fishing dock with her uncle, she eyed the tall masts of the merchants' ships coming and going from the harbor. She knew ships were already gathering for the fall tobacco fleet, when some 200 or more ships took the colony's crop to England. There would be few ships heading from Hampton to the Caribbean right now.

On the way home, she'd dawdle along the harbor, almost invisible in her sailor slops – the short-legged pants, canvas jacket and shapeless wool cap she wore when out on the water with Joe. She seemed to be just another young fisherman, listening for any word coming up from the south, from the tropics.

One September afternoon she was walking down the pier when she passed three young men launching a skiff. She paid no attention to them until she heard a voice call out loudly.

"Anyone smell fish? A really strong fish smell? Oh, never mind. It's just *her*."

It was Arne Wharton, one of the local youths. She'd known Arne all her life. The son of a successful Hampton merchant, Arne was as stupid and as mean as his parents were wealthy, and he never tired of bullying anyone he considered smaller, weaker or less advantaged. Chrissie knew if she reacted he'd sense weakness. She kept walking.

Getting no response, Arne spoke out louder as she passed.

"Look at her! She even looks like a flounder. Can you imagine someone marrying her?"

Chrissie kept walking.

Even louder, he shouted out, "And then there's her father."

Chrissie stopped dead.

"You know what everyone's saying about him, don't you boys?"

She heard Arne's friends snickering behind her. She turned.

"If he wasn't killed by them pirates, he's turned pirate. I guess that'd be better than comin' home to a daughter looks like that. Either way we've seen the last o' him. He ain't comi ..."

He didn't get to finish the sentence, because he suddenly found himself face to face with a very angry Chrissie, her right fist cocked.

"YOU TAKE THAT BACK!" she shouted.

The boy's look of smug superiority turned to alarm.

"Take it back!"

The boy retreated a step. He was taller than Chrissie, who was considered tall for a girl, and his stocky frame gave him a good thirty pounds on her. But one glance at her face warned him he couldn't match her in fury. This wasn't a normal girl. She was dressed like any of the fishermen on the dock, and she was mad. He took another step back.

"I didn't mean nothin'," he stammered. "I just said what everyone in town knows – your pa ain't comin' ..."

He didn't get to finish the sentence before he found himself sitting in the dusty street, his cheek stinging. She stood over him scowling, her left hand ready to deliver another blow.

"Say that again and you'll get worse," she said.

The boy scuttled backwards, crablike, but she stayed with him, looming over him, ignoring his two friends, who fled the scene at a dead run.

"C'mon Chrissie," the boy protested, trying to make himself enough room to get back on his feet. "Everyone knows he's either a pirate or..."

"Say it and I'll black your other eye!"

She was interrupted by a gruff voice shouting from the pier.

"Oy! Chrissie! What d'you think you're doin' there?" the man shouted.

She shot a glance at her uncle's wiry figure approaching her.

"What would Mrs. Garrity say if she caught you brawlin' in public?"

"Should I take him somewhere private to finish this?" she asked, not taking her eyes off the boy at her feet.

"You know what I mean, now let him up."

"All right, Joe," she said, stepping back.

Joe reached down, hoisting him by his shirtfront to his feet.

"Arne, I shoulda known," he said. "Now what's all this about?"

Arne looked as if he wanted to be somewhere else – anywhere else – but he screwed up his courage and jerked his head towards Chrissie.

"It was her fault. I wasn't even talkin' to her. I just told my friends what everyone in town knows – her father's a pirate, or dead."

Chrissie tried to throw herself at Arne, but Joe held her back while he withered the boy with a look.

"And I'm sure the fact that my niece was in earshot when you said it was just a coincidence, right?" he said. "Look, Dan Warren may be a lot of things, but never a pirate. No one knows what happened when the ship got taken 'cept them what was there, and you weren't one of them. So I'd like to know exactly how you know he's dead."

The boy looked at his feet and stammered inaudibly.

"I thought so," Joe said. "Now Chrissie, apologize to him."

"What?" she snorted. "Me apologize to him?"

"You heard me. Apologize for hittin' him. It's not his fault he's an idiot."

Chrissie took a deep breath, then blurted out, "I'm sorry you're an idiot."

Joe tried unsuccessfully to suppress a grin as he turned toward the boy.

"That's as good as you're gonna get, so be off with ye, or I'll let her loose."

Arne Wharton didn't wait to be told twice. Before Joe could change his mind, Arne was running down the waterfront.

Chrissie trembled. The fiery anger disappeared and she was cold. Her knees trembled and she shot a hand toward her uncle for support.

Joe engulfed her in his arms.

"'S'all right, Chrissie girl, 's'all right," he said.

"I'm sorry Joe. I know I shouldn't have ..."

The fisherman cut her off.

"You know Mrs. Garrity will hear about this, don't you?"

"You won't tell her, will you Joe?"

"Course not, but she'll hear about it just the same. Maybe already has."

"But you heard what he said!"

"You're not responsible for what he said. You're responsible for what you do," Joe said. "I know it's hard, but you have to ignore fools like him. People will say what they say, and you can't do anything about it. That's not why I taught you to defend yourself, you know that. You certainly can't give 'em all black eyes."

"I can try," she muttered, shaking herself free of Joe's embrace.

"And what would your father say about that?" Joe asked. "When he asked me to watch over ya, I don't think he meant he wants me to have yer back in a fight. I do have it, but I think what your father wants is to come home and find you've grown into a fine young lady. After all, next week you'll be 14 years old, Chrissie."

"What if I don't want to be a fine young lady?" she snapped back. "What if I just want to be me?"

She could feel her uncle looking at her, but she didn't make eye contact, breaking away from him and turning her back.

"And who is that?" he asked gently.

She shook her head. Joe sighed.

"I'm going home to head off Mrs. Garrity, who has probably heard all about it already and will be fixin' to tar and feather the both of us," he said. "Take a few minutes to collect yourself, then come on home."

He waited for her reply. She nodded silently and started to walk away, back down the pier. Joe watched her for a moment, then turned and headed home.

Chapter 7

Trapped

Chrissie wandered the town before finally turning for home as dark began falling. A half dozen paces from the small, tidy house, she stopped as she caught sight of a figure waiting out front. It was Joe.

"Storm warning," he said.

"Mrs. Garrity's heard about the fight?"

"Aye, but that's not the worst. She heard because Mrs. Wharton is inside. C'mon," Joe said. "We'll take a walk. She can't wait forever."

"No," Chrissie said. "If she wants to talk about me, I'll have plenty to say about her son."

"I don't think that's ..." Joe started to say, but Chrissie pushed past him and walked in the door.

"There you are, you slattern," a voice snapped at her.

"Lucy Wharton!" Mrs. Garrity said, shocked. "There is no need for that kind of language!"

"Slattern, wench, call her what you will," said Mrs. Wharton. "Arne told me all about you, your language and your uncouth behavior and your violence!"

30

"Did he tell you what he said to me?" Chrissie demanded.

"He didn't say anything to you, and even if he had that doesn't excuse you striking him," Mrs. Wharton said. "I should call the constable and swear out a complaint. But I guess I shouldn't be too surprised. Like father like daughter, I'm sure."

Chrissie's voice turned cold and flat.

"What did you say?"

"You heard me. I can't expect much from the daughter of a pir..."

"He is not a pirate!" Chrissie shouted.

Chrissie was now toe to toe with the older woman. Mrs. Garrity tried to get between them, but Chrissie pushed her away.

"My father will come home because he promised he would," Chrissie said. "As for your imbecile son, he can't be much of a man if he needs you to come over and fight for him. I pity the girl who listens when he comes calling!"

Mrs. Wharton's mouth hung open for a moment, then snapped shut with an audible click as she stormed away. At the door, she looked back at Chrissie and snarled, "Arne Wharton has plenty of prospects, which is more than you ever will. You just stay away from him or I'll see you before the magistrate."

With that she left, slamming the door behind her. Chrissie stared after her. It wasn't until she felt Mrs. Garrity's arms around her that she began sobbing.

Mrs. Garrity soothed Chrissie until the tears stopped.

"Dear," the housekeeper said, "would you do me a favor?"

Worn out with the emotion of the day, Chrissie just looked at her.

"The next time you decide to spar with Arne Wharton, would you give me a couple of day's notice? I'd like to limber up, so I can give his mother a matching eye."

Chrissie stared at Mrs. Garrity, then suddenly both of them were laughing and couldn't stop. Uncle Joe stuck his head in the door, looking perplexed, but the older woman waved him away.

Later in her darkened room, Chrissie heard the housekeeper talking to her uncle in the sitting room.

"It can't go on much longer, Joe Riley, and it's your fault," Mrs. Garrity said.

"My fault? How is it my fault that that boy acted like a..."

"Not the boy, though lord knows he's bad enough. It's Chrissie. She's almost a grown woman and you treat her like one of your crew, parading about the waterfront like just another fisherman. In case you hadn't noticed, she's turning into a woman, and those sailor slops she wears won't hide it much longer."

"Maybe she'll take after her mother and not be so ... curved, at least not right away," Joe said.

"Aye, maybe, but she'll be 'curved' enough, soon enough," the woman said sternly. "And if you don't notice, there are plenty of young men in this town who already have. That big oaf Arne Wharton might be the first, but he won't be the last. It won't be long before they start calling on her. By next summer she could be married!"

"So what do you want me to do?" her uncle asked.

"Well it's obvious what we have to do, isn't it? Chrissie is going to become a woman, and we have to help her learn to be one. That means no more fishing. She has to learn some skills, learn a trade."

"Fishing's a trade," Joe grumbled.

"Not for a young woman," Mrs. Garrity said. "She needs to find a job, maybe go into service in one of the big houses."

"Not the Whartons," Joe said sharply.

"Well of course not the Whartons," Mrs. Garrity said. "But if you won't think of her future, Joe Riley, then I will. I'll start asking around and see what prospects there are in town, maybe if anyone's hiring kitchen help. We've got to get the girl situated in life before it's too late."

Chrissie knew what the older woman meant. She looked, with alarm, at the slight swelling of her chest. Now, in her darkened room, she realized there wasn't much she could do about it except hurry. She couldn't face life as a scullery maid in one of the big houses, she wouldn't. She couldn't care less about boys "calling on her," and couldn't even begin to think about a life trapped in a marriage. For some girls, that was fine, it was all they wanted. Not her.

Trapped. That was it. She could feel it closing around her, all the tentacles of life in the town and the expectations of what a girl could do or be. She was trapped, just as she believed her father was trapped in the Caribbean. And the fact that she was a girl was part of that trap. But she couldn't let it get in the way.

She knew what she had to do.

Chapter 8

Plans in Motion

Over the next week Chrissie helped Mrs. Garrity around the house. The housekeeper seemed delighted that she was showing an interest, and Chrissie used the opportunity to rummage through the sewing basket, where she found a long strip of undyed cotton cloth left over from when they'd made curtains. When Chrissie was cleaning up after the mending, the cloth disappeared into her room. So did a couple of items from her father's old sea chest – a clasp knife, a cap and an old tarpaulin jacket, stiff with age but serviceable, and an old seabag. Into that she also put her spare fishing clothes. She stowed the bag under her bed, out of sight.

Mrs. Garrity was mollified, and didn't object too much when Chrissie went out on the bay with her uncle. Returning home after those outings, she walked the waterfront on her own, keeping her ears open. It wasn't long before she overheard two sailors talking about a ship. Running back down the pier she found it. It was just what she'd been looking for.

She arrived home as evening was coming on.

"Sorry I'm late," she called out as she hurried in the door. "They were really running today; we filled the hold. Joe took care of business and he's down at the Dolphin now, but he'll be along soon."

Mrs. Garrity grumbled, but told Chrissie to clean up and get to the table.

"Your dinner is cold and your uncle's will be even colder if he dawdles too long at the tavern 'taking care of business.'"

Chrissie scrubbed herself clean, dressed and came back to the table. As she ate, she said casually, "Joe's going to need me again tomorrow."

The housekeeper sighed.

"Chrissie, don't you think you're getting too old for this?" she asked.

"But Joe needs the help," Chrissie answered. "The bluefish are running in big schools and it's hard for Joe to find help this time of year."

"But it's not proper for a girl your age," Mrs. Garrity complained.

"Tell you what," Chrissie said. "I'll take care of things here tonight. You get to bed, and I'll clean up, get Joe his dinner when he comes in, take care of all those domestic things you've been teaching me."

"Are you sure you can ..."

"Of course I'm sure," Chrissie said firmly, taking Mrs. Garrity by the arm and leading her toward her bedroom. She ran down the list of chores that needed to be done, convincing the housekeeper that she could take care of them.

"You'll see, everything will be fine," she assured her.

Mrs. Garrity stood in the doorway to her room, looking hesitant.

"You won't forget to ..."

"I won't forget," Chrissie said firmly. "Now get to bed and I'll take care of it. You look tired."

"Well, I am, and that's a fact. It's nothing that being twenty years younger couldn't cure, but I wouldn't mind a little extra sleep."

She turned to go, saying, "Well, then, good night Chrissie."

The girl stopped her.

"Goodnight Mrs. Garrity. I love you," she said, throwing her arms around the older woman.

"Well of course, and I love you dear," she said.

Chrissie got to work on the chores, and half an hour later was finishing the dishes when her uncle Joe came in. She pushed him into his chair and put his dinner in front of him.

"Well Chrissie, what's this? You doin' the cleanup after a whole day on the water?"

"Mrs. Garrity looked tired, so I sent her to bed," Chrissie said, returning to her chores.

Joe ate quickly, and in silence. As he finished and Chrissie took his plate, she said, "If it's all the same to you, I"m going to stay home tomorrow and help her out around here."

Joe looked surprised.

"Are you sure?" he asked.

"Yes, Mrs. Garrity has plenty of work tomorrow, and she's not getting enough rest. She's not getting any younger, you know."

"Who is? Well, if you're sure. I can always find one of the lads on the dock who're willing to go out."

"I'm sure. Here. I'll leave something for your breakfast right here. Don't make any noise getting up – I don't want you to wake Mrs. G."

"Well, alright then," Joe said. "You're a good girl, Chrissie."

Chrissie felt a moment of guilt, lying to her uncle, but thought about what needed to be done and steeled herself.

"Thanks Joe. Get to bed now. You have to get back on the water soon enough, and I have work to do here."

"Good night Chrissie."

"Good night to you. I love you. Now go."

"I love you too. See you tomorrow."

Chrissie choked back a response, smiled, and said, "Good night. I'll see you."

Early the next morning, before the eastern sky had begun to show the first hint of dawn, a slim figure wove through the waterfront, heading toward the dock where a ship, with the name *Skipjack* painted on the stern, was taking on cargo. The figure climbed the gangway, sea bag over one shoulder, until challenged by the bos'n.

"What do you want here, boy?"

"Heard you were looking for a few more hands. I came to sign on."

The bos'n looked penetratingly at the slim figure before him.

"How old are you?" he asked.

"I'll be 17."

"I'm sure you will, but when?"

"My birthday's in two days time."

The man grunted.

"Ever sailed?"

"Been on fishing boats all up and down the bay."

The bos'n looked the newcomer over. Young and slim, couldn't possibly be 16 years old. A runaway, obviously, although the bos'n didn't hold that against anyone. Hadn't he run away to sea when he was younger than that? And there was something about this one – the garb, the casual way the bag was balanced, the wool cap pulled down low over the eyes – that spoke of the sea. The bos'n finally nodded.

"Welcome aboard, boy. Stow your bag forward. Ask for Farmer, he's with the starboard watch. He'll get you settled. Captain's name is Naughton, a hard man but a fair one. Do your job and you'll have nothin' to complain about."

The man took a pen from the makeshift desk from which he'd been working and dipped the point in the ink jar while opening a logbook.

Pen poised over the page, he asked, "What's your name, boy?"

The youngster nodded, giving the short salute of obedience.

"Name's Chris Warren, sir."

Chapter 9

Aboard Skipjack

The man scowled at her.

"Don't call me sir. I'm Mr. Connelly to you. Now get below, Farmer'll take care of ya.."

Chrissie made her way quickly across the deck toward the bow. She was aboard ship, but until they left the harbor, the wrong eyes happening by and recognizing her could put an end to everything. She didn't waste any time gawking like a lubber at the activity going on all around, and tried not to stare up at the three masts that rose at least three times higher than the single mast of Joe's fishing boat.

One step at a time, she reminded herself. Maybe she could let down her guard later, when she was in the Caribbean and had found Pa.

She found herself in a dark passage below decks with a tiny bit of light filtering down from the gathering dawn. Chrissie was temporarily blinded before her eyes adjusted to the dimness below. The space was small, the passageway narrow and the ceiling not far above her head.

An opening appeared on her right and she turned into it, then bounced back.

It was as if she'd run straight into a solid wall, only this was a wall of flesh. Looking up from the floor, she could see a pair of bandy legs topped by a torso as thick and solid as an oak tree, and as hairy as a bear. If it hadn't been wearing pants – and Chrissie thanked God it was – she might have assumed it was some kind of animal.

The shape turned around and extended a hand down towards her, his face showing a broad grin with a gap in the jagged white teeth. Two bright eyes peered out from a huge mass of bristly black hair that covered his head.

"Sorry mate, didn't see ya there," he said, grabbing Chrissie by the hand and propelling her back to her feet with no more effort than if she'd been a kitten.

Chrissie dusted herself off and picked up her sea bag, nodding at the man, a little intimidated by his bulk. He was stripped to the waist, but the hair on his chest and shoulders was so heavy and dark he could have been wearing a shirt. His forearms were thick, and a series of tattoos ran up his arms, disappearing into the thick mat of hair.

Standing now, she realized he wasn't as tall as she'd thought, only a few inches taller than she was. But what he lacked in height he more than made up for in width. From his broad shoulders his body went straight down without tapering to his hips, with no sign of a waist, as if he were a walking barrel.

"I'm Charlie Stickle," he said, engulfing her hand in a giant paw. "And who would you be?"

"Chris Warren," she said, making sure to keep her voice pitched low. "Just signed on. Mr. Connelly said to come below and find Mr. Farmer."

"Mr. Farmer?" the man said, grinning even more broadly. "Did you hear that, Jack? You're 'Mr. Farmer' now! How's that sound to ye?"

"Ridiculous," came another voice.

"C'mon Jack, take a look at this," he called out. "Captain's takin' 'em awful young. New hand here hasn't even got his growth o' beard yet."

"I can handle myself," she said.

"Oh, aye, I've no doubt. And what you can't do your mates'll teach you quick enough," he said with a smile.

"Welcome aboard," the second voice said. Chrissie craned her head around Charlie and looked into the bluest eyes she'd ever seen. His eyes locked onto hers and she felt a flutter in the pit of her stomach.

"Are you all right?" the man asked, looking concerned as Chrissie struggled to breathe normally.

"Oh, yeah, I'm fine," she said. "Just got a little dizzy."

The man cocked his head in puzzlement, then shrugged. He was younger than Charlie, probably in his late teens or early twenties, and his face was clean-shaven and bronzed by the sun. He was taller than Charlie by several inches, with broad shoulders that tapered to his trim waist. His red hair had been bleached to a light copper by the sun; his shirt was open at the neck.

"Jack Farmer," he said, holding out his hand. "If Connelly told you to ask for me, you must be on the starboard watch with us."

Chrissie realized she was staring at the young man and took his hand, shaking it vigorously. Don't be stupid, she told herself sternly. You're a boy finding work in a man's world. You're a boy!

But she held his welcoming handshake just a moment too long, then pulled her hand away awkwardly.

"Well, you're enthusiastic I guess," he said. "Drop your bag; we'll settle you in later. There's plenty of work before we sail, so let's get topside and see what you're made of."

Chrissie took a deep breath and followed the men to the deck.

"You from around these parts?" Charlie asked over his shoulder as they joined the tumult of activity on deck.

"Raised on fishing boats around here," Chrissie said.

"Family in these parts?"

"Some," was all she said, uncomfortable with too many questions.

"Enough jawing," Jack said. "We've got work to do. All right, Chris? Stick with me and Charlie. We'll look out for you."

Just like that she was part of the bustling throng, racing behind Jack and Charlie as they found their places. A flurry of orders flew from the quarterdeck, which were then repeated in a bellow by the bos'n, Mr. Connelly.

Chrissie did her best to follow Jack's lead, hauling or heaving or belaying in rhythm. The brig was modestly sized, but even so, she was so much bigger than Joe's boat that she was a whole different world. Chrissie grabbed lines that were pointed to her and hauled when told to, rarely certain what she was hauling or heaving or belaying.

They finished with seconds to spare, then were called up on deck by the ringing of a bell and Connelly's barked orders.

"All hands! Ready to set sail!"

Lines that tied Skipjack to the pier were cast off while men vaulted into the rigging to unfurl sails. Chrissie remained on deck, coiling lines that were tossed to her, following the example of those around her.

Almost at once she could feel the difference underfoot. Tied to the dock, the ship had been an extension of the land. It bobbed some, but had been lifeless. Now, free of the mass of land, tugged by the racing tides that pulled it away from the pier, then driven by the breeze blowing from offshore, the ship began to sway, to plunge on the currents.

As the land receded behind them, *Skipjack* began to heel over slightly as the sails caught the freshening wind. It became alive.

Chrissie Warren – now Chris Warren – was on her way.

Chapter 10

Hiding in Plain Sight

Chrissie stared behind her as the land grew more distant by the moment. Of course she'd been out many times before, sailing with her Uncle Joe all over the huge bay that spread out north of town. But this was different. The ship turned south, towards open sea, and she knew she wouldn't be coming back for supper. A pang of fear and loneliness shot through her as the enormity of what she had done struck her, but only for a moment. She was snapped back to the present by the booming voice of Mr. Connelly, who apparently had been reading her mind.

"Warren! Too late for second thoughts! You'll see Hampton again, but not tonight! Don't worry, you won't have time to get homesick."

"Yes sir," she said.

"I told you, don't sir me! I work for a living!" Connelly snapped. "Let me fill you in on a couple of things real quick. You call the officers 'sir.' That's the captain and mates. I'm Mr. Connelly to you. Not 'sir.' There ain't nothin' 'sir' about me."

Chrissie had never heard anyone put as much contempt into one syllable as Mr. Connelly did with the word "sir." He looked thoughtful for a moment, then shook his head

"Listen up, 'cuz I'll only do this once. You don't speak to your betters unless you're spoken to, and in your case, that's pretty much everyone aboard 'cept the cabin boy and the nippers. When an officer speaks to you, you say, 'Yes sir,' and you never offer your opinion 'cause you don't know enough to have one, and if you did have one, it'd be wrong. You make your obedience, like I seen you do when you came aboard," he said, imitating the thumb-to-forehead salute, "and wait for him to say whatever he needs to say to you.

"And now I'm done bein' teacher. Any questions you have, your watch captain can answer. There's plenty for ye to learn, and we'll keep you busy, sure enough."

Mr. Connelly was as good as his word.

The days passed in a blur of activity. Land was a distant memory as *Skipjack* drove southeast. Scrubbing decks and polishing fittings, picking apart frayed bits of rope and mixing them into oakum, which was shoved between the cracks in the deck planking to keep water out, were just a few of the daily tasks. One afternoon she was part of a crew that slurried the masts – coating it with a greasy mixture that allowed lines, pulleys, halyards and the other bits of rigging to slide up and down more easily.

Somewhere in that blur of activity, Chrissie realized, her birthday had come and gone. She was fourteen. It was certainly a different birthday than her thirteenth, but if she wanted anything like that again she'd have to follow through and find her father.

As he'd promised, Jack made sure Charlie or one of the other members of the starboard watch was always at hand to make sure the "new boy" was able to do the job. She was quickly becoming adept at all the skills required at sea, even becoming at home in the rigging. It was a good thing, too, because there was always work to be done, under the watchful eyes of Mr. Connelly, Captain Naughton or one of the other officers.

Chrissie couldn't let her guard down, and had to avoid any situation that would expose her. That wasn't easy in a ship barely more than 100 feet long and 26 feet wide at its beam. Sleeping in the crew quarters amid dozens of snoring, smelly men, Chrissie felt more than ever how alone she was. Under other circumstances, her worry might have made it impossible for her to sleep. But every night, within minutes of climbing into her hammock, she was out, exhausted from the day's exertions.

Chrissie almost didn't notice at first, but realized after a few days she avoided working with Jack, always volunteering to work with Charlie. It wasn't that she didn't like Jack, he was thoughtful and a good teacher, and compared to the other sailors a soft-spoken, interesting person to listen to. But Chrissie found it difficult to pay attention when he was talking. She'd be following his explanation and suddenly realize she wasn't following his words, just the sound of his voice.

"*Stop that Chrissie!*" she'd silently command herself.

And she would – until the next time.

She and Charlie were polishing the brass fittings along the railing when she felt a tug at the back of her head.

"Nice braid," Jack said, pulling on the blonde hair sticking out from under her cap. "Did you tie it yourself?"

"Aye," she said, flustered at his touch.

"Not bad for someone so young," he observed. "Charlie, who was that fella we met in Bristol, had the braid down to his waist?"

"I remember him. Billy somethin' or other. Swore he'd never had it cut in his life."

"You've got a ways to go to catch up with him," Jack observed to Chrissie, "but you've got a good start."

Chrissie pulled away nervously as Jack tried to examine her braid, stuffing the hair back up as best she could.

"Think you could retie mine?" Jack asked, turning his head so she could see the hair hanging down his neck in a pigtail. He pointed to Charlie. "This fella is a fine sailor, but he doesn't know the first thing about braiding."

"I know all about it," Charlie protested. "It's just my fingers are too big to do it."

"Are those fingers, or sausages?" Jack asked, laughing as he pulled a small book from his pocket. Charlie snatched it away before he could open it.

"Whaddaya reading now? I can't tell the title, but I'm sure I've seen you reading this'n before."

"It's essays by Montaigne," Jack said, reaching for the book, which Charlie held just out of reach, "and yes, I've read it before."

"Essays about a mountain?" Charlie asked. "Why would you need that at sea? No mountains here."

"Not mountains, Montaigne, Michel de Montaigne, a French philosopher from ... Never mind. Just give me my book please."

"Of course," Charlie said. "A Frenchie, huh? Here you go, monsoor."

He tossed the book back to Jack, who gave it a quick look to make sure it was still intact.

The ship's bell rang eight times, signaling the end of the watch.

"Dinner! I'm starved," Charlie said, getting to his feet.

"Follow me!" Jack shouted over his shoulder to Chrissie, who stared numbly after him for a moment.

"I'm a boy named Chris Warren," she told herself sternly. "And I'm hungry. That's all. Just hungry."

Chapter 11

Sea Stories

Chrissie was slumped against the railing with yet another plate of salted beef and ship's biscuit on her lap. She warily eyed the unpalatable-looking mass on her square, wooden plate, but she knew that – good or bad – she'd need the fuel.

A figure appeared beside her, taking a seat to one side.

"Gonna watch that or eat it?" Charlie asked, tending to his own plate.

"In a minute. Just keeping an eye on it so it doesn't scuttle off somewhere while I get up the energy to eat it," she said.

Charlie shoveled a giant quantity of beef into his mouth and chewed, his face thoughtful. Finally, he swallowed, and looked at Chrissie with a smile.

"Don't worry lad, you get used to it."

She returned his smile, then started eating. The sticky mass took some effort to get down, and the crew was silent as they chewed, swallowed and washed it down with water.

Charlie, not surprisingly, was the first to finish, and he scraped his plate over the side – not that there was much left to scrape – then turned to another sailor.

"How 'bout a song, Mickey?" he asked.

The man he addressed, a tow-headed Irishman with a sweet tenor voice, just looked at Charlie, his teeth still working on his own salted beef, his plate still half full.

"No?" Charlie said, undeterred. "How 'bout you, Sid?"

Sid Stevens was also still eating, and called back, "Why don't you sing, Charlie."

Everyone seated nearby laughed, Charlie not the least.

"Me sing? While you're eating? Well, if you don't mind me chasin' away the fish and making birds fall outta the sky, sure I'll sing!" he said to even more laughter.

"How 'bout a story, then?" someone called out.

"Yeah, something to take our minds off this food," someone else said, and there was a general chorus of agreement.

Charlie shrugged.

"Sure," he said. "What do you want to hear?"

"The Barbados brawl?"

"The earthquake in Port Royal?"

"The pirates!"

There was a sudden hush, as if the mere mention of pirates carried menace. Then several heads nodded agreement, and someone called out, "Tell the pirate story, Charlie!"

He cocked his head.

"You sure?" he asked.

"Aye! Tell the pirate story!"

"Alright then, settle back."

Charlie's voice dropped to a dramatic timbre.

48

"It was seven – no, eight! – eight years ago. The worst week of me life. I was aboard *Atkins*, an old lugger runnin' between Charleston and Boston. Now you might think most pirates and the worst o' them buzzards would be down in the Caribee, but don't tell that to the boys roamin' from the Carolinas up to Newfoundland. They know their business right enough. Our captain, Hiram Knickerson – you ever heard of him? No? Well, he was a good man, but stubborn, and it cost him.

"We were rounding Cape May in good shape when a boat came scootin' outta the inlet. A two-master, she was, and fast. Within half an hour she was right behind us and gaining. The captain had us put up more sail and soon we had us a race going. Then the other ship dropped its colors. It threw up a black flag and fired a shot. You know what that means – heave to and give 'em what they want – or else."

Charlie raised his eyebrows suggestively, allowing his growing crowd of listeners to imagine what "or else" might include.

"But Captain Knickerson, he don't want to heave to. Not sure what he was thinkin', but he had us throw every stitch of canvas we had up on the spars. It made no sense, there was no way we were going to outrun 'em, loaded down like we was.

"They chased us for an hour, popping away at us with a bow chaser to remind us they were back there, as if we'd forget.

"But the wind started dying and they pulled within range and let us have a broadside from about a hundred yards. Chain and grape went whistlin' into us like – well, like chain and grape! Bloody mess. Our mainmast went down, men were dead and dyin' all over the deck. Captain Knickerson was the first man to fall. I saw him layin' on the deck with a sliver of oak like a bayonet stickin' out of his chest. He was just starin' up at the sky like he was wondering what he'd been thinking, trying to outrun pirates."

49

Charlie had the crew's attention and he knew it. He could see the gaping eyes, the jaws hanging open, the last remnants of dinner forgotten on men's plates. Even some of the officers, Captain Naughton and the mate, Mr. Mason, were leaning down from the quarterdeck, listening. Chrissie was as rapt as any of them.

"That took the fight out of us, you can be sure. They stormed aboard, cuttin' and hackin' as they came, on account of bein' so mad at us for trying to run. Not one officer survived, and a lot of the rest of the crew as well. I got this" – he pointed to a livid scar on his calf – "and this" – pointing now to a round scar on his shoulder – "just for bein' there and following the captain's orders. The only fellas on the ship who didn't get somethin' were the two who jumped overboard and swam for the beach. It weren't more than a half mile to shore and I guess maybe they made it, though I never did see either o' them again. I didn't try 'cuz of course, I can't swim.

"When they was done there was only six of us aboard drawing breath, and we were all bleeding somewhere. They left us with nothing – besides our cargo they took all the sailcloth, all the stores, all the charts and instruments, all the line. Stuff they didn't want they threw overboard. They busted up the water butts for sport. They even took the one jolly boat that hadn't been shot up by their guns. The masts were down and we were shipping water from one end to the other. And when they sailed away, leaving us to our fate, they was laughing at us! Laughing!"

"How'd you make it?" asked one of the surrounding sailors.

"Just barely, I can tell ye that. If the tides had been out to sea at that point I wouldn't be talkin' to you now," Charlie continued. "As we drifted that hulk kept settlin' lower in the water until we were almost awash, and there wasn't nothin' we could do about it. But just before we went under the ship settled on a sand bar. Looked over the rail and there was the beach, not more than a hundred yards off. We wrestled the least damaged boat overboard and hung on as we pushed it in to shore.

"It took us another day to find a town, and one of the fellas died overnight. We were weak, hadn't eaten in two days. That's why I eat so much now. I still haven't satisfied that powerful hunger from that day to this," he said, a grin spreading across his face.

"And that was the story of the pirates of Cape May. Countin' officers there were twenty four of us aboard, men and boys, and five lived to tell of it. My only meetin' with pirates – and I hope the only one I ever have!"

There was a hushed silence.

As Charlie told his story, three sailors had been chasing each other through the rigging. Now they hurtled down the ratlines, racing to be the first to touch deck. Seeing he was going to lose if he kept climbing down, one sailor leaped out and grabbed a backstay, dropping hand over hand.

"Watch it there!" Jack shouted.

"What?" Charlie said, turning.

He didn't make it all the way around. The man dropped to the deck, bowling Charlie over. The big man reeled, bouncing against the rail. Jack raced over to grab him, but missed.

With a surprised look on his face, Charlie Stickle waved his arms, trying to catch his balance, then toppled over the railing, crashing into the waves with a splash.

Chrissie threw down her plate and raced to the rail. At first she saw nothing, then Charlie's head broke the surface. The ship was already pulling away, leaving Charlie bobbing in its wake.

She leaped onto the railing.

"What are you doing?" Jack asked.

"He said he can't swim," Chrissie shouted.

She took a breath and jumped.

Chapter 12

Man Overboard!

The cold water of the Atlantic closed over Chrissie's head as she plunged beneath the waves. With a kick and a thrust of her arms she halted her descent, sped upward and broke the surface.

Spluttering, she turned in the water. The ship had already passed beyond her, still moving south, though Chrissie could hear noise from the deck and caught a glimpse of a sail flapping in the breeze as it was lowered.

But her attention wasn't on the ship; it was on Charlie. She struck out with a long overhand stroke, keeping her head out of the water to search for him.

For a moment, a head and hand broke the surface less than a hundred feet from her. It was Charlie, splashing, gasping for breath, frantically trying to keep above water.

"Hold on, I'm coming!" she started to shout, but a rolling wave caught her and filled her mouth. By the time she had coughed and cleared her throat, Charlie had disappeared again.

She put her head down and dug in, swimming hard for where he had been. When she got in the general vicinity, she treaded water and called his name.

With another great flailing crash he broke the surface again, sputtering and thrashing ten feet from her, his eyes wide with terror.

"Hold on, I'm coming," she shouted.

Then Charlie's fear betrayed them both. As Chrissie reached out to him, his hand grabbed hers and pulled her towards him. He wrapped his arms around her, almost pulling her under.

She tried to wrench free but the big man held on, struggling. Chrissie strained against him, calling his name to get his attention, to get him to loosen his grip and relax, but his only response was to lock one arm around her neck, cutting off her breath. They were going under.

Chrissie could think of only one thing to do. One of her arms was pinned to her side, the other struggled desperately to keep her above water. She cocked her head back, then reared forward, her forehead striking Charlie square in the face. Stars exploded in her eyes, but his grip slackened as he rocked back, blood spurting from his nose. She broke his grasp and pushed him away. Then, before he could sink again, she swam around behind him and reached her arm around his neck. The other hand grabbed his hair, pulling his head back.

"Stop fighting!" she shouted at him. "Charlie Stickle, stand down! It's me, Chris Warren. Stop it or I'll hit you again!"

His hands grabbed the arm around his neck, but he stopped thrashing. She kept the one around his neck and her other free to swim with.

"Just relax; take it easy," she said more calmly now. "Lay back. I've got you."

His movements became less jerky as she kept talking, trying to relax him. She tried to sound casual, acting as if this were no big deal.

She heard a splash beside her and then Jack bobbed up alongside her. "What kept you?" she asked.

"Wanted to make sure I didn't jump in with my book still in my pocket," Jack said, treading water. "Besides, it looks like you've got everything under control."

In fact, Chrissie was tiring. It hadn't been a long swim, but the burst of energy that had propelled her across the water to him was dissipating after the struggle, the water's cold seeping into her, numbing her muscles. And Charlie was heavy.

They shifted positions so that Chrissie and Jack were both able to get a grip under Charlie's arms and keep him afloat. Chrissie could see the ship, now about a quarter mile away, almost motionless as it turned back toward them. There was a flurry of action on the deck and a moment later a longboat was lowered.

"Hold on, they're coming for us," she said. "They'll be here in a minute. Take it easy."

She didn't know how much longer she could keep it up, but she and Jack kept treading water, trying to move in the direction of the boat. It seemed an eternity.

Then she heard the sounds of rowing, voices calling from the boat. The sailors cleared the side and hands reached out for Chrissie.

"Take him first; he's pretty much spent," she said. She was able to shift Charlie's bulk toward the boat, and ready hands pulled him over the side. Chrissie clung to the boat as Jack threw himself over the side and reached back for her.

He had a smile on his face as he pulled her aboard, then a look of surprise. The other sailors were huddled around Charlie.

"Sit here," Jack hissed. Grabbing a blanket, he quickly draped it around her shoulders and pushed her onto a bench in the bow. "Keep covered up until you fix your shirt."

Chrissie glanced down and realized with horror that, in her struggle with Charlie her shirt had been ripped open and the cloth wrapped around her chest was visible, and askew.

"No, no, it's not ..."

"It's not what?" Jack asked, a blank look on his face.

"All well, Farmer?" came the voice of Mr. Connelly.

"Aye, Mr. Connelly," Jack called. "We're fine. Let's get back to the ship."

The sailors jumped to the eight oars and began pulling back toward *Skipjack*, with Connelly at the tiller.

Charlie had struggled to a sitting position, and grinned over at Chrissie through a face that was a mask of blood from his nose.

"Thankee, boy. I owe ya, and I'm not one to forget."

Chrissie just shook her head.

"No, seriously. Charlie Stickle is in your debt."

"Shipmates," Chrissie said with a shrug. "That's what we do. Right?"

Charlie stepped between two rowing sailors and settled onto the bench in the bow, facing Chrissie and Jack.

"Aye, shipmates," he agreed. "But why'd ya have to hit me so hard?" His hands gingerly probed his nose. "I think ya might have broken it."

"Had to do something or you'd have drowned us both," Chrissie said. "Saw my uncle do that once when he was helping pull another fisherman out of the drink. Come to think of it," she added with a grin, "Joe broke that fella's nose, too."

"Well, I guess it was worth it. I couldn't have held on long enough for that boat to get to me. You saved this old salt from gettin' a lot saltier, and that's a fact. But I'm gonna have a hard time livin' this down. Got my nose broke by a young slip of a lad."

Jack shot a look from Chrissie to Charlie and back.

"You might have a harder time livin' it down than you think," he said, staring hard at the girl.

"Please don't say anything," Chrissie said.

"About what?" Charlie asked, a puzzled look on his face. "If you think I'm not gonna let people know how you risked your life to save my worthless skin, you don't know Charlie Stickle."

"No, not ... Jack."

Charlie turned a confused face to Jack, who just shook his head.

"I'll hold my tongue, for now, but we'll have to talk."

"What are you two going on about?" Charlie asked.

"Nothing, nothing," Chrissie said.

"Later," Jack said to Charlie, with a look over his shoulder. The other sailors were hard at their tasks as the boat pulled close to *Skipjack*. No one appeared to listen, but on a crowded ship there could be few secrets.

"We'll talk, but not now," Jack replied. Chrissie gave a short nod in reply. Charlie stared at them both, and looked about to say something when the crew started to toss lines down from above.

Jack grabbed one and turned to Charlie.

"Think you can manage it without falling back in? Or should I have them send down a bos'n's chair?"

Charlie looked offended as he grabbed the line.

"The day I need a lift to get aboard ship is the day I give up the sea and become a pig farmer," he said.

Swinging a leg over the side of the longboat, Charlie scrambled up the side of the ship, where waiting hands pulled him aboard.

Jack passed another line to Chrissie.

"You alright?"

"Aye," she said shortly.

"Keep that blanket wrapped tight around you and get straight below," he said.

"Alright, I ... Thank you," she said.

"For what? I should thank you. You were quick off the mark, and saved his life. If he'd had to wait for me, I wouldn't have got there in time. The world's a cold enough place without losing a friend," he said.

Her heart raced as she followed Charlie up the side, surprised at how tired she was. It was all she could do to reach the rail and swing over. When she stood on the deck, her legs wobbled.

Jack was right behind her and caught her before she could sink to the deck.

"All right then boy, steady there," he said.

"Is that them?" came a voice. Looking up, Chrissie saw Captain Naughton standing in front of her.

"Aye sir," Jack answered, one arm holding onto Chrissie and the other giving a salute.

"Damn brave thing to do," the captain said. "Foolish, could have lost three crew members there instead of one. But brave. Mr. Connelly! An extra ration of rum for Farmer and... what's your name, boy?

"Warren, sir."

"And Warren. I'm gonna have Mr. Wells take a look at you, just to be sure you're well," the captain said, indicating the sail master, who doubled as the ship's doctor.

"That won't be necessary sir," Chrissie said quickly.

"I don't know, there's an awful lot of blood," the captain said.

"All Charlie's," Jack said quickly. "The boy here had to get his attention."

"Really? You did *that* to Charlie Stickle? There's more to you than meets the eye," the captain said, admiration in his voice.

"I don't know about that, sir," said Chrissie.

"Captain, can I get the boy below decks to his berth? He's plum wore out and that's a fact."

The captain looked skeptical, then relented.

"Well, if you're sure you don't need to see the sawbones, then get below and grab some hammock. And Warren?"

Chrissie looked up into his bearded face.

"Good work, boy."

Chapter 13

Everyone Has a Secret

Jack hustled Chrissie forward and down into the fo'c's'le.

In the crew quarters, Chrissie turned to him.

"Thank you for not ..."

Jack shook his head and put his fingers to his lips. Chrissie looked perplexed.

"Small ship, lot of men. No privacy," Jack said quietly. He pointed to the vent that brought fresh air below decks. "Never know who might be polishing the brass up above and hear anything said below. We'll talk later. Right now, I'll leave you alone so you can take care of ... " He waved vaguely toward her chest, then dropped his hand.

Chrissie just nodded, muttering thanks.

"Don't thank me yet. I haven't made up my mind. There's an extra shirt in my sea bag."

He rummaged for it, but she stopped him.

"No, thanks. I've got a spare."

"Alright then," he said. "Straighten yourself and get some sleep."

He left her alone in the middle of the crew quarters. From the sounds above she knew the ship was getting under way again and she might not have much time before some of the crew was dismissed and came down.

She quickly stripped off her shirt and examined it. The tear was along a seam and was easily fixable. She adjusted the cloth bands more firmly around her chest and slipped on a shirt she'd made during the last make-and-mend day. It was a good fit. She smiled at herself and thought of Mrs. Garrity teaching her to sew.

"She'd be horrified if she could see me," Chrissie thought. Then with a stab of guilt, she wondered for a moment what Mrs. Garrity was thinking right now. But she put it out of her mind – she was doing what she had to do.

Moments after she'd crawled into her hammock several sailors came down to the crew quarters. They called out to her, congratulating her for her heroism, joking about Charlie's clumsiness. She pretended to be asleep, and soon the sailors had crawled into their hammocks and were snoring.

Sleep didn't come as easily for Chrissie, whose mind was racing. What was Jack going to do? And what would happen to her if the captain found out she was a girl?

She finally drifted into a sleep troubled by dreams. She was swimming, trying to catch up to the ship, which was slowly pulling away from her. In the dream she called out for it to stop, to wait for her, but there was no response. She could see Jack at the stern, staring at her with pity in his eyes. She tried to shout to him, but a wave engulfed her. Looking up, she saw the dream Jack wave once to her from the boat, then turn his back and disappear. The waves closed over her head, and she sat up, suddenly awake and slick with sweat.

"Somethin' the matter?" asked a voice in the dark. It was Charlie. "You was talking and thrashing in your sleep. Everything alright?"

Chrissie's ears could hear the sound of other sailors snoring, the gurgle of water passing the hull. She took a deep breath.

"No, I'm ... I had a dream. What did I say?"

"Nothin' I could make out. Look, go back to sleep. You're with your mates. Ain't nothin' gonna happen to you here, not with Charlie Stickle on watch."

Chrissie lay back with a sigh.

"I'll be fine," she said.

She closed her eyes and within seconds was back asleep, this time untroubled.

In the morning she awoke as always to the sound of bells, the shouts of Mr. Connelly and the sound of feet on the deck overhead. *Skipjack* was sailing south under a brisk breeze, the crew working the usual routine chores. The captain was on the quarterdeck and everything seemed normal. But now more of the crew and officers seemed to notice her, smiling and nodding. Did any of them know? Were the smiles and nods of the other crewmen directed at her for what she did for Charlie or did they know her secret?

Jack was here and there during the day; he and Chrissie were not on the same work detail but she was acutely aware any time he was near. There was never a chance to speak with him, though, and she was sure he'd wave her off if she tried.

It wasn't until the evening meal that he sat down beside her, his plate full of the usual salted beef.

"Make sure you rest during the dogwatch," Jack said. "We've both drawn night watch tonight, midnight to eight bells. Not much to it," Jack said. "Unless weather comes up or something, we're mostly making sure the ship keeps pointing south and doesn't sink before sunrise."

"Alright then."

"It'll be you, me, Theissen, Stevens, one of the officers," he said, then added pointedly, "It'll be quiet. About the only time on a ship that you get anything close to privacy."

Chrissie nodded.

"See you then." Jack stood and walked away.

The ship was dark when, at midnight, eight bells rang, signaling the end of first watch and beginning of middle watch. Most of the sailors were below. Mr. Kite, the second mate, had command and Stevens had the helm under his watchful eye.

The others made a walk of the deck, checking the ship before starting various tasks. Chrissie felt a tug on her elbow.

"C'mon," Jack said. "We're going aloft."

Chrissie started climbing. A pit of dread formed in her stomach, but it had nothing to do with the height – she'd been in the rigging almost daily since signing aboard. It was what might come next.

Jack led the way up to the first trestle on the mainmast, then scuttled out onto the spar to make room for her.

"Keep your voice low," he said. "We'll only have a few minutes to talk."

Chrissie stared at him through the darkness. She could make out his shape and the general outline of his face, but couldn't read his features.

Finally Jack broke the silence.

"You're a girl."

Chrissie nodded, then said quietly, "Yes, I am."

"How old are you?"

"Fourteen."

"Not sixteen?"

"I didn't say I was sixteen," she said. "I said I'd be seventeen, and I will – someday."

"What are you doing here?"

"It's a long story."

"Make it a short one."

Chrissie took a deep breath, and then started. Jack was silent as she told him of her father, of her uncle and Mrs. Garrity, of the story that had come back to Hampton about pirates taking *Gladys B.*

Chrissie couldn't see his face, but the way he leaned in made it clear he was listening intently. She finished the story with her climbing the gangplank and signing on to the crew of *Skipjack.*

"I have to do something," she said. "Pa is down there, and I have to do something."

There was a long pause while Jack digested it. Finally he released a long, low whistle.

"That's quite a tale. And you saved Charlie's life to boot. Your loyalty does you credit, even if you haven't done much actual thinking."

"What's that supposed to mean?" she asked.

"What are you going to do on Nevis?"

"Find my father."

"How?"

"I'll get down there and start asking questions. I'll figure it out."

"What ship did you say he was on?"

"*Gladys B.*"

"I think I've heard of her. And I've certainly heard of Leech. With Blackbeard gone north, Leech is all anyone talks about down in the Caribbean. But that's not much to go on."

"I'll worry about that when we get there. What are you going to do now?" Chrissie asked.

"Do? What should I do?"

"I'm a woman ..."

"A girl."

"Fine. I'm a girl. If you tell the captain, won't he put me ashore?"

Jack pointed to the dark endless ocean that surrounded them.

"Shore? By now, putting you ashore means tossing you from the boat at Nevis, most likely. Cap'n won't waste time stopping somewhere to put you off. So you have little to fear from me. One way or another you'll wind up on Nevis."

"They say females are bad luck on a ship," he continued. "I don't know anything about that. I've seen you work. You've the makings of a good sailor. You were sure good luck for Charlie, saved his life. Charlie thinks he owes you, and if he does, I do."

"Why?"

"He saved my life once."

"So you won't tell the captain?"

There was another long silence before Jack spoke again.

"There's lots of secrets on a ship – everywhere, really. We all have the person we are, and the person we want the world to think we are. Some of us there's not much difference between the two, it's little things. Charlie's got a secret too, and it doesn't matter really. It's not my job to ferret 'em all out and report to the captain. It isn't any of my business. Do your job and keep your head down and I don't see why it's any concern to me."

"How about you?" Chrissie asked. "Do you have a secret?"

He rose and reached out for the rigging.

"If I did, that'd be a secret, wouldn't it?"

He leaned out, ready to climb down, then turned back to her.

"You know, you're a damn fool," he said. "There's not much chance you'll find your father. It's impossible odds. He could be anywhere in the whole Caribbean."

"If he's with Leech it should be easy. You said yourself, everyone's talking about him. I just have to track down Leech and get my father."

"Perhaps, but that's not a plan. 'To be prepared is half the victory,' as that Spaniard said."

"What?"

"Cervantes. A Spanish writer. Never mind."

Chrissie shook her head, her voice taking on a stubborn tone. "I'll find him," she said.

"Well, if we can help, we will. Charlie and I owe you that much."

Jack slid down the line and out of sight.

Chapter 14

Thunder on the Water

The next day at noon, the ship's company was called out on deck, forming a circle around Mr. Mason, the mate. He stood behind one of the guns, its heavy barrel resting on a wheeled oaken carriage. The crew murmured excitedly. Few of them had fired one before.

Mr. Mason called them to attention.

"Stand easy," he said. "We're sailin' into the Caribbean, and that means a nest o' pirates. With luck and the good Lord's protection we won't run into any of 'em. But if we do, I'd rather be prepared, wouldn't you? That's why I was hired on as part of this crew, and why we brought along these beauties," he said indicating the guns.

"Before I joined up for this cruise I learned my sailing – and my fighting – in the Navy. If you listen to me and pay attention, we'll do alright if the time comes. Now, I'm not going to ask if any of you have fired one of these before," he said. "I don't care. If you weren't trained by me, you don't know anything about it. Forget anything you think you know, because you're going to do it my way. That way, there's a chance most of us will live through it."

Live through it? Chrissie thought.

"This," he said, patting the gleaming gun, "is a four-pounder, but don't let the name fool you. Gun and carriage weigh right around 500 pounds. If you've loaded it properly and managed not to blow up the ship doin' it, it'll fire this," he held up an iron ball, "straight at whatever you're aiming it at, fast enough to smash it."

"We'll divide some of you into gun crews to man the guns," he said. "Of course some of you will be needed to work the ship if we get in a scrape, but every man is going to learn how to fire them."

Mr. Mason gave a grim smile as he saw the crew's growing excitement. He held up his right hand for silence.

Then, as the crew focused on him, he held up his other hand. For the first time the crew noticed his left hand was missing three fingers – only the thumb and index finger remained.

"Aye, and I was the lucky one," he said, letting the men get a good look. "Two other men were killed, and one lost an eye and an arm. You make a mistake, bad things happen and you don't usually get a chance to fix it. So listen close. In the next few days, we'll practice loading and firing every day until you can do it in your sleep. It's easy enough. The trick is to do it fast – load and fire in under three minutes – and do it safely. Oh, and do it while someone else is shooting at you. If you make a wrong move, stand in the wrong place, do the wrong thing, this" – he waved his injured hand – "is the best that's likely to happen to you. At worst, you could kill some of your crewmates as well – maybe all of us."

He paused and could see his words had their effect.

"This is serious business, as serious as anything you'll undertake at sea or on land," he said. "This is business, and I'll not have any carelessness or sloppiness. Am I understood?"

"Aye!" the crew shouted.

"Very good, then, let's get to work."

For the next two hours they drilled. Though some clearly had fired guns before, Mason made no distinctions. First he showed them, step by step, each task involved in loading and firing the big guns. Every man took a turn performing each step. Then two dozen men were designated as the four-man crews for each of the guns.

Jack and Charlie were both picked for a gun crew. Chrissie was not, along with four other sailors whose disappointment was clear on their faces. Mason smiled.

"Now, before you get all teary about being left out, let me explain. We need four men to each gun. We need the rest of you lot to sail the ship. We can't slug it out with a well-armed pirate. Best we can do is surprise 'em and run away, so we'll need enough crew to man the ship. That's you. The guns can keep 'em off for a while. The sailors will save our lives. But everyone on the ship will learn. If someone goes down," he waved his injured hand in the air again, "and some of you will go down, someone else can step in."

Mason was soon putting them through their paces.

They didn't fire the guns, but they went through the actions, swabbing and sponging and loading, all in pantomime, then shoved the guns up to the gun ports.

"Fire!" Mason shouted.

The six men designated the captains of their crew clapped their hands down to the touch holes.

"Hold right there. Nobody move!" Mason shouted. He walked down the row of guns to the port and starboard sides of the ship, pausing now and again, his eye critically examining everything. At the end of the line he stopped, turned back to the men, and spat over the railing.

"Stevens, you're dead. Look where you're standing!"

The skinny sailor at the second starboard gun looked embarrassed as he realized he'd stood directly behind the gun.

"That gun would've crashed right into you. You'd be dead. You too, Theissen, you're dead. Bending over to line up your shot that way, your head got turned into jelly. You're dead!"

"Bryant! Nebergall! Swinton! Stickle! The four of you probably wouldn't have lost more than your legs, standing that close to a bucking gun. Should I send you down to the surgeon now? Let him get to work fitting you all for pegs? Or do you think you can do this right?"

The men who had been singled out hung their heads. One of them managed to mumble that they'd like another chance.

"Really? Then let's do it right! Then we can try it for real, if I think you can do it without killing everyone on board."

The men smiled at this. Pretending to load the cannons under the hot sun was no fun, but the chance to really fire gave them something to look forward to. The guns were quickly pulled back away from the railing.

"By the numbers! One!"

They did it again, this time under the watchful eyes of the captain and Mr. Connelly, while Mason called Chrissie and the two cabin boys to follow him below.

The powder magazine was two levels down, amidship, a small room with a glass door.

"Never bring a light in here, covered or uncovered. Never, unless you really do want to blow the whole ship to hell," Mason told them sternly. "The light outside that glass is all the light you get in here. Am I understood?"

Chrissie nodded, her eyes wide. The young boys looked as if they'd rather be anywhere else.

"Good. These are the cartridges," Mason said, picking up one of the canvas bags stacked neatly to one side and passing it around. "Take a look."

Chrissie picked one up. It was a little more than three inches in diameter and somewhat more than eight inches long, sewed closed.

"That's the powder," Mason explained. "It's a smaller charge, no point in wasting any. I made these up for practice. Get six of these up to the guns, then come right back and get another six."

Each of them grabbed two and raced back topside, where they saw the gun crews, cheered on by their shipmates, shoving the guns back against the rail under Captain Naughton's command. When all were in place, the captain shouted, "Fire!"

Again there was no noise other than some of the sailors shouting "Boom!"

"Mr. Mason," the captain said, "Three times, and they've got it down to just under four minutes."

Mason spat over the rail again.

"Not good enough, but better," he allowed grudgingly. "Now let's see how you do with live cartridges. Powder monkeys, pass 'em out."

Chrissie handed a cartridge to Jack, who was captain of his crew, then to the captain of the gun beside his. Both took them gingerly, as if they might explode in their hands.

Most of the men had stripped off their shirts while working in the blazing sun, making Chrissie keenly aware of their bare chests. She glanced at her own shirt. Obviously she couldn't take it off. The voice of Mr. Mason saved her.

"What are you waiting for? By the numbers now! One! Powder monkeys! Get below like I told ya! And if you blow up the ship while you're down there I'll stop your rations for a week!"

Chrissie took off below with the two cabin boys, so she wasn't there to watch the gun crews carefully, deliberately, load their guns under Mason's stern eye. She hurried back to the powder locker, opened the door and snatched up six more practice cartridges, handing two to each of the boys. Overhead, the wheels of the gun carriages rumbled across the deck as the men shoved them toward the railing. She carefully closed the door behind her and headed toward the deck.

As she emerged on deck she heard Mason shout, "Fire!"

Six hands clapped six sputtering pieces of slow match down on the touch holes of the guns. There was a sizzling noise, then a roar.

It wasn't just the noise, although it was certainly loud. It was as if the air was suddenly compressed, squeezing tight all around her, almost knocking her back down the hatchway.

A huge cloud of white smoke swirled over the deck. The last thing she saw was the guns recoiling, straining against the ropes that held them. Then everything was lost in the acrid white smoke.

There was a moment of stunned silence, then Mr. Mason's voice cut through the haze.

"What are you waiting for? By the numbers! One! Powder monkeys, pass those cartridges!"

Chapter 15

Here They Come!

Skipjack had been alone on the wide ocean since setting sail from Hampton, but now they began to see other ships as the sea lanes narrowed down towards the Caribbean.

But though each sighting brought intense study from the officers and an excited rush of seaman to the rails, they never came within more than a few miles of each other, which brought a snort of disgust from Charlie.

"Five years ago – No! – eighteen months ago, we would have hove to. It's a big ocean and when you see another ship this far out, it's exciting! We'd trade news, maybe pass along any mail we happened to be carrying."

He shook his head.

"Now we stare out to sea, scared as kittens that a sail on the horizon might be a pirate. They're probably as scared of us. Either ship so much as changes a sail and the other will fly away like a frightened bird."

"Less chatter, more work!" Mr. Connelly called to them, "Put your backs into it!"

And the crew went back to work. And part of each day's routine was practice with the guns, and it was paying off. If they weren't quite up to Mr. Mason's standard, they were at least getting better.

This gave Chrissie a new worry as she carried cartridges up to the gun crews. She had come to the Caribbean to find pirates, but she was awakening to the problem – if she found them in the middle of a fight, people would die. And if the other ship was Davy Leech's and her father was aboard, what if he died from a gun she had helped load? She couldn't bear the thought.

After breakfast yet another ship was spotted, this one off the portside. The call went down, and the second mate, Mr. Kite, leaped into the rigging to give the ship a look.

"About five miles off, two masts, seems to be running parallel to us," he called down.

"What colors is she flying?" the captain asked.

"None I can see," the mate shouted down.

The captain paused, then shouted back up, "C'mon down, Mr. Kite. Leave your glass with the lookout."

The crew went about their work and had almost forgotten the interloper. They'd had plenty of company on the ocean the last day or two, and each ship had passed without incident.

It wasn't until about 10 a.m. – four bells of the forenoon watch, as Chrissie had come to think of it – that the lookout called down again.

"Ahoy the deck!" he shouted. After Mr. Connelly acknowledged him, he shouted down, "The ship off the portside, she's closed to three miles."

All eyes instantly turned aloft as they watched Kite race up the ratlines again to stare long and hard at the other ship. Finally, he came sliding down, his brow furrowed.

"She's slid toward us, true enough," he told the captain.

"Mr. Wells, two points starboard," the captain ordered the helm.

"Two points starboard, aye sir," the sail master said.

"Gently, Mr. Wells. I don't want any sudden moves."

"Aye, sir. Gently."

The helmsman made the slight course change, bringing Skipjack ever so slightly to starboard.

"Keep a close eye on her, Mr. Kite," the captain said. "Let me know what she's up to. There's enough breeze for the top gallants today, so run 'em up. See if we can't leave this fella behind ."

"Aye sir."

"I'm going below. Mr. Kite, you have the deck."

"Aye sir, I have the deck."

The captain went to his cabin as the crew raised the topgallants, which billowed out in the wind. But it wasn't long before he was called back. Every crewman strained to hear the conversation on the quarterdeck.

"Ten minutes after we made the course change, she matched us," Kite told the captain. "Still no obvious interest, but she's closing."

"Still no flag?"

"Nothing yet, sir." Kite said.

"Very good. Mr. Mason! My cabin please," the captain said.

The crew was all alert now. Something was up.

"Next step will be early supper," Jack said.

"Why?" Chrissie asked.

Before he could answer, Connelly shouted out, "Port watch! You're on supper!"

"How did you know?" Chrissie asked.

Jack shrugged.

"They don't want the galley fires lit if there's gonna be a fight," he said. "They'll feed us early and shut everything down. And of course, that way if there is a fight, at least we'll be well fed. I'd hate to die on an empty stomach, wouldn't you?"

Chrissie tried to muster a smile, but suddenly found it hard to do so.

By noon the other ship was about two miles off, still running on a nearly parallel course, slowly edging closer and slightly ahead of Skipjack while feigning a lack of interest in the merchantman. Naughton had the crew run up a signal flag asking the ship's identity, but there was no reply.

"He means no good," the captain said. "Mr. Mason, Mr. Connelly, clear for action!"

The call went out through the ship. Any stray gear and cargo was swept below so that, from bow to the quarterdeck, the ship was an open expanse. Nets were strung across the rigging to keep spars and other debris from falling on the crew below.

At Mr. Mason's direction all six of the guns were trundled to the starboard side of the ship, a move that surprised the tense crew.

"What's he playing at?" Stevens asked. "That other ship is over there," he said, waving to port. "Why are we putting all the guns starboard?"

"I 'spect he's got his reason, 'though he didn't tell me," Charlie said, securing one of the two swivel guns to the starboard bow.

Chrissie looked at the swirl of activity, all purposeful, all carefully carried out, and all meant to lead to battle and death. She fought a growing feeling of panic, turning to the task at hand. Right now she was placing buckets around the deck, each with a sputtering length of slow match that would be used to fire the guns if it came to that.

Muskets and barrels of cutlasses were stacked around the deck. Chrissie brought up the cartridges, which were loaded into the barrels and tamped down by the ramrods. Then the cannisters of grapeshot were loaded, along with a fistful of cotton wadding, and that too was rammed home. All that remained was for the captain of each gun to pierce the cartridge with a long, heavy needle through the vent, and prime it with fine powder from the powderhorn, and the gun would be as lethal as any manmade thing on earth. The barrels were run out the gunports.

"Let them get a little farther ahead of us," Naughton ordered, and the sails were slackened just a hair, enough to bring a tiny bit of speed off *Skipjack*. The other ship jumped slightly ahead, Naughton and the ship's other officers closely watching it.

"She looked a little slow in answering," Mr. Kite commented. "Shall we try it?"

"Aye, let's see how they handle their ship."

At that moment, a single gun fired from the approaching ship, and a ball skipped over the water across their bow.

"I believe that was for us," Naughton said calmly.

"Aye, and take a look at their stern."

From the stern rail of the other ship, a black flag was breaking out.

"Well, that settles that. Mr. Connelly, hard a'port! Let's see what they do."

"Hard a'port, let haul!" Connelly shouted.

The crew, well-trained after hard days of drilling, leaped to action. Sails were swung about and drawn taut, and Skipjack wheeled in a tight port turn, now heading almost straight at the other ship.

"Here we go boys, strip for action!" Mr. Mason said.

Most of the sailors on the gun crews pulled off their shirts and tied bandanas around their heads. Earlier, Mr. Mason had a barrel hauled out of the hold and pulled open. From it, sailors began spreading sand across the deck, especially around the guns.

Chrissie looked a question at Jack, who tried to smile encouragingly.

In his tension, the look was more sick than supportive.

"Better footing," he said. "In case the deck gets covered with ... liquid."

"You mean blood."

Jack shrugged.

"Liquid," he said. "It could be other things. Water or something."

"All hands, stand by. Gun crews, at the ready."

Mason motioned Chrissie over to him.

"All guns loaded and have two reloads?"

"Aye, sir," she said. "Should I go below and get more?"

"No, this'll be fast. We won't have time for more. But stand by."

The other ship was slowly turning to answer Skipjack's maneuver. On the quarterdeck, Naughton grunted with satisfaction.

"They handle their boat like a cattle ship. Mr. Connelly! Two points more to port!"

With that slight change, Skipjack was now on a course that would cut across the path the other ship had taken, putting them directly across the stern of the pirate ship – which is what the black flag proclaimed them to be.

"They're a small target," one of the sailors said, eyeing the other ship.

"They'll look a lot bigger right quick," Mr. Mason assured him.

"Steady, men!' Mason shouted. Then, to Chrissie, he said, "Keep an eye on her heads'l. Let me know when they start hauling that around; it'll mean they're turning to get off a broadside at us."

Mason and the captain were rapidly calculating in their heads, measuring the distance between the ships, their respective speeds, the angle of the wind.

"C'mon now, fella!" Mason said. "Let's get a little closer. A little closer before you turn."

The oncoming ship loomed bigger and bigger in front of Chrissie. Dozens of men lined the opposite railing, waving cutlasses and shouting. Several of the pirates shouldered muskets, puffs of smoke showed they were starting to fire.

"Don't worry; they're not close enough to hit anything," Mason said.

They were now about four hundred yards apart, and *Skipjack* had crossed the other ship's path. The pirates had to keep turning to get inside *Skipjack's* course. That slowed them even more.

At one hundred yards, Chrissie saw the other ship's headsail go slack and flutter in the breeze. She pointed it out to the gunnery officer.

"They must all be drunk over there, look at that." Mason shouted with glee. "They forgot where the wind is and they're dead in the water!"

Indeed the other ship seemed to be hanging in its turn, the sails slack.

"Captain?" Mason shouted to the quarterdeck.

"Aye Mr. Mason. Mr. Connelly, bring her around!"

The maneuver had put the pirates on *Skipjack's* starboard side, and the enemy ship was hardly moving. Men on the pirate ship were firing handheld weapons at them, chanting and jeering, and a swivel gun barked out, sending a spray of grape high over the deck. Chrissie could hear the balls whistle overhead, a few cutting through sails.

"Steady as she goes lads!" Mason said.

"Mr. Mason!" the captain called down. "You may tell the men to open fire."

"Aye sir!"

The enemy ship was now less than fifty yards away and Skipjack was coming around to her side.

"Ready lads!" Mr. Mason shouted. "On my command ...

"Fire!"

Chapter 16

Battle at Sea

To Chrissie, everything seemed to go into slow motion. The roar of the six guns, combined with the fire of the oncoming pirates, wasn't just sound – she felt a giant hand squeeze the air around her as tongues of flame and white smoke erupted from *Skipjack's* guns.

Looking across the water she saw ragged, bloody holes torn in the mob of pirates who moments before had teemed the railings. The ship's headsail was ripped to tatters, and spars and lines dangled from rigging of the stricken ship.

And all Chrissie could think was – *My god, what if Pa is aboard that ship?*

"Let's go, men! Reload!" Mr. Mason's voice snapped Chrissie back into the present. For now, all she could do was reassure herself that the odds were against her father having been aboard, and worry about what needed to be done right now.

She looked at Mason for orders.

"Not yet boy," he said. "I'll let you know when ..."

He was cut off by the sound of something plummeting. It was the body of Thomas Swinton of the port watch. He lay on the deck, his limbs splayed at grotesque angles, his open eyes staring without seeing at the bright blue of the cloudless sky, a red stain covering his bare chest.

Chrissie stared in shock. She couldn't remember ever even speaking to him; his was just another face in the crowd of sailors. And now ...

It took a moment to realize that someone was shouting her name. He was shaking her shoulder.

She looked up and saw it was Mr. Mason.

"Wake up! No time for that now!" he shouted. "Get to the number four gun. Man down. Go on, get to work."

Chrissie stumbled to the gun where the downed man – Abernathy, she remembered his name was – lay on the deck clutching his leg. The other three men were struggling to reload as *Skipjack* continued coming around the pirates, now only twenty yards away. Johnson was working the wormer, the long corkscrew-shaped tool that removed any leftover, smoldering bits of wadding from the barrel.

Chrissie saw the sponge, a long sheepskin swab on an iron handle, lying on the deck near Abernathy, and snatched it up. As Johnson pulled out the wormer, she plunged the swab into the water bucket, spun the excess water off, then ran it down the barrel to extinguish any remaining sparks and embers before the gun was reloaded. She rammed it all the way down, felt it hit home at the end, pulled it part way out and, with a twist, shoved it back. That would do. She pulled it out.

Balls from the pirates' muskets and pistols whizzed through the air around her, and she could hear as one or two hit the railing in front of her. She couldn't attend to them. There was no time to think about anything but firing the cannon. *Skipjack* was clear of the other ship's stern and coming into range of her broadside.

The captain of Chrissie's gun, Cotton Nebergall, was lowering the cartridge into the barrel and another man rammed it home. Another cannister and some wadding were added and that rammed down. Then Nebergall ran his piercing iron down the touchhole, tearing open the canvas.

He reached for the powder horn, ready to pour a little of the fine grain powder down the touchhole, when all hell broke loose.

The pirate ship opened fire, nine cannon blasting a wall of smoke and fire at *Skipjack*. Chrissie was knocked off her feet. She could hear the balls rip the very fabric of the air. Lines snapped, spars dangled loose, debris rained down, the railing in front of her turned to splinters, and Nebergall went down.

She could hear Mr. Mason's voice cutting through the cloud of gun smoke.

"On your feet men! Load and fire! Load and fire!"

Some of the other crews were working their guns, but at least one that she could see was out of commission, the gun tilting crazily on its smashed carriage, blood and something worse smeared across the deck.

She pulled herself up. The gun was loaded. It had to be fired.

The rest of the crew was gone, she couldn't see where. She pulled herself to the gun and dragged herself up. There was no powder in the touchhole. She looked around but couldn't find the powder horn.

Chrissie turned to the gun on her right. That crew was shoving it into position to fire again, heaving against its 500-pound bulk. Even though she screamed to be heard over the din, she couldn't get their attention to use their powder.

To her left was the ruined gun. She scrambled over and saw an arm sticking out from under the smashed carriage, a leather strap in its hand. She tugged on it and it came loose, then stopped. She pushed on the carriage to raise it slightly, but it didn't budge. Throwing her shoulder into it, she heaved, her feet scrabbling against the sandy, bloody deck, and pulled harder on the strap. It was caught on something.

With one more convulsive effort, she heaved against the carriage and pulled.

The powder horn came free.

She grabbed it and raced back to her gun. The horn was cracked, grains of gunpowder spilling out in all directions, but she directed most of it down the touchhole.

Done. Now the gun had to be manhandled back into firing position.

The gun to her right fired, and another roar and cloud of smoke spat death at the pirates. She turned to that gun's crew, tugging on sleeves and gesturing to make it clear they needed to push her gun to the railing.

Two of them came to her aid, and she collared a third man who was wandering by in a daze, blood oozing from a cut on his scalp.

Together they pushed the gun hard against the railing, drawing tight the lines that held it in place. Reaching into the bucket, she pulled out a piece of slow match and ran back to the gun. *Skipjack* was moving slowly but she was moving, and was now off the rear quarter of the pirate ship. The pirates were struggling to get their boat turned. Some stopped to raise muskets and fire.

Standing carefully to the side of the gun, Chrissie arched her back and leaned over, sighting along the barrel. The ship leaned into the swell, so she waited – and waited, blowing on the end of the slow match to keep it hot.

Finally the ship began to roll back. Looking along the barrel, she saw green sea, then slowly the side of the opposing ship rose into view, then the deck. She waited until *Skipjack* reached the top of its roll and began setting back toward the ocean, then clapped the slow match onto the touchhole. As it sputtered, she and the gun crew jumped back.

The gun roared and bucked – if she hadn't leaped back she'd have been crushed. Her ears rang, and the noise of the battle vanished.

Chrissie shook her head to clear it, but the ringing persisted. Mr. Mason had drilled them not to stare at the target – whether they'd hit it or not couldn't be changed now. All that mattered was getting off the next shot. But Chrissie couldn't stop herself from glancing over to the other ship, which was so close she felt she could have hit it with a rock.

The pirate ship's quarterdeck was a mess. A tangle of canvas, cord and spars dangled crazily. The crowd of men who'd been swarming the railing seemed to be gone, their place taken by smashed woodwork and a nasty red stain smeared across the hull. Blood oozed from the ship's scuppers.

In a daze, Chrissie looked back along her own deck where one more gun was being loaded, another about to be fired. Though the rigging had been somewhat shot up and the woodwork and hull had been pounded, the sails were still full, and the wind began increasing the distance between *Skipjack* and the pirates.

The other ship was wallowing in the ocean swell, unable to turn. With the wind behind them, it looked as if the battle was over and *Skipjack* was getting away.

Chrissie leaned back against the still-smoking gun, her knees giving out as she slid to the deck. Her head was swimming, her ears still ringing.

She let her eyes wander into the sky. The sun was still high, apparently the whole affair had taken less than half an hour, though it had felt like an eternity while she was in the middle of it.

The sunlight was warm on her face, but she shivered. Closing her eyes, she let the tension and worry fade out of her.

A deep, deep sigh. And, for a moment, Chrissie was unconscious.

Chapter 17

Picking Up the Pieces

Chrissie became aware that someone was tugging her sleeve and calling her name, though the sound seemed to come from a great distance. She wanted them to stop, but they persisted.

"Chris! Chris!"

Her eyes fluttered open. Peering down at her was the hairy face of Charlie Stickle. Behind him was another figure. Chrissie couldn't focus on him, but the coppery hair led her to believe it was Jack.

"Chris? Are you alright?"

Her ears were still ringing and suddenly she had no strength. Her whole body ached. She tried to talk, but could manage only a feeble wave of her hand and a thin smile.

Charlie took a knee beside her, and Jack leaned in.

"You alright? You don't look like you're bleedin' anywhere," Charlie said.

That was reassuring.

"Let me fetch you below to the doc."

"No, no. Hold on, just give me a second," she managed. "He's probably got enough to deal with without me getting in the way."

Charlie looked doubtful. Jack took her arms and ran his fingers up and down them, then pulled her legs out straight in front of her and checked them.

"Don't seem to be broken. You hurt anywhere?" he said.

"Everywhere. Hold on, help me up."

"No, just sit," Charlie said.

"I've sat long enough."

She pulled her legs underneath her and, with a steadying hand from Jack, forced herself to her feet. With a great deal of effort, she managed to stand straight, without swaying.

"See," she said. "I'm fine."

"Right, you look fine too," Charlie said, standing next to her. "Better than some of the lads, and that's a fact. C'mon, Mr. Connelly wants everyone front and center."

Leaning heavily against Charlie, she made her way to where the crew was assembled. It was a smaller crew than it had been less than an hour ago. Instead of more than thirty sailors, officers and ship's boys who had answered roll call when the ship set out, there were twenty one men on the deck, and many bore signs of the trial they had passed through.

The quarterdeck was a tangle of cords and spars. The captain and bos'n were there, but Mr. Kite and Mr. Mason were not in sight.

"As many of you as can climb, get aloft and clear the rigging," Connelly shouted. Whatever else had happened, Chrissie thought, the bos'n's voice hadn't lost any of its power. She could hear him clearly over the ringing in her ears.

"Four of you – Stickle, Farmer, Stevens, Warren – get below and bring out the canvas. We need to bring down that mains'l and get up somethin' that'll hold wind," he said. "But first the cap'n wants a word."

Captain Naughton stepped forward, limping slightly as he approached the crew.

"Well done, lads," he said. "They weren't expecting us to fight back. They were sloppy, they were slow and they mighta been drunk. But don't think they're finished. They're shot up; we're shot up. I can still see them back behind us, and if they get fixed up before we do, I know which way they'll be headed – right at us."

They men stirred uneasily.

"We're in better shape than they are, but I reckon they still have more hands. So I need every able man and most of you who ain't so able to pitch in and get us moving again. And if they catch up to us again, we'll bloody their nose again. Am I right?"

The crew answered with a cheer and went to work with a will. The rigging wasn't in bad shape, but as Mr. Connelly had observed, the mains'l had been pierced, torn and shredded, and would hold no more wind than a fork would soup. The new canvas was wrestled out of the hold and quickly bent to the spar and unfurled. Some lines could be spliced back together; others had to be replaced. The woodwork had been heavily shot up, but the hull was mostly intact, with no damage below the waterline. The pirates had been firing to cripple the ship, not sink it. Cosmetic matters like the railings and brightwork could wait. Right now, they needed to be able to sail, and fast.

And they had to do it with fewer hands. When Chrissie went below to fetch the canvas she got a glimpse of the carnage in the officer's wardroom, which was doubling as the surgery since it was the biggest open space below decks. Mr. Wells, the ship's doctor as well as the sailing master, was working with a saw on a sailor's leg while two of the wounded man's friends held him down, his screams muffled by a leather strap clenched between his teeth. On either side of the room men sprawled on the deck or leaned against the wall, reddened bandages clutched to their wounds.

On deck, the mute forms of six shrouded figures lay in the sun. As soon as time could be spared, they'd be given a burial at sea, Jack assured Chrissie, but in the meantime, there they lay.

To Chrissie, the flurry of working at breakneck speed was a godsend. It gave her no time to think, no time to feel, except, of course, for physical pain. Every time she lifted or hauled, her right side from shoulder to knee screamed in protest. She ignored it and kept working.

Skipjack moved south, her speed increasing as repairs proceeded. The other ship disappeared behind them as the sun slid down the sky toward the horizon.

"By the time they get themselves sorted out, we'll be lost in the dark," Jack said, glancing back.

"Sounds good to me," Chrissie said.

"I was watching. You did well back there," he said.

"I did what I needed to do."

"That's what that means. You did well."

She paused, looking back along the path *Skipjack* had sailed since the battle. Finally she turned back to Jack.

"I was scared."

"Good," he said. "If you weren't, I'd have said there was something wrong with you."

"Were you scared?"

"Terrified," Jack said without pause. "People died. You could have died. Me. Any of us. We all could have died. We got lucky; they weren't ready for someone willing to fight back. And thank God for Mr. Mason. That was a clever plan of his."

"What about the next one?"

"We'll see," he said. "Look, there might not be a next one. If there is, they might be more drunk or more stupid or more cocky than this lot, Or they might be sharp and lethal and they'll have us for breakfast. We knew when we signed on what the score was."

"Aye, that we did," she said. "In fact, that's why I signed on, to find the pirates who ..."

She stopped herself, unsure who might be listening. Jack nodded slowly.

"Exactly. Now you've found some. How do you feel about 'em?"

She let out an incredulous snort.

"How do I feel? Like I want them all dead! Like I hate them for what they did to my Pa and tried to do to me. Who are they, that they're willing to come out of nowhere and try to kill me? Bunch of animals."

"Well, some of 'em are, sure enough. But it wasn't all that many years ago the British crown paid those men and others like 'em to do what they're doing now, only to Spanish ships. It was a good job, a patriotic job, they were good at it and some of 'em got rich. Most of 'em just got drunk and quite a few got themselves killed. But then England settled its war with Spain and said, 'Sorry mates, don't need you anymore, go back to your other life. No more privateering.' To these lads, there is no other life. It's all they know. Only now they do the job they were trained for and they're criminals."

Chrissie listened, fascinated and perplexed at the same time.

"So are you saying it's the king's fault we're being attacked by pirates? We're English! That doesn't make sense."

"No it doesn't. None of this does. All I'm saying is, if you're going to go looking for pirates, you're probably going to find 'em, and it's best to know what kind of men you're likely to find. As the philosopher said, 'Knowledge is power.'"

Chrissie looked at him, waiting.

"Francis Bacon," Jack said, with an "of course" tone.

"Well, the knowledge I need is where Leech and his crew are hiding out, and I can't find that out 'til I get to Nevis. Until then there's not much I can do about it."

Jack smiled and pointed to where the setting sun was painting the sky a deep red and gold.

"Well, you'd best start thinking about it, because that smudge on the horizon ..." he indicated a dark mass to the southwest, "is probably Puerto Rico. You're almost there. By this time tomorrow you'll be in the Caribbean. A couple of days after that you'll be on Nevis. So, what are you going to do?"

Chrissie was brought up short by the question. When she started out, she thought she knew what came next. Once in the Caribbean she'd find her father, Simple.

Now she was nearly there, and it wasn't so simple.

What *was* she going to do?

Chapter 18

A Fight in the Dark

Chrissie didn't have a lot of time to ponder the question. The passage through the Caribbean had everyone on their toes, keeping a sharp lookout for sails.

Still, whether working in the rigging or laying half asleep in her hammock, she turned it over in her mind. First, she needed to find out approximately where Leech was. If he was close to Nevis, find him. If he wasn't, find out where he was. And then ... Well, she wasn't sure how she'd track him down, but she knew she would do it. She had to.

The sea lanes became much more crowded. After having seen hardly a sail for weeks, the crew suddenly found themselves in crowded waters, with commerce from all up and down the North American colonies and England heading in toward St. Kitts, Dominica, and especially towards Nevis, the island renowned throughout the world for the quality of its sugar cane.

The double watch was out the first night as they sailed by Puerto Rico. The wars between England and Spain were at an end, but that didn't mean the Spanish suddenly loved British sailors. Plenty of sailors on that island had adopted the ways of the buccaneers who had brought the Spanish empire down, making a living by raiding the ships that passed by their island.

Skipjack kept well out to sea, her tops'ls reefed close to keep her from gaining too much speed in the dark waters. The masthead light had been doused so the lookouts could see better, and the only light that shone from the ship was the lamp on the quarterdeck. From her perch high in the foretop, Chrissie strained her eyes to pierce the dark as *Skipjack* plowed steadily forward. It was two hours until sunrise, and the eastern horizon had yet to show the first telltale blush of dawn.

"If only there was a moon," said Stevens, who was laying out on the yard. "Can't see a blasted thing."

Chrissie glanced up. The stars were bright, reflecting off the calm waters, and she marveled at how the familiar constellations changed their positions as the ship sailed south. The Hunter was low in the eastern sky, but instead of standing, as he did in the sky above Virginia, he seemed to lie on his side, taking his rest. Hardly the posture of a hunter, she thought. More like The Napper.

Suddenly there was a stir. She couldn't tell if the sound had come from the deck or out on the water, but it had sounded like a muttered, angry oath.

"Did you hear that?" she asked Stevens.

"Something," he muttered. Sitting up, he grabbed a backstay and leaned out, peering into the gloom.

Chrissie scanned the waters. There was no sign of a ship, but as her eye swung from east to west a dark shape moved across the surface, the reflected starlight suddenly obscured.

"Out there," she said urgently, pointing. "Something's moving!"

"Where away?" he asked.

"Just off the starboard bow, maybe two hundred yards."

Stevens stared hard. He was notorious for having the worst eyesight on the ship and as the seconds ticked by Chrissie grew increasingly nervous. Suddenly he started and called below.

"Ahoy the deck!" he said in a whispered call. "Something moving on the water, a cable length off the starboard bow!"

A voice spoke quietly on the deck, and sailors raced up the ratlines while others made for the bow railing. The rest were being roused from their hammocks.

A large dark form appeared in the cross trees beside them.

"What are we lookin' at?" Charlie asked.

"Out there, starting to close."

Charlie peered out at the night for a long moment, then nodded.

"Might be a fishing boat, might be something else. We'll know in just a minute," he said. "You spot it, Sid?"

"Can't take the credit," he replied. "The boy here saw it first."

"Good work lad," Charlie said in the dark.

Chrissie heard a metallic click and realized Charlie had brought a musket aloft with him.

"Get down on the deck and get yourself something to fight with," he told both of them as he adjusted his footing and shouldered his weapon, bracing against the mainmast. "Smartly now."

Her heart pumping, Chrissie grabbed the shroud lines and slithered quickly to the deck, which bustled with suppressed but urgent activity. Men spilled from the fo'c's'le hatchway and were quietly issued weapons. Almost as she hit the deck, Chrissie found herself with a cutlass pressed into one hand, a pistol in the other, then sent forward to the bow where she stood shoulder to shoulder with nine other sailors, staring down into the water.

There was the slightest sound of splashing from below them, and suddenly it was right before them, a long, low canoe with the shape of many arms – impossible to count in the dark – propelling it forward with paddles.

"Avast ye!" Mr. Connelly shouted. "Heave to and declare yerself!"

It might have been Chrissie's imagination, but the smoothly moving shape seemed to falter for a part of a second. Then, with a cry of "Drive boys!" the boat shot forward toward *Skipjack*, and the flare of musket shots lanced out at them as the distance shortened.

"Hold fire," Connelly's voice barked, "Hold ..."

The canoe thumped hard against Skipjack's hull, and Chrissie could see a tangle of men standing, snarling at her as they tossed ropes up. Several raised pistols and fired at the mass of sailors on deck, but from their unstable perch their shots all flew over the heads of the Skipjacks. Still, the firing had its intended effect, many of the sailors broke ranks and ducked, giving the attackers a moment to climb up the sides of the ship.

"Fire!" Connelly roared.

A blaze of pistol and musket fire poured down into the attackers and in the sudden stab of gunfire Chrissie glimpsed men falling back into their comrades still in the canoe. She leveled her own pistol and pulled the trigger, but nothing happened.

A hand reached over her shoulder and grabbed the pistol, pulling back the hammer and firing over the side.

"They work better that way, " Jack said in her ear. He pressed another pistol into her hand. "Try it."

She pulled back the hammer with her left hand, heard it click. As she did, a face appeared at the railing, a scowling, furious face topped with a wild tangle of hair. Chrissie pulled the trigger.

Whether she hit him or not she couldn't say; the recoil jarred her arm and the flare of the gun blinded her momentarily. But when she looked up, the face was gone.

A second round of pistols was passed around and more *Skipjack* sailors were crowding the deck, eager for their chance.

"Take that, you whoreson dogs!" shouted a *Skipjack* crewman, who craned over to aim his musket into the mass of men aboard the canoe. Chrissie heard the crack of a pistol from below and the man reeled back, his musket clattering to the deck as he clutched his chest.

A roar and bright flash from the waist of the ship showed where Mr. Connelly manned the swivel gun. Its load of grapeshot poured down on the unlucky canoe, and Chrissie could imagine the carnage below.

Heart racing, she tossed aside the pistol and bent to scoop up the cutlass she had left against the railing. As she did, she heard the crack of a gun and a furious howl from behind her as a pistol ball ripped through the air where moments before her head had been.

"Port side! PORT SIDE!" yelled a voice from above. "They're coming up the port side!"

It couldn't have been the men who were lying below her in the bloody shambles of the canoe. A second canoe, unseen in the dark, must have come around the other side and its occupants had quickly, quietly clambered up the side.

With savage screams the attackers bowled into the defenders lining the starboard rail. Chrissie saw one man knocked clean over the railing, landing with a thud in the ruined canoe below. A second man on her right went down with a scream. A man rushed towards her, his cutlass swinging overhead. She ducked to her right and the blade hit the railing, biting down deep into the wood.

Without thought she kicked out with her foot and caught the man on the side of the knee as he struggled to free his blade. The joint gave way with the sickening pop of tearing cartilage, and he fell with an oath. He turned towards her, teeth bared like an animal and lashed at her with a knife.

Chrissie dropped to the deck and rolled, the cutlass falling from her hand. She leaped to her feet, but her adversary was almost as quick despite his ruined knee.

The deck was a tumult of noise and chaotic activity, but all Chrissie could see was the man's ugly face and the gleaming blade he thrust at her; all she could hear was his rasping breath.

She turned into the knife thrust, spinning like her uncle Joe had taught her. Doing so made his arm shoot past her on the right, as she suddenly stood with her back to her adversary, his chest bumping into her as he went off balance. She grabbed his arm at the wrist and brought it sharply down against the railing, hanging on with all her might.

She heard and felt a bone crack and the knife fell over the railing into the sea. But as she tried to spin away again, his left hand caught her collar, lifting her off her feet.

She could smell his reeking breath as his eyes glared at her, and she felt him shifting his weight to hurl her overboard.

That's when his head exploded. One moment she faced a snarling fiend ready to kill her, the next she was dropping from his lifeless fingers, covered with his blood and brains as he toppled over.

Staring up at the spot where he had been, she had the briefest impression of Jack Farmer tossing aside a smoking pistol, then wheeling around with his cutlass and plunging into the fray.

Shaking aside the horror that almost paralyzed her, she searched for her own cutlass, pistol, anything she could use as a weapon. Nothing came to her sight but the pirate's cutlass still lodged in the railing. Throwing her weight against it, she felt it budge, then break free.

It was heavier than the one handed to her earlier, but felt more solid. She hefted it. It felt good in her hand.

"Skipjacks! Skipjacks!" Mr. Connelly's voice bellowed like a bull. "On them boys!"

The pirates had tried to take them from both sides, and if they'd succeeded they'd have made short work of the merchant's crew. But with the starboard attack foiled early and the element of surprise gone, the remaining pirates soon found themselves pressed against the railing. They took no quarter, and they received none. The crew of *Skipjack* cut them down until there were only two left.

The press of sailors stepped back, offering them the chance to surrender. One dropped his cutlass, holding out his hands. The other, with a growl of contempt, whirled with his own blade and before the crew could stop him had lodged it in the surrendering man's throat. Three pistols barked out from the deck and the last man jerked, then toppled over the railing.

There was a long silence, broken by the cries of wounded men.

Finally, Captain Naughton's voice spoke out from the waist of the ship, where he'd been as deeply involved in the fighting as anyone.

"Welcome to the Caribbean, boys!"

Chapter 19

Reporting for Duty

Charlie found Chrissie on deck after the fight and was horrified at the sight of her, dazed and bathed in blood. He was certain the lad must have suffered a grievous wound.

"I'm fine!" she protested.

"You're bleedin'!" he cried.

"No, that's not mine. That's from ..."

She paused, a catch in her voice. In her mind, all she could see was the pirate's head bursting open like a deadly flower, blood and brain and splinters of bone gushing onto her from what had been his face. The world swam in front of her for a minute, but she caught herself.

"It was one of them," she said. "He ... I got some of his blood on me, I guess."

"You guess? Look's like you've been swimmin' in it," Charlie said. "Best get those bloody rags off. Go stand under the pump and wash off."

He steered her forward to where the pump had been rigged and pumped the handle. Water washed over her, the cold tang of it bringing her a little closer to her full senses. Then he hustled her below, where she found her one set of spare clothes – a pair of canvas slops and a blouse with the broad black and white horizontal stripes so often seen on sailors.

"I'll be fine," Chrissie assured Charlie as she looked for a private place where she could change.

"Are you sure you don't need anything?" he asked.

"No, no, best get back on deck, Mr. Connelly's calling. There's work to do. I won't be a minute."

Charlie nodded and slipped back above deck. Chrissie quickly went to the far corner of the crew quarters and stripped off her blood-soaked clothing. She looked at the cotton strips bound around her chest and realized they were bloody too. It was awkward, but she pulled the last strip she had out of her sea bag and quickly wrapped it around her, cinching it tight.

"Everyone will just assume they're bandages," she said to herself as she pulled on her outer garments.

She turned to leave, but realized she was shaking again. Leaning against the hull, she sank down to the planks beneath her.

The visions from the fight closed in on her. Suddenly she was staring again into that face of death – her death – and then the man's head exploding from Jack's pistol shot. Then she saw the face that had popped over the railing and disappeared as she fired her pistol. Then the jerking death dance as the last pirate killed his mate seconds before dying himself.

"I can't do this," she whispered, tears coming to her eyes. "I can't."

She could barely breathe for the shuddering sobs that wracked her.

What made me think I could face down pirates? Why did I think I could do this?

She gasped a ragged breath as the tears poured down her cheeks.

It's too hard. Not because I'm a girl. It's too hard for anyone.

It would be so easy, she thought, to go up on deck and admit to the captain that she was a girl. She'd be relieved of duty and put ashore at

Nevis. Maybe they'd send her home, or else she'd have to find work a woman could do on the island until she could get back to Virginia. But she'd be out of this.

Whether she sat there for a few seconds or a few minutes, she didn't know. But her reverie was broken by the sound of a voice calling from the deck, and the rapid patter of feet above her head. The voice was Mr. Connelly, of course.

"All hands on deck!" he was shouting.

And she could hear the footsteps of the crew running to their places, Charlie and Jack and the others. It was hard for them, too, but together they managed.

Without even thinking she responded to the call, pulling herself to her feet and staggering toward the stairs. The soreness in every part of her body matched the heaviness in her heart, but she kept moving one foot in front of the other.

For just a moment she was shocked to realize that something had happened to her in the weeks since she'd left port, something she hadn't even been aware of. She was no longer pretending to be Chris Warren. That's who she *was*. And Chris Warren was needed on deck.

She took a deep breath. From above, she heard Mr. Connelly shout.

"Warren! Warren! Shake a leg boy, toe the line right now!"

She ran to her place.

"Glad you could join us, boy," the bosun said. "Are you all right? Ready to get to work? Or should I get the lads to find a feather bed for ya?"

"I'm fine. Chris Warren, reporting for duty!"

Chapter 20

A Familiar Face

The first order of business was dealing with the dead and wounded. Two more of the crew had been killed and eight were injured badly enough to have been carried below. Everyone else had been knocked about; there wasn't a man among them who didn't bear a few marks.

The two fallen crew members had been wrapped in their hammocks and friends of the men were sewing them in with cannon balls at their feet to keep them from floating, When there was time there'd be a small ceremony, the men standing at attention while the captain read a verse of scripture, then the shrouded bodies would go over the rail and sink to the ocean floor, just like the men killed in the earlier battle had been.

The pirates weren't given the same consideration. Their bodies were tossed unceremoniously over the side. But they weren't all dead despite the defiant final act of the last pirate. Five of the attackers were still alive, injured, some barely drawing breath, but alive for the moment. Their wounds were quickly dressed and they were locked in chains.

"Put 'em in the cable tier," Captain Naughton said curtly.

"Farmer, Theissen, Warren, Jamison, Stickle, come with me," the second mate, Mr. Kite, said. "We got to get these vermin below and out of the sight of God's eyes."

"Let's go, you curs," he added with a kick at the closest one, who was nursing an injured leg. "Get below."

"But I'm not a pirate, not one o' them," one of the men pleaded. "Please, you've got to listen to me."

Chrissie looked at the man, who was talking through teeth clenched from the pain of a pistol ball in his thigh. His hair was a wild, filthy tangle of black, his haunted eyes sunken into a face that wore a deathly white pallor. But for all that there was something familiar about him.

The other captives turned from him in disgust, starting to shuffle sullenly below.

"Save your breath and get below," Kite snarled. "You can tell it to the court on Nevis."

"But they'll never listen," the man said. "They'll hang me for a pirate, and I was a forced man. Never meant no harm, but they forced me to join 'em or they'd have killed me!"

Kite kicked at him again and the man climbed painfully to his feet, hopping on his right leg to spare the agony to his injured left. He looked from man to man among his captors but saw no sign that anyone was willing to believe him or even listen.

"Move out now, smartly," Kite said.

With *Skipjack* sailors standing guard, they hobbled painfully below. The man who claimed to have been forced stood at the top of the steps, looked around hopelessly, then started to hop down, leaning heavily on the railing. Halfway down he tripped and tumbled the rest of the way.

"Pick him up, I won't have such filth fouling the deck," Mr. Kite ordered.

Charlie bent and wrapped his thick arms around the man's chest, heaving him up. The man cried out in pain as he was set roughly on his feet.

"Here, give a lean," Charlie muttered, half carrying, half dragging the miserable creature the rest of the way below to the dark of the cable tier.

"We should be in Nevis in two days," Mr. Kite said. "If any of you are still alive, you'll see the sun again when we turn you over to the authorities there, and may God have mercy on your souls."

They turned to go, Chrissie and Jack the last to leave. As she passed the man, he tried to reach out to clutch her pants leg, but Jack knocked his arm out of the way.

"Please, someone's got to listen to me," he begged. "It's true. If you turn me over, I'm a dead man and you might as well pitch me overboard right now with them other corpses."

Chrissie just stared at the haggard form on the bench. Jack shrugged and motioned for her to follow.

"You believe me," he said, looking at Chrissie. "It's true! I'm not one of them!" the man cried out. "I'm Silas David, an honest seaman until they took my ship and told me to sign articles or they'd kill me."

She walked to the door and started to step through so that Jack could close and lock it, then stopped dead, bumping into Jack. He looked at her with surprise, thinking she had stumbled, and put a hand on her shoulder to steady her. She swatted it away and turned back.

"What did you say your name is?"

"David, Silas David."

"What ship did you sail on?"

He looked confused, but answered without hesitation.

"*Gladys B.*"

A thrill shot through her and she could hear her blood pounding in her ears.

"When were you taken?"

Jack, standing behind her, tried to interject.

"Doesn't mean anything, doesn't prove anything," he said. "If this man were a pirate, he'd have come up with the name of any ship they'd captured."

From farther down the line another captive piped up.

"Me too, I was on the *Gladys*, what he said."

"I sailed on *Ocean Swift*," another pirate called out. "They forced me to sign articles."

"See?" Jack said. "There's no truth in 'em. They're all liars. Now c'mon."

"Wait," Chrissie said, thinking back to a night more than a year past. "Who was the captain?"

"Captain Williams."

"Aye, that's right, I remembers him well," one of the other pirates said. "Good ol' Cap'n Williams."

"Chris," Jack said. "They're just making it all up."

She ignored him.

"Who led the mutiny?"

"I ... I don't like to say." The man gave a haunted look at his fellow captives, then repeated, "Don't like to say his name."

"Three nights before *Gladys* sailed from Hampton, what did you do?"

"I was in the pub," a pirate said, laughing. Another snorted and said, "I was wiff a girl I know in port!"

"Not you," she snapped, then turned back to Silas David, staring at his face. It'd been more than a year since she had seen the man, but the name was right, and his face bore the look of someone who had suffered much in the intervening months. Still ...

"Tell me," she pressed. "Three nights before you sailed, what did you do?"

The man looked confused, then screwed his eyes closed as if thinking. Then he sighed and shook his head.

"Think!" Chrissie pushed. "Did you go anywhere, talk to anyone."

"I don't know, I ... Wait, three nights before... The captain, he needed someone to let the crew know when we'd be sailing. He gave me a list ..."

"Where did you go? Who did you talk to?"

"Several of the lads. Most were in the pubs drinking. But there were a couple of fellers who ..."

"Who lived in the town?"

"Aye, right. Had to track 'em all down."

"Close your eyes and think. You're knocking on the door. Who opened it?"

The man thought a long time. Jack shook his head and reached for Chrissie's shoulder. She shrugged him off. Finally the man opened his eyes again.

"An older woman, then she went and got the man. Dan Warren, the ship's carpenter."

"Was anyone else there?"

"Don't remember. They were ... Wait, that's right. There was some kind of a party or something. I felt bad about interrupting."

"That's right," she said at last, tears forming in her eyes. "It was a party."

"Did you know...?"

Chrissie looked up at Jack, who was staring at her, then back to the ruined man chained in the cable tier.

"Yes, I know him. He's my father."

"You're Danny Warren's boy?" the man said with wonder in his voice. Then a confused look came over his face.

"That's enough for now," Jack said sharply. "Chris, we've got to go."

"Chris, that's right, his boy Chris," David said. "But ... no."

"Don't speak of this to anyone," Jack told him. "I'll be back. Chris? Now!"

"But Jack!"

"Now! Out of here. We don't want to talk among this lot."

"I'll be back," she told David, who had sunk back against a coil of rope as if too tired and confused to think any more. His eyes showed little comprehension, but he nodded slightly.

Chrissie rose and ducked through the opening. Jack followed her, dogging the hatch cover. Then he turned to her.

"Jack, he was with my father! He can help me find him!"

Jack put a finger to his lips.

"We don't want to share any of this information with anyone, especially those pirates in there," he said quietly but firmly.

"But Jack, you heard! He's the man who came to my house!"

"And what if he is?"

"Then he's telling the truth about being forced."

"Maybe he is and maybe he isn't. We'll have to think about this, and about what we're going to do next."

"What *we're* going to do?"

"You know what I mean. What you're going to do, and what I'm going to do about what you're going to do?"

"Why should you do anything?" Chrissie asked.

"Depends on what you do," Jack said with a shrug.

She started to say something, then shook her head stubbornly. All the fear and irresolution from last night's fight were gone, at least for now. She faced him in the narrow passageway, focused only on one thing – and it wasn't those blue eyes so close to her own.

"I'll tell you what I'm doing. I'm doing whatever it takes to find my father and bring him home. Right now that man in there seems like my best chance to find out. And there's nothing you or anyone else can do to stop me."

Chapter 21

Darkness Below Deck

The wind turned against them as they entered the Caribbean and it took four days to reach Nevis instead of the predicted two.

But though they fought headwinds the whole way, tacking endlessly into the breeze that blew from exactly the wrong quarter day and night, the time was put to good use. The two separate attacks had left plenty of cleanup work to do, and the remaining crew had been hard at it, painting and repairing, patching sails and splicing lines. By the time they drew in sight of St. Kitts, with Nevis just a few hours away, the ship – battered and patched though it was – looked as neat and trim as the crew could make it at sea.

Chrissie hadn't wasted her time either. By the time they drew in sight of Nevis, she had the first bits of information she'd needed and the beginnings of a plan.

She had to wait until the second night after the attack to get another chance to talk to Silas David. The first night, Cotton Nebergall was posted outside the cable tier. He'd been wounded in the first attack and was only just returning to duty. Unable to perform any work, he had been assigned to guard the prisoners because, as Mr. Connelly said, "You can sit up, and you can yell if there's trouble. Not much more to it than that."

He recognized Chris Warren, of course, and was happy to see him and talk about the fight and his wounds, but he wasn't going to let him pass.

"Sorry, boy, I can't let anyone in. Got my orders," he said.

Chrissie gave in, and instead pumped Nebergall for any information he had about the prisoners.

"The doc just came out and said two of 'em for sure ain't going to make it to Nevis, and he ain't too sure about a third."

"What about the fella with the leg?" Chrissie asked.

"He's one of the ones in a bad way, Mr. Wells said. Probably just as well, if you think about it. A wound like that, how they gonna stand 'im up to hang 'im? It'd be a botched job for sure. He's a lot better off if he slips off down here. Then it'll just be over the side for 'im, and he won't even have to climb to get back on deck. One of us'll have to carry him. Guess that'll be his last laugh on us."

Chrissie didn't find it funny.

The second night, Charlie Stickle had drawn guard duty. It had been a long, hard day and everyone was exhausted. Chrissie crept from the crew deck down to the cable tier and found him slumped against the wall, his head jerking up as she approached down the passageway.

"Chris," he said. "Thank the Lord it's you. Wouldn't do to have Mr. Connelly or Mr. Kite catch me nodding off, but I just can't keep my eyes open, I'm that tired."

"They'll never hear it from me," she assured him. "Mind if I sit with you a while?"

"Trouble sleeping? After the day we've had?"

"I keep thinking about the fight," Chrissie said. That much was true. The images of blood and death still forced their way into her mind whenever she wasn't occupied, and sometimes even when she was.

She glanced at the door into the tier.

"Do you suppose I could go in and see them?"

"Ah, now Chris, I'm supposed to keep everyone out."

"I know," she said. "But I need to talk to one of them."

"Cap'n don't want no one talking to them pirates," Charlie said, "and I think he's right. Can't help them, and it can't help you."

"But it can," she said. And it all spilled out. Not the part about her being a girl, but all the rest of it, her father, *Gladys B.*, the man who had interrupted the party and the fact that he was right on the other side of the partition, maybe dying.

Charlie listened, a troubled look on his face.

"Jack let me in on some of this," he said. "I don't rightly understand it all, and I don't see what you can do about it."

He hesitated. She pushed.

"Please Charlie. Let me talk to him for twenty minutes and we'll be all square," she said. "Then I'll stand the rest of the watch with you. We can take turns waking each other up."

He looked more uncomfortable, his duty as a sentry struggling against the sense of responsibility he felt for the boy who'd saved his life. She looked him in the eye until he finally grimaced, then glanced up the passageway.

"All right. Twenty minutes. If you're caught in there, the cap'n'll think we're both plotting something. If you hear me whistle, it means someone's coming."

He got up, went to the door and pushed it open, glancing inside.

"All's quiet. Don't get near enough that any of 'em can lay hand on you. Four bells was just a few minutes ago. If I haven't called you out, get out when you hear five bells."

"Thanks Charlie."

He smiled.

"If nothing else, this'll keep me awake, worrying on you."

Chapter 22

Staring into Eternity

The first thing that hit Chrissie inside the cable tier was the smell. The small, confined space was always rank, with a smell of tar and foul bilge water. But now it was much, much worse. It reeked of sweaty bodies left to stew in their own waste, mingled with something worse – the smells of putrefying wounds, of decaying flesh, of blood and pus and rot and urine. Of death. If these men were marked to die, as everyone aboard assumed, they were well on their way.

Chrissie gagged, it was all she could do to draw breath. She almost backed away, but Charlie had already closed the door behind her. Besides, this wasn't about her nose or her horror. It was about her father.

In the dark, she shuffled down the tiers to where she remembered Silas David had been chained. There was a shape huddled in the blackness between the two coils of cable. She started to reach out a hand to shake his shoulder, then drew back, afraid.

"Silas," she whispered. "Silas David."

The lump moved slightly and there was a break in the rhythm of the shallow breathing, but other than that there was no response. She heard someone else stir farther down the line.

"Silas," she said again, a little louder. She reached out her hand until she felt the greasy clothing covering the figure and shook it slightly.

"Silas David, it's me. Chris Warren. I talked to you when you came down here."

The figure pushed itself up slightly with a groan.

"Who?" he said.

"Chris Warren. Dan Warren's ... child. I need to talk to you about what happened to my father."

"Your father?"

"Dan Warren."

"Oh, Danny. What do you need to know? And what's it worth to you?"

With a tremble, she asked the question that had been uppermost in her mind all year.

"Is he alive?"

"Who? Danny?

"Yes! Dan Warren! Is he alive?"

"Sure, yes."

Chrissie let out a breath.

"At least he was when I saw him last."

"When was that?"

There was silence, a silence that lasted for a dozen heartbeats.

"Well? When did you last see him? How long ago?"

"I'm trying to think," he snapped. "We were together after the pirates took the ship and forced us to join. They wanted him because he's a carpenter. They even let him keep his tools."

"Where is he?"

"Hard to say."

"Why? What happened?"

He was silent again.

"You've got to tell me," Chrissie said.

"What's it worth to you?"

"What do you mean?"

"You want information."

"Of course I do."

"I want out of here. I want to live."

"But ..."

"Get me out of here and I'll tell you what you need to know to find your father."

Chrissie pulled back, gasping.

"How can I do that? I can't! It's impossible."

The man coughed, a low, rumbling cough that seemed to come from deep inside. It shook his entire body.

"I'm dying down here."

"I'll get you some water."

"Don't bother. Get me out of here."

Chrissie wanted to shake him. So close to an answer, and he wouldn't talk. She wanted to pummel him, and might have if she weren't pretty sure it would shake him apart.

Another voice spoke from farther down the tier.

"I can tell you what happened to him, boy," said one of the other pirates.

"What?"

"I'm like ol' Silas there. I'll tell you when we're free and away from this boat."

Silas David spat.

"That ain't gonna happen Royce, you scabrous dog, you're going nowhere 'cept the gallows," he said. "This is between me and the boy."

The other voice chuckled.

"The boy?" it asked. "What boy would that be?"

"This fella, Danny's son."

The other voice just laughed. David coughed again, long, wracking spasms that shook his body. Finally he caught his breath.

"You want to know about Dan, you'd better come up with a plan," he said. "I don't think I've got much time."

There was another long pause, and Chrissie began to wonder if the man had passed out again.

"Mr. David?" she asked. "Mr. David?"

He stirred.

"Look, Mr. David, you know as well as I there's nothing I can do. This isn't about you. It's about saving your shipmate from the same fate."

The man didn't answer. In the dark, Chrissie could feel his eyes boring into her. Then he gave a long, shuddering sigh.

"You're right, of course. I been a dead man since the day those fellas took our ship. It was just a matter of time. I shoulda let them kill me then."

"If they had, you wouldn't be able to help my father," Chrissie answered. "Maybe that's why God let you live."

"Dan was alive two months ago, last time I saw him. We'd been taken, along with a dozen others. That was back in February, when they took *Gladys* and forced us to sign the articles."

"Ye damned dog!" cried another pirate nearby. "You were happy enough to join us when you thought it'd make you rich!"

"Oh, stow it, Royce. You'll be damned yerself soon enough. At least I'll meet my maker with a clear conscience," David sputtered, before breaking out in another spasm of coughing. Chrissie waited impatiently until the coughs subsided and, with another shuddering breath, he continued.

"They took over the ship just north of here coming up out of the Antilles. Killed half the crew. They took the ship and killed the captain. I saw his body; they kept it stretched out in the rigging for weeks, like a warning. We sailed - I don't know how long it's been now; seems like forever."

"Why isn't he here now?"

"The crew got too big. So did Royce there. He thought he oughta be captain. Half of the crew went with us, half with the other fella. They took the boat and left us."

"Why didn't you stay with Pa?"

"Wasn't given a choice. Don't know why he'd taken offense at me, but the captain wanted me gone. He's a man if, he wants you gone, you'd better go or he'll send ya straight to hell. But he took Dan with him, on account of him bein' a carpenter, ya know."

"Where's Pa?" she asked when he seemed recovered.

"Pa? Oh, Dan, right. The cap'n wanted to keep him because he's a good carpenter. So they took the ship and left us on the coast of Puerto Rico. We built us a canoe and stole two more, and we've been hitting fishing boats and small merchants. The Spanish are onto us, though, and Royce here figgered it was time we took a ship and moved off south. That's what we were looking for when we attacked you."

"Where did the other ship go?"

"I swear I didn't mean to hurt anyone when we attacked," David said. "I'm sorry. I've been wicked, not as wicked as some but I've done things I don't want to think about. And I repent 'em all now, and ask God to forgive me."

"Sod off," Royce snarled in the darkness.

"I do," David said, clutching feebly at Chrissie's sleeve. "I repent myself of my sins."

Chrissie was going mad with frustration, but she forced herself to stay calm.

"I know God forgives you," she murmured.

"He does?"

"Aye, I'm sure of it. As he forgives all poor souls who ask. He made us what we are, how can he blame us for that?"

A smile spread over David's face.

"Aye, that's right. And I do repent, I do."

"Good," Chrissie said. "Now, the ship, with my father, where'd it go?"

"South," David said. His strength was fading and Chrissie could barely hear him. She leaned over, almost gagging at the smell that rose from him, but intent on hearing what he had to say.

"South? South where?" she asked. She realized that David had no idea where *Skipjack* was, so any compass directions he came up with couldn't mean much.

"Not far," he breathed. "The Island of the Holy Cross."

"Holy Cross?" She'd never heard of it, but if she had a name and got a chart, she'd find it.

"Aye, just south of Puerto Rico. That'll be their base and they'll work east and west from there."

"And the ship? "

It took him three or four breaths before he could make himself answer.

"*Sea Devil*," he finally breathed.

"*Sea Devil?*"

He nodded weakly and his eyes closed.

"It's the same ship, isn't it? *Gladys B.* ... Silas!"

She shook his shoulder and he stirred again.

"It's the same ship?"

"Aye," he said, barely audible.

"The captain. What's his name?"

"Davy Leech. And a worse fiend you'll never meet. He's an evil, evil man. You steer clear of him, as you value your soul."

From above Chrissie heard the sound of five bells. She stood to go, but paused. There was a sound at the door – Charlie peeking in.

"Boy! Time to go! Can't let anyone find you here."

"Just a second Charlie," she said. "Just one second."

She leaned in close to the man, who was clearly dying.

"Is there anything I can bring you, anything that'd help ease this for you?"

Another longish pause, then in a surprisingly meek voice, the man asked, "Could pray with me for just a bit?"

"I could."

Charlie looked nervously over his shoulder.

"Chris, c'mon! No time."

"There's time. All the time in the world, isn't that right Silas?"

"Aye, eternity."

Chrissie started reciting the Lord's Prayer, Silas whispering along with her. Halfway through, she heard the rumble of Charlie's voice join in behind her.

As she neared the end, Silas nodded off, but his breathing seemed less labored.

She finished, ducked out, and Charlie locked the hatch behind her.

Chapter 23

We're All Fish Food

Chrissie was on her knees the next morning, scrubbing the deck, when she heard a clatter come up the hatch, two sailors lugging something up from below. They tossed it onto the deck not more than ten feet from where she worked, and she gasped.

It was the body of Silas David, his limbs splayed out at odd angles. The eyes in his ravaged face were open, staring blankly at the sky.

Chrissie stared as the men bent over the corpse, struggling for their grip. One of them swore as they tottered to the railing with their load. Without speaking, the men swung it once, twice, then lofted the mortal remains of Silas David, sailor and repented pirate, over the side.

Chrissie rushed to the railing in time to see him hit the water. The body sank, then surfaced, bobbing on the swell. She stared as the ship began to leave it behind.

Chrissie felt a hand on her shoulder. She turned and saw Jack, gazing out astern at the body.

"It isn't fair!" she said, trembling.

"No, probably not."

"He repented."

"Charlie told me," Jack said. "Sounds like he made his peace with God, and has you to thank for it."

"And we just toss him overboard like garbage," she said.

"For what it's worth, it doesn't matter much to him now. He was done with his body. What difference does it make if it's tossed overboard, or sewn up in canvas and slid over the side with ceremony, or buried in the dirt? He's just as dead."

She stared at the deck and fought the tears welling up inside.

"None of that, now," Jack said in a low, urgent tone. "Don't want anyone wondering why the boy is crying over a pirate. Besides, it ain't that different an end than any of us is likely to have."

Chrissie looked up at him reluctantly.

"Oh, aye," he said, smiling. "Any man who spends his life at sea will most likely end up fish food. You, me, the captain, even ol' Charlie. And Charlie, big as he is, is gonna make a whole school of fish happy when he goes."

It was a gruesome picture, but Chrissie couldn't help smiling at the comparison.

"Right, then," Jack said. "We'd best get back to work before Mr. Connelly takes an interest. You alright?"

By the time *Skipjack* arrived off Charleston, Nevis's one big city, two more of the prisoners had died. The ship docked the next morning and the last two pirates were taken off the ship in chains, turned over to the port authority. Captain Naughton would have to testify at a trial the next day, but that was a formality. The two would be hanged before *Skipjack* cleared port on its homeward voyage.

Now the crew gathered on the deck, eagerly gazing out at the city, anticipating shore leave.

"There's a place I'll show ya, a great tavern," Charlie told Chrissie. "She's got the best rum in the Caribbean, and cooks like an angel."

"She?" Chrissie asked.

"Aye, Maggie's her name, and she owns the best tavern this side o' the Atlantic. Both sides of the Atlantic, and that's a fact. Oh, Maggie, she's ..."

Jack cut him off.

"She's the love of Charlie's life, and *that's* a fact," he said, smiling.

"Maybe that's so," Charlie admitted with a sheepish grin. "She's a fine woman and no mistake. And the fact she has the best rum in the Caribbean doesn't hurt. Wait'll you meet her."

"All hands!" bellowed Mr. Connelly, and the sailors too took their places on deck, waiting for the captain.

It was a much smaller group than had gathered on the deck after leaving Hampton. Only eighteen crew members reported for duty the first morning in Nevis. Ten were dead and eight were still recovering from injuries. On the quarterdeck the officers all looked the worse for wear, and Mr. Mason was making his first appearance on deck since the attack, his head still swathed in a heavy bandage and one eye swollen shut.

The captain looked over the crew, then nodded to Mr. Connelly, who called them to order.

"Well that was an eventful trip, eh lads?" Naughton asked, a wry smile on his face. "When we get back to Hampton, you'll all have some stories to tell, and there'll be a bonus for every man aboard."

The crew gave a delighted whoop at the news and the captain let it play out before holding up a hand and regaining their attention.

"Right now there's work to do. The sugar wagons are due in the morning so I want those hatches opened and the yards rigged. We'll have the holds emptied and flogged clean by this afternoon or there'll be no shore leave for anyone. And there's plenty more work to be done setting this ship to rights. I don't want to hear a word from any of you birds about going into town until *Skipjack* is shining again. Mr. Connelly has the job details, so get to work."

The men turned toward the hold, where Mr. Connelly stood on the hatch cover, ready to get started. Charlie hustled directly to him, then turned and called impatiently to the rest of the crew.

"C'mon boys! The sooner we start the sooner we're done, and the sooner I'll see Maggie!"

The crew worked with a will, and the hold was soon emptied and cleared, ready for the cargo of sugar that would be delivered in the morning. Meanwhile, another work detail began painting. The damage done in the pirate attack had been repaired, but the fresh wood stood out like scars. Four men, led by Jack, were hanging over the side, repainting the bright yellow stripe that ran around the ship just below the railing.

"Well, you know the proverb," he said, popping his head over the rail to chat. "'Idleness is the root of mischief.'"

They both looked at him blankly. He sighed and shook his head.

"Chaucer," he said. "Anyway, the devil won't get any time for play here. If he shows his face here, Mr. Connelly will put him to work, you can bet."

Charlie suddenly froze, looking out to sea.

"Jack!" he called. "Whaddaya make of that?"

The three of them looked out into the offing, where ships came and went on their way to and from foreign ports.

"Ship coming in," Jack said. "Don't like the look of this."

A trim sloop rounded the point and turned into the harbor. The ship glowed in the midday sun, and from her mainmast fluttered the Union Jack.

"Is that Royal Navy?" Charlie asked.

"Looks like it," Jack said, scowling at the newcomer.

The sloop turned into port, showing its starboard side to the sailors at the rail of *Skipjack*.

"Anyone have a glass?" Jack asked. Someone handed him a small brass telescope and he trained it on the ship. He stared for a long minute, then swore. The ship fired a single gun, a salute to the garrison manning the dockside port. A single gun fired from the fort in answer.

"His Majesty's *Lark*," Jack read. "Hmm. Things might have changed; it's been three years since I heard anything about him. But it might be a good idea for me to lay low."

Chrissie was puzzled.

"What ...?"

"Unless there's been a promotion or change of command, her captain is someone I can't afford to run into," Jack said, handing back the scope and turning back to work before Chrissie could ask any more questions.

Throughout the morning, whenever his work had him on deck or up in the rigging, Jack kept one eye on *Lark*. Before the ship dropped anchor in the harbor there was a flurry of flag signals between the ship and the fort, and a steady parade of boats began going back and forth. Then, just before noon there was a squeal of ship's pipes from across the water and a longboat was lowered. Jack pointed out the activity to Chrissie.

"There goes their captain," he said, pulling a spyglass from his pocket and ducking below the railing so he wouldn't appear obvious. He gave a long look at the officer.

"That's him all right," he said in a low voice. "Hasn't changed a bit."

"Farmer!" boomed Mr. Connelly's voice. "Did I call a break or did I put you on paint duty?"

"Paint!" Jack answered, straightening up and saluting.

"Then quit starin' out to sea and get painting, or I'll put you on rat duty!"

"Aye aye!"

Jack picked up his brush and got back to work without a word.

Chrissie looked at his retreating back, then turned to Charlie. His normally jovial face was furrowed in a serious frown, but he wouldn't talk either.

They'd been back at work two hours when Jack scuttled over to Charlie and pulled him aside. The two began talking, quietly but earnestly.

"Are you sure he saw you?" Chrissie heard Charlie ask.

"He couldn't have missed me," Jack said ruefully. "My own fault. I was out on the stern just finishing that god forsaken stripe when his boat came back from the fort. It was the captain's gig, sure enough, and he passed almost under our lee."

"And he saw you?"

"He must have. I was right there hanging over the stern, like an idiot, not even thinking of keeping an eye out. He was close enough I could have hit him with a rock, and I should have, too. Not more than twenty feet."

"He might not have recognized you, it's been more than six years and you've changed a lot. You're a man now."

"Maybe, but I'm sure he noticed and it must have gotten his attention."

"So what do you want to do?"

"Stay out of sight, for starters, and start thinking about where to go if he comes looking. And it might be a good idea if I was ready to be someplace else."

"But that means ..."

"Aye, it means I might be leavin' *Skipjack*. But if he saw me, that probably means the same thing, and a lot less pleasant, to boot."

The two men didn't notice Chrissie edging closer, taking in every word.

"I'll get my gear ready," she heard Charlie say.

"Not you. I'm the one what's gotta go."

"I'm not letting you go alone," Charlie said.

"I can't let you do that, Charlie," Jack said.

"You can't stop me. The only question is, are we gonna lay low? Or are we leavin', and if we're leavin' how are we getting off the island?"

Chrissie took a step forward, pushing herself into the conversation.

"I've been thinking about that very thing," she said. "I know where I'm going, I just have to find it. And I admit, I could use some help."

Jack just looked at her.

"Tell us about it," he said.

Chapter 24

If You Want to Be a Man

Chrissie's entire wardrobe consisted of two pairs of sailors' slops and three blouses. She was wearing the best set, and threw on her tarpaulin jacket, cramming its deep pockets with everything else she owned, including her flute, her clasp knife and the spare, blood stained cloth she bound around her chest.

For Jack and Charlie, it was a little more difficult. They didn't want to advertise that they were leaving the ship, so they couldn't take their sea bags with them. They didn't own much, but what they did own they'd mostly have to leave behind. That was harder for Jack than Charlie. Charlie was going on shore leave, so he was already wearing his best clothes, and he filled his pockets with a change of clothes and a couple of other items.

Jack, on the other hand, had amassed a small library. Most of his nine books were small volumes, but collectively they were bulky enough to be a problem. Unable to choose, he finally slipped the eight smaller books into various pockets and carried the large, leather-bound collection of essays under his arm.

"I don't need the rest of this," he said. "It's just things. They can sell my clothes at the mast, and there's not much else here worth worrying about. But my books ... " He stopped, a little self-conscious, and shrugged.

"Are we ready to go?" Chrissie asked. Now that the decision was made she was eager to be away.

She watched with affectionate amusement as her crewmates primped and straightened their clothes, trying to look their best for their night on the town. All were wearing their finest outfits, or at least their cleanest. They'd dusted off their shoes and brushed their hair. She realized, with a lump in her throat, that she was going to miss them, miss being part of this odd, ocean-going family.

Chrissie found herself braiding Charlie's thick black hair for him, tying it at the end with a faded blue ribbon he'd found. Then Jack asked for her help and she found herself braiding his red hair, her fingers trembling ever so slightly. He in turn offered to re-braid hers, but she said she was fine.

"I'll just keep it tucked in here," she said, sticking a few stray wisps of hair under her cap.

"Ah, but if you want to impress the ladies you've got to put on a better show for 'em," Charlie said. "A woman sees a sailor with a thick, long braid, she knows he's manly enough."

"And why would I care about that?" she asked. "We're looking for a boat leaving the island, not a woman."

Charlie just looked at her perplexed, shaking his head.

"Boy, there's a lot of holes in your education that we need to fill in," he finally said.

"But maybe not tonight? We have other business tonight."

"Well, if you insist," Charlie said with a shrug. "But just cuz we've got business doesn't mean we can't enjoy the pleasures of the harbor. And there are a few things you'll need to learn if you want to be a man."

Then he turned and headed toward the deck, passing Jack, who required all his effort not to break out laughing.

"That's right, Chris," he said a moment later, vainly fighting the grin that spread across his face. "If you want to be a man you'll have to ..."

"Stow it, Farmer!" she snapped, turning red.

"Of course. But you know, there's some big holes in your education and ..."

She punched him in the chest and stalked past him, her cheeks burning.

Chrissie had her own reasons for wanting to get ashore that had nothing to do with becoming a man. A portside tavern, where the crews of dozens of ships from all over the world mingled with local sailors, would be the perfect place to ask questions. And there ought to be a few local fishermen who might be willing to talk about the local islands.

"All right you lot, listen up!" Mr. Connelly's voice roared from the head of the gangway. "When you go out into the town tonight, ye'd best remember two things. You're Skipjacks, not a bunch of lopers off some old coaster. You've earned your fun, but anyone who tarnishes the name o' this ship doesn't have to bother reporting back, because I won't let you aboard. And second, you'll be back aboard by four bells of the midwatch. When it's time to work in the morning, don't expect me to go easy on anyone just cuz they drank too much. Do I make myself clear?"

They all yelled their agreement, and the bos'n stepped aside.

"All right then. Have at it! And may God have mercy on this town."

The men thronged towards the gangway, jostling and shoving as most were unwilling to wait their turn. Chrissie, Jack and Charlie hung back and were among the last to reach the head of the gangway.

Mr. Connelly gave them a penetrating stare as they each leaned over the crew list and initialed their names.

"Looks like it'll be a nice night," he said.

Chrissie hoped that in the russet sunset the bos'n wouldn't be able to see her embarrassment.

"Aye sir, that it does," she said.

"Kinda warm for that jacket, I'd have thought."

"Well, I ... Maybe, sir," Chrissie said, flustered. "I just ... if it gets too hot I can take it off, but ... you know. I just like to be prepared."

"I can see that," he said.

Charlie and Jack finished signing out and started heading down the gangway, but Connelly called out to them.

"Doing some reading while you're in town?" he said, indicating the tome under Jack's arm.

"You know me," Jack replied.

"Aye, that I do. Navy's in town, keep an eye out for the press gang," he said.

"We will, you can be sure o' that," Charlie said. Jack nodded.

Connelly started to turn away, but as they stepped onto the gangway, he turned back. "Farmer?"

"Aye?"

"A pleasure sailing with you. All three of you. Now be careful."

"Aye, that we will," Jack said. "You be careful too, sir."

They all saluted him, then turned and headed down the wharf.

"How did he know?" Chrissie asked.

"He's not a stupid man," Jack said. "He sees everything that happens on board, and is smart enough to put two and two together."

Charlie had the lead as they ambled down the pier. They had almost reached the end, ready to turn onto the main street that ran down the harbor front when Chrissie's eye caught a flash of red, and she stopped, pulling herself and Jack into the shadow. Charlie stopped, looking confused.

"What're you two doing?" he asked.

"Look down the street," Chrissie said, her voice hushed. "Did I just see a couple of soldiers?"

Charlie walked to the end of the pier, whistling, trying to look casual. After a moment he took a few steps back to where his friends were hiding.

"Three fellas in red uniforms, sure enough, just outta the lamplight," Charlie said. "They look like they're waiting for somebody, but they were keeping a close eye on our mates as they passed in the light."

Chrissie peeked around the corner and saw what he meant. The soldiers were in the shadows, positioned so they got a good look at the sailors from *Skipjack* passing under the lamp.

"Press gang? Idlers? Or are they lookin' for someone in particular from the ship?" Chrissie asked, with a glance at Jack.

"Well, let's not find out," he replied. "If we go straight ahead, then cut around ..."

"Sure, but if they're looking for someone in particular, say, somebody their captain saw hanging from the stern of *Skipjack*, they're probably not the only soldiers in town looking for him," Chrissie suggested.

"Well, we have to try something, don't we?" Jack retorted.

"Sure, but let's try to even the odds a little bit." Chrissie glanced at him. "What's your most prominent feature?"

"It's hard to say," he said, grinning. "My noble nose? My bold chin? My stern, uncompromising brow? Or my generally pleasant personality?"

"Your hair, you idiot," Chrissie said, whipping off her cap. "You're the only red-headed man on the crew. Cover it up with this. I'm going to go out and talk to them. While they're distracted by me, you two head up the street. Charlie, stay between them and Jack so they don't see him."

"What if they're the press gang?" Charlie worried. "What if you end up in the Navy?"

She gave Jack a quick glance, then told Charlie, "I have less to worry about on that score than either of you. And they'd have to catch me first."

Chrissie shook her head so that her own straw colored braid hung down her back, then tucked the last wisps of Jack's hair under the cap.

"Keep it pulled low," she warned.

"Aye, over my uncompromising brow."

"Over your idiot face," she snapped. "Wait 'til I get them focused on me, then move down the street like you don't have a care in the world, just two tars out for a night on the town."

Without giving them time to object or herself time to be afraid, she stepped out boldly from their hiding place and started marching down the street, at first acting oblivious of the soldiers. Just as she reached the pool of light she turned and looked at them as if startled. She peered into the shadows, then let a big grin spread over her face.

"Hello general!" she shouted as she ambled towards the three uniformed men, who straightened up, startled by her approach. "What are you gents doing out here on such a fine night?"

They looked up and down the street, not sure what to do, but Chrissie didn't slow down.

"C'mon general, let me buy you a drink! There's a pub just down ..."

"Get lost boy, or we'll drag you down to see the captain," one of them growled.

"See the captain? Why? Is there somethin' funny lookin' about him?" she asked, wide eyed.

"There's nothin' funny about it, see? Just be on your way."

She walked past the trio, then stopped and turned back to them. To keep an eye on her, they had to turn their backs on the street.

"You know, my pa was a soldier, and in his memory I'd like to buy you all a drink. C'mon!"

She reached up to tug on the man's arm, but he shook her free and shoved her back. She tumbled into the dust of the road.

"I said be on your way, boy."

The soldier glowered down at her. He was a tall man with a bald head and a beaked nose. Staring up at him, Chrissie felt like she was being watched by a bird of prey trying to decide if it was worthwhile swooping down and seizing her.

"Now, there's no need to be like that, general."

"I'm no general, I'm Sergeant Thorne, and if I didn't have work to do this night, you'd be on your way to servin' his majesty the king as a loyal member of the navy for the next twenty years or so. Now I've told you to clear off! So clear off!"

Chrissie crabbed away from the men before turning and taking to her heels. The sergeant kicked at her as she scrambled away but barely connected. Running up the street, away from the tavern, she heard the men laughing. Stooping down to pick up a loose stone, she turned and hurled it at the men. She didn't wait to find out if she hit anything. She bolted straight up the road leading uphill, then turned left at the first corner.

Pausing to catch her breath, she hoped that Jack and Charlie had gotten past alright. There was no sign she was being pursued, so with luck she'd meet them in a few minutes at the tavern Charlie had been talking about, the Lamplighter. She jogged down the street, then cut back down the next street and found the two of them waiting for her.

"That was brilliant!" Charlie said. "I knew you could do it."

"Great job," Jack agreed. "When that soldier pushed you I thought Charlie here was going to storm in to rescue you."

"Nah, I knew he could do it from the first," Charlie said. Then he paused, and with a grin, added, "And if they'd tried anything more I probably would have taken 'em apart. Now let's get on to that tavern! It's just up here."

With that he led the way up the street toward a building where ruddy light was flooding through the windows. Jack pulled Chrissie aside.

"Good work, but we probably haven't seen the last of those soldiers and their friends. Keep an eye on this fella, won't you?"

"Charlie? What do we need to watch him for?"

"You'll see. All I'm saying is we all need to watch each other's backs."

Chapter 25

Too Many Questions

The room was clouded with smoke and chatter, with a heavy overlay of alcohol as they walked in. The customers who crowded around the tables paid them no mind, but there was a shriek from the woman behind the bar as they came through the door.

"Charlie!" she cried. She slammed down the mug she'd been filling with ale and ran out from behind the bar, pushing through the crowd toward him. He let out a laugh and roared, "Maggie!" and she flew into his welcoming embrace with a very public display of affection, one that might have gotten both of them arrested in more puritanical cities.

The greeting lasted some minutes. Chrissie was becoming uncomfortable about the display before the woman began to unwind her arms from around Charlie's neck and glanced at his companions.

"Jack! Good to see ya," she said, greeting him pleasantly but with considerably less ardor than she had Charlie.

"And who's this?" she asked, glancing at Chrissie.

"Chris, I wants you to meet an old friend, Maggie Irons, owner of the best alehouse on either side of the Atlantic! Maggie, this here is a new shipmate, Chris Warren. Believe it or not, this slip of a boy here saved my life on the voyage down, pulled me right out of the drink he did, when I'd all but given myself up as drowned!"

"And what were you doin' *in* the drink is what I'd like to know," she said, swatting him across the chest. "Didn't I tell you to be careful and make sure you come back to me in one piece? How can I convince you to marry me if you're drowned?"

"Long story," Charlie said. "The point is, I thought I was a goner until this lad jumped in and kept me afloat until the boat arrived. Broke me nose, but it was worth it to get back to you."

Maggie studied his nose from front and profile, then smiled.

"It's an improvement," she said, giving it a small kiss. Then she turned to Chrissie.

"That was a good bit of work you did, boy," she said, throwing an arm around Chrissie. "This old lug might not be much, but I'm fond of him all the same. Now, how long are you in port?"

"Well, that's kind of hard to say," Charlie replied as Chrissie extracted herself from Maggie's embrace. "But what does a man have to do to get a drink around this place?"

"In your case, not much," she said. "Rum?"

"What else would a man drink?"

Maggie looked over at Chrissie.

"And you?"

"No rum for me, thanks," she said. "Ale?"

"C'mon lad," Charlie said. "You're a sailor, you've gotta drink rum. The best rum in the world is here in the Caribbee, and Maggie's got the best o' the best."

"Might not be a bad idea to keep a clear head," Jack cautioned Charlie. "At least one of us needs to stay alert."

"Ahh, you worry too much," Charlie said. He turned back to Maggie and said, "Two rums, both for me, and ale for Chris. And Jack, you'll probably want something?"

Jack ordered ale. Maggie told off a group of men who seemed asleep at one of the tables, clearing a space for the three friends, and within minutes, Chrissie found herself sitting, sipping very cautiously from a tankard of ale. She wrinkled her nose against the bitterness of the brew – it was not unusual for people younger than she was to drink regularly, but Chrissie didn't like it. She took a small sip, then waited for Charlie to look away and surreptitiously poured some out on the floor, smiling and nodding when he turned back to her.

Charlie began a circuit of the room, talking and laughing with everyone he met. The noise in the packed room was loud, a cacophony of chatter and laughter and singing, but Charlie's laugh boomed over the tide of sound. Often he pointed to his nose, laughing, then back toward her at the table. Chrissie couldn't tell if everyone knew him, or if he was so naturally outgoing that he just made friends, but in the next hour he seemed to share a word or two, or a story or two, with everyone there.

Chrissie turned to Jack and found him with his back to her, chatting with a couple of sailors at the next table. Chrissie watched him laugh and talk, and again felt that lurch in her stomach. What was it about him, she asked herself? He was such a know-it-all, always quoting dead writers and making convoluted arguments, but he was also such a devoted friend to Charlie. He'd certainly protected Chrissie's secret and hadn't taken advantage.

Chrissie got up and wandered to the bar to talk to Maggie.

"So this your first voyage?" the bar owner asked.

"Aye! I've worked on fishing boats most of my life, but this is a whole new world."

Maggie eyed her keenly, then asked, "How old are you?"

"Sixteen."

"Really?"

Chrissie reddened.

"Well, fourteen, but I said sixteen to get the berth."

"Do Charlie and Jack know?"

"My age? We never really talked about ..."

"Not your age. Your ... "

Chrissie stared at her. Maggie just smiled and made a gesture that indicated a woman's curves.

"Look, it's nothin' to me. The rules about who can and can't work on a ship are stupid, I says, and if you want to be a boy and sail the seas, fine, no difference to me."

Flustered, Chrissie leaned across the bar until she was inches from Maggie so that her next words wouldn't be overheard.

"How did you know? What did I do? Is something showing?"

"No, no, don't worry dear," the older woman said. "It's just – well – men can be real sweethearts, and they're dead useful at times, but sometimes they can be a bit thick. Like old Charlie there. He's a wonderful man, but he sees what he expects to see. You tell him you're a boy, dress the part, and that's what he sees."

"You're not going to tell him, are you?" Chrissie asked.

"Who, me? I'd water down me rum before I'd tell tales out of school. You don't have to worry about Charlie, either. You're his shipmate, and that's all that matters to him. But I wouldn't go spreading it around."

"I've been careful. Only Jack knows."

"Ah, Jack. He's deep, that one. Lays it on like he's a regular salt, but there's more to him. Haven't figured out what yet, but I will."

A pause. Then Chrissie asked, "You've been in the Caribbean long?

136

"A fair time. Nigh on twenty years. Came out with me husband; he's long gone."

"When did he die?"

"Didn't say he died! Said he was long gone, and good riddance to him," Maggie retorted, laughing. "He certainly might be dead by now, haven't heard from him in a dozen years."

Chrissie glowed with embarrassment, but Maggie waved it off.

"He was a sailor. You know how they are," Maggie said.

"But you've been here a long time," Chrissie said. "You know the islands?"

"Ain't been to any besides this one and St. Kitts, but I knows of 'em pretty well. With the customers I get through that doorway I hear all the stories. Why?"

"Do you know of a place called Island of the Holy Cross?"

"Can't say I've heard that name, but wait." Her brow furrowed in concentration. From behind her, Chrissie heard a raucous chorus of laughter as Charlie finished a story. He looked at his empty mug, and then came back over to the bar for more rum.

"Just wait your turn, you big oaf," Maggie said. "You've gone and driven it right out of my head."

"But the rum ..." Charlie said.

"And don't you know where I keep the rum? Can't you go in the back room and help yourself as you've done a time or two in your life? I was talking to Chris here."

Charlie meekly accepted the dressing down, then pointed to his empty mug. Maggie pointed firmly to the kitchen. Charlie shrugged and went through the door.

"No now, what was it? He can be infuriating, that man. Always talking when you're tryin' to think of something. Island of the Holy

Cross? Well, no, I can't say I've heard of it, but there's an old fella often in here, knows all the islands. Nathan, his name is. Fisherman. They say he's been sailin' these islands since before Columbus. He might be able to help you. I don't see him here tonight, but he was in just a coupla days ago, so he's probably still on island. I'll keep a lookout and give you the high sign if he comes in. There might be some others here who know something about it. But watch yourself. They ain't all amiable as Charlie. Couple of 'em look like right bad 'uns."

She cocked her head toward the back. Through the haze Chrissie saw five men holding a huddled conversation around a table as they nursed glasses of rum.

Maggie had a tavern full of people to tend to, so she left Chrissie, who looked back at her own table and saw Jack now deeply engaged in conversation with several other men.

She turned to the man sitting next to her, a sailor with a grizzled beard and glassy eyes.

"Evening!" she said. He made no response. She tried again.

"Evening! Have you ever heard of an island called Holy Cross?"

The man didn't so much as blink. She extended a finger and poked him, and the man toppled face first onto the bar.

"Alright then," Chrissie said, "Good talking to you. I'll just try someone else."

Over the next ten minutes she introduced herself to the men around the tavern, trying to emulate Charlie. She'd give her name, slap someone on the back and say she was just in on *Skipjack* and wondering if anyone had ever heard of the Island of the Holy Cross. Most told her they hadn't, a few looked at her with curious or even hostile stares.

She found herself standing at the edge of a dice game, waiting until she could get the players' attention. Finally one of the men told her to put her money down or get out, so she fished a coin from her pocket and put it down. She didn't know what the rules were or what her bet signified, but it seemed to satisfy the men. The dice were rolled, there was much yelling and laughing, and her coin disappeared. One of the men looked at her.

"Well, are ya gonna stand there or you gonna play?"

"Actually, that was all the money I had," she said. The remark immediately cost her any interest the men might have had in her. They turned away and resumed talking among themselves.

"But I'm new in port and I was just wondering if any of you had heard of the Island of the Holy Cross."

The men clammed up immediately, staring at her with unmasked hostility.

"Why do you ask?" one of them said.

"No, I'd just heard of it on the voyage down and it got me curious."

"Well forget about it," the man said. "Don't stick your nose places it don't belong or it might get cut off." He turned back to his game.

"What are you up to?" a voice asked in her ear.

She spun to find Jack at her side. He took her elbow and led her away.

"What are you ...?" she protested.

"You've attracted some attention," he said quietly. "Just come on back and sit quietly. What were you doing?"

"Trying to get information," she said.

"And walking up to strangers and asking for it was the best plan you could come up with?"

"What do you mean? How else am I supposed to get it?"

"Look at Charlie," Jack said, pointing to their friend across the crowded room. "He's talked to everyone in the place practically, and probably picked up all kinds of information he doesn't even realize he has. See, he doesn't act like he's after anything. He's just talking, having a good time. He doesn't care. Whereas you seem desperate for information, which makes people not trust you. Speaking of which, we ought to get out of here. There's several other taverns we can check on, and I'm not comfortable with the attention you've stirred up here. I'll get Charlie. You stay here. Don't go anywhere – and don't ask anyone anything."

Chrissie watched him work his way through the crowded room until he arrived at Charlie's side. He waited while Charlie finished saying something to the sailors he was talking with.

She didn't even notice the man slip up alongside her until he spoke in her ear.

"C'mon outside real quiet like," he said.

"What?" she asked in surprise.

"If you want to know about the Island of the Holy Cross, come along right now. Don't make no fuss. Don't tell those friends of yers. Just go."

Chrissie looked at the thin, sallow man with long, greasy brown hair. "Who are you?"

"I said go – right now." The man smiled and nodded down. Chrissie realized he was pointing a small pistol at her under his arm.

As warm as the night was, Chrissie suddenly felt ice cold. She shot a glance at Jack across the room, but he didn't seem to notice. He was too engaged in explaining to Charlie that they needed to go. The man noticed her glance.

"Never mind your friend. He couldn't possibly get to you as fast as the ball in this here pistol could. Now go. Side door."

Chrissie rose and felt the man push her toward the door. She tried to look back, to do something to get Jack's attention, but the man crowded behind her, not giving her a chance.

He pushed the door open, and pushed her through. As she stumbled out, someone grabbed her and swung her around, crashing her into the side of the building. Rough hands turned her around and pinned her to the wall.

"Well what have we here?" said a voice.

There was little light in the alley and Chrissie couldn't see her attackers as more than dark shapes against the Caribbean night sky. There were at least three of them, maybe more, she thought. One man was on either side, holding her in place, and the third, a smaller man, stood right in front of her. There was nowhere to run, even if she weren't being held.

"Who are you, eh?"

"I ... I ... No ... " Chrissie stuttered.

"C'mon boy, out with it. Or we'll get it out of you."

The man held something out, and moonlight glittered off the blade of a knife. The man chuckled, then suddenly drove it forward. Chrissie shrieked as the blade dug into the wall just inches from her head.

The man stuck his face forward. She caught the glimpse of gold in the man's mouth, then was overcome as the stench of his breath hit her.

"You!" she managed to gasp.

The man in front of her was one of the men from the alley back in Hampton, the smaller one. One of the Leech brothers.

Chapter 26

Danger in the Alley

The man cocked his head as if puzzled. He grabbed Chrissie by the front of her jacket and pulled her away from the wall, trying to get a better look at her.

"Do I know you?" he asked.

"No. I was just ..."

"You was just about to tell me why you're so all fired interested in an island that you ain't got no business with," he said, pushing her back again.

"I'm not. I'm ... I just heard about it and wondered."

"Where did you hear about it?" he asked.

"From someone on ship."

"What ship, boy?"

Chrissie didn't know what to do. Should she tell them anything? These appeared to be some of the men who had her father. The only thing she knew about them was that they were dangerous, and their leader even more so. Her mind raced as she tried to decide if she should admit knowing who they were.

She had taken too long to answer. The man stepped in and suddenly she was on her knees, gasping for breath. He had punched her square in the chest, driving the air out of her. The men holding her released their grip and laughed as she toppled over into the dirt of the alley.

The leader squatted beside her.

"You're gonna tell us. You're gonna tell us everything. So why not make it easy on yourself? It doesn't have to hurt. Well, no, that was a lie. It's gonna hurt. But it might not hurt as much if you just tell us. So let's start again. Why are ya lookin' for our island? What business is it of yours? Who are you?"

Chrissie could see the wolfish look on the man's face, and heard the low chuckle from some of the other men.

"I'm looking for someone," Chrissie blurted out.

"Now who would you be looking for?"

"Someone told me he'd be on the Island of the Holy Cross."

"Then someone told you wrong, boy," the man said. "There ain't nobody there but us, and you'd better hope you're not lookin' for us. We're not real friendly. But maybe you guessed that already."

"I'm just trying to find someone, and that's what I was told. Now that I've talked to you," she struggled to a sitting position, "I can see I was given bad information, and I'll sure remember that."

"Well, now that's the problem, in'it?" the man said. "That you might remember." He looked up at one of his men and said, "Get me my knife."

"Aye, Seth," one said. Chrissie heard the sound of the knife being wrenched out of the wood. The one called Seth reached over his shoulder and the other man slapped the knife into his palm. He held it out so she could see the blade clearly. Her eyes locked onto it as he passed it slowly back and forth in front of her. Five inches of cold steel, honed to the sharpness of a razor.

"Listen close, young fella. I'm gonna ask you again who you're lookin' for, and if I don't like your answer, I'm gonna give you your first shave. Only since you don't seem to have much whiskers, it's your ears I'm gonna slice off, unnerstan'?"

Before Chrissie could answer, another voice interrupted.

"Hey! What you boys doin'?" demanded a voice thick with the accent of the islands. "Why you makin' trouble for that little fella, all five o' you big men?"

Chrissie looked up and saw a wizened old black man approaching down the alley from the street, leaning heavily on a walking stick.

"Ol' Nathan, he say five against one ain't fair. You let dat boy alone."

"Quiet, old man, or we'll make trouble for you next," one of the men said, reaching out to push him away. Instead, he found himself sprawled face down. The old man had twirled his walking stick high in the air, and brought it whistling down on his assailant's arm. Then the old man swung the stick around and shot it forward like a spear, catching the man in the gut, sending him sprawling face first in the dirt, gasping for breath.

"You shouldn't a'done that, Nathan," Seth Leech said, rising and brandishing his knife as he and his comrades advanced. The man on the right side jumped at the old man, but met the walking stick with his teeth and fell to the ground, whimpering and spitting blood. Seth looked startled for a second, but recovered quickly. He gave a low, short whistle, then he and his two remaining friends spread out like a hungry pack of wolves, covering the entrance to the alley. She heard the rasp of steel being drawn from scabbards; at least some of the men were carrying cutlasses.

The old man took another step back and Chrissie struggled to her feet and stood by his side. She looked about for something, anything, she

144

could use as a weapon, but the alley was empty. In answer to the whistle, three more shapes joined the men closing in on them, and began advancing slowly.

The side door Chrissie had been dragged through burst open, sending one man sprawling as Jack and Charlie stormed into the alley.

"What's going on here?" bellowed Charlie, picking up the nearest man and hurling him back into the others.

Seth Leech squared off with Jack as Nathan stepped forward brandishing his stick. Chrissie followed on his heels.

Leech feinted at Jack's eyes, then switched the blade to his other hand and brought it down in a high arc. Jack ducked and swung. There was a sharp "thunk" as the heavy book he had been carrying slammed into Leech's forearm. Enraged, the pirate switched the blade back to his right hand and sprang forward, driving the blade straight toward Jack's heart. Jack tried to pull back but the blade found its mark.

Everything froze. Looking on in horror, Chrissie saw Jack staring down at the hilt of the knife sticking out of the front of his coat.

Chapter 27

Enter, the Marines

Leech's face held a look of smug satisfaction as he waited for his opponent to fall. It changed to surprise as Jack reached down and pulled the knife free, then reached into his inside pocket and pulled out a small, leather book, which now showed a great gash from the knife.

"You Philistine!" he shouted. "That was Sir Thomas More!"

He tossed the book over his shoulder and held out the knife as if it was his turn to attack. But before he could, there was a shout from the head of the alley and the sound of muskets being cocked.

"Stand down in the king's name!" shouted a voice that could have taught Mr. Connelly a thing or two about volume. One of the figures brought out a lantern, and the light reflected off the dress uniforms of a squad of Marines. Even at that distance, in the dim light, Chrissie recognized the shape and the sharp, pointed nose of Sgt. Thorne.

Chrissie elbowed her way forward, shouting, "Sergeant! Thank God! These men tried to kill us."

She would have said more, but she was jerked back by Jack, who glared at her and pointed toward the side door.

Thorne had barely gotten a glimpse at the speaker, although his eyes widened slightly, as if he recognized the voice as the young person from earlier on the street. Scanning the crowd he also noticed Jack, who had lost his cap in the scuffle. Even in the dark, it was apparent what his hair color was. The sergeant turned to the Marine on his left.

"Corporal, arrest all of these men. We'll sort 'em out back on the ship!"

Without waiting for the Marines to take another step, Jack pushed Chrissie through the side door back into the tavern. Charlie was already moving in that direction and Jack snagged Nathan's arm and pulled him after. He slammed the door just as one of Leech's men grabbed for it, and they heard the man bounce off the mahogany panel and fall back into the alley. As Jack shoved a barstool into place to help secure it, they all heard the sound of a musket shot from the alley and the howl of pain from someone.

"Back door!" Charlie shouted.

"No good, They'll be right behind us." Jack said and whisking them back towards the barn. Turning to Maggie, he asked urgently, "Maggie, you have a basement?"

"Better'n that," she said. "I have a basement that connects straight through to most of the buildings on this street. Get movin'. Door on the left."

She hustled them through the kitchen door, turning and shouting at her alarmed clientele. "Press gang!"

Those two words were all that was needed to start a frightened rush out the front door, which blocked the Marines from coming in that way.

She led them to the basement entrance and told them how to access the passage between buildings.

"I'll be back as soon as I can, love," Charlie promised. "There's

147

something about you that just keeps drawing me back."

"My rum!" Maggie snapped.

"Aye, and your wine," Charlie said with a smile.

"Enough you big oaf," she said, pushing him away. "Right now you've gotta run. Just come back in one piece. And don't you touch my bottles down there when you're goin'!"

"I'll be back, you know it," he said, and clattered down the steps. As she started down after him, Chrissie nodded her head in thanks to Maggie, who winked in return. The last Chrissie saw of her before the basement door closed was Maggie opening the rear door and stepping out into the alley, shouting, "You there! Get back here! You haven't paid for my rum," as if yelling at fleeing sailors.

"What a woman," Charlie said as they crept down the stairs. "It's a damn shame I'm not the marrying kind."

"As long as you're the running kind," Jack said. Let's see what this passage looks like."

Jack and Charlie shifted crates that blocked the entrance, revealing an opening into a dark passage that appeared to run down the front of the block in either direction.

"Which way are we going? East or west?" Jack asked.

"My boat is tied up not far west of here," Nathan said. "Not a bad place to start, on the water, away from all those men."

Jack grabbed a lantern off the wall, and after a few moments with flint and steel had managed to light it. They followed its sputtering flame through the dank passageway. The tunnel ran right against the waterfront, so its walls were damp, the ground slimy and in some places puddled. Above them they heard occasional footsteps, and once even heard the sound of horse hooves clopping overheard.

They walked in near darkness for what seemed miles, although

Chrissie knew it could only have been several hundred feet. Jack had apparently been counting, because he suddenly stopped and peered at the wall on their right.

"We ought to be right at the edge of town," he said. "There has to be an opening around here, back into the basements."

He held the lantern up. It was Charlie who spotted the rubble strewn opening that led them into a cluttered room. At the back a flight of stairs led up, and Jack pushed the door open a crack. As no light came down, they all went up.

"Some kind of office or merchant," Jack said. "Keep quiet, someone may sleep upstairs. Charlie, Nathan, go check out the front window and see where we are."

Jack, meanwhile, unlatched the back door. "In case we need to run," he whispered to Chrissie.

Charlie and Nathan came back and told them they were within a few hundred feet of where the boat was tied up.

"And there's no sign o' them Marines," Charlie added.

"Right. Well, let's chance it, shall we?" Jack said. They all nodded agreement and stepped out into the back alley.

Chapter 28

Away from Nevis

After being trapped down in the damp tunnel, Chrissie thought the outdoor air smelled sweet, with the tang of salt and a hint of flowers. It was warm, and countless stars were shining in the sky above them. Fortunately, the moon wasn't out, and this far down the waterfront they were out of the glare of any lanterns.

"Lead the way," Charlie urged Nathan.

They dashed across the street and down the seawall to the rocky beach. A line of fishing boats was just ahead. Nathan signaled them to wait, then cautiously approached the third in the line. Chrissie had just begun to relax when they all heard a voice from in front of them, on the boat.

"Good to see you Nathan," said a voice that was all too familiar to Chrissie.

Leech and maybe some of his friends had beaten them there.

Jack immediately stopped, crouched low and signaled for the others to pause. He slipped between the two nearest boats and a moment later they could hear movement in the water.

"You shouldn't have gotten involved, Nathan," Leech said. "It's gonna cost ye. The lobsters got three of my men, and I don't take kindly to that. So tell me who those fellas were and where I can find 'em. I've got a score to settle."

Chrissie moved stealthily forward. She could hear the faint sound of Nathan's voice replying, but couldn't make out the words. Then there was a slapping sound, and Leech spoke again.

"That won't do, Nathan. Just tell me where I can find 'em." Then his voice shifted, as if speaking to a different person. "Keep an eye forward. I don't want no surprises."

So there were at least two of them, maybe more.

As Chrissie groped on the ground for something to use as a weapon, a second voice spoke up.

"It's no use, Seth. He either don't know or he's not saying. Let's cut his throat and be gone."

"Last chance, Nathan," Leech said. "You want us to leave you on the beach without a boat, or without a head?"

Chrissie's hand closed on a piece of coral – a bit small but all she could find. She was straightening up to make a run at them when she felt Charlie rush by.

He was on them so fast they didn't see him coming, and over his head he held his own piece of coral, this one big enough so that when it came down on the lookout's head, it left him slumping to the beach.

Chrissie ran up beside him and fired her chunk of coral in a tight overhand throw that flew true, hitting another man between the eyes, sending him reeling back to fall at the water's edge.

"You!" Seth Leech said. "How handy."

Charlie didn't bother with banter. Instead he whirled on the spot and sent a roundhouse punch whistling past Leech's chin. The narrow miss threw him off balance and Leech swung a punch that toppled Charlie over into the surf, gasping for breath.

Leech turned toward Chrissie, but before he could take a step, he was slumping to the sand. Standing behind him clutching an iron boat hook was Jack, dripping from his short swim to the stern of the boat. Meanwhile, Charlie was getting back to his feet, wet but otherwise undamaged.

"Get some line," Jack snapped at Charlie. "Chris, make sure Nathan's all right."

Chrissie found the old man propped against the side of his boat.

"T'ank-you, t'ank-you," he said, putting his head to his hand where blood was trickling down from a gash in his forehead. "Dey some bad men."

"Stand still here and let me see to that," she said.

Nathan protested that he was fine, but Chrissie forced him to stop moving. She rinsed the blood away, drawing a gasp from the old man, and satisfied herself that the wound was long but not very deep.

"Do you have any spare strips of cloth?" she asked him. "We should bandage this up."

"In de back," he said.

As she helped him to the small covered area in the stern that served as his home, Charlie came back down with spare lengths of rope. By the time Chrissie had covered Nathan's wound, Charlie and Jack had bound the three unconscious men. They were on their bellies in the sand, firmly trussed up with their arms behind them, their wrists bound to their ankles.

"That ought to hold them for a while," Jack said. "Nathan, I suggest we don't want to be here when they wake up. Is there anything you need from shore?"

"No, no. Nathan lives on de boat; everything I own is right here. So you can bet I was plenty worried when those men said they were gonna take her. Even more worried when they said they was gonna slit ol' Nathan's throat. If they took my head, I wouldn't need these t'ings, but if dey took my t'ings, I'd feel like I lose my head anyway!"

"What will happen to those men?" Chrissie asked, worry in her voice.

"Someone'll find 'em," Charlie said as he started freeing the bow line. "We left 'em above the high tide line, so they won't drown, but close enough that they'll worry. Maybe the Marines'll find 'em," he added with a sudden thought. "Press 'em right into the navy and they'll be one less thing to worry about."

Nathan slapped Charlie on the back.

"Ol' Nathan stopped worrying the moment you three came to his rescue. But now that we're ready to go, he's got a question. Where we goin'? And are we all goin' together?"

"It's your boat, and a fine one, too. So it's really your decision," Jack said. Then with a glance at Chrissie, he said, "But we were looking for an island, and if you don't want to go there, we'd sure appreciate if we could get us to a place where we could find a boat bound for the Island of the Holy Cross. Do you know it?"

"Sure, Nathan know all the islands round here. Holy Cross two, maybe t'ree days due west. But you won't find no boats going to Holy Cross. Nobody lives there. If that's really where you wanna go, Nathan will take you. After all, you saved my life. I guess I owe you. But we should get going. Those men might have friends who'll come looking for them.

"Men like that don't have friends, just accomplices," Jack said." But yes, let's move."

"But wait!" Chrissie said. "I haven't even told you the important part! Jack, the one in charge, the one who stabbed you – or stabbed your book, I guess. That one? He's one of the Leech brothers! They're here somewhere!"

Jack and Charlie both stopped and stared – Jack because he knew what that might mean, Charlie because he didn't.

Jack reacted first.

"All the more reason for moving fast," he said.

"But don't you see? If they're on Nevis, my father must be too."

"We don't know if they are, just that one of them is. There was no word about *Sea Devil* at the tavern was there Charlie?"

"No, couple of lads mentioned pirates, but no one mentioned Davy Leech."

"Maybe because they were too afraid to," Chrissie argued.

"Or maybe Leech is at his hideout, like that Silas person told you, and sent his brother ahead to scout things out. We just don't know."

"We could ask him," Chrissie insisted.

Jack looked thoughtful, then nodded.

"You're right," he said. "I don't expect him to say much but ..."

A voice shouted from down the beach.

"Marines?" Charlie asked.

"Do we want to stay around and find out?" Jack asked.

"But what about Leech?" Chrissie asked.

"He wouldn't tell us anything, and if he did, what good would it do if we're all in the brig?"

Chrissie sighed in frustration, but nodded.

"Cast off," she said.

Jack and Chrissie jumped out and pushed the boat away from the beach and out into the water. By the time they scrambled back aboard and got the sail rigged, they were moving away from the shore, but they could see forms running down the beach toward where they had cast off.

"That was close," Charlie said as he manned the tiller.

"But he could have told us where my pa is!" Chrissie said.

"*If* he had told us anything, which is unlikely. But it wouldn't have done us any good. If those are his crewmates, he's free now. If they're the Marines, he'll be in chains soon enough."

"Who are they anyway?" Charlie asked.

"Remember what I told you about her father?" Jack asked.

Charlie nodded, Chrissie took over the story.

"He's the pirate – well, not this man, his brother, Davy, Davy Leech – He's the pirate captain – and he has my pa."

"He *took* your pa," Jack said. "We don't know if he still has him."

"Stop being so cautious," Chrissie said.

"Considering what your lack of caution almost got you, it seems like somebody needs to be."

"You can argue about that later," Charlie said. "Right now, I just want to thank Nathan for stepping in and taking care of the boy back there."

Nathan stopped and looked at Chrissie, then back to Charlie.

"What boy?" he asked.

Charlie looked surprised.

"Why, this one here. Chris."

Nathan shook his head in surprise.

"Dis ain't a boy! Dis here is a girl. I figured that out right away."

Charlie laughed, but then caught himself, a puzzled look on his face. He turned to Chrissie, looked at her, started to smile, then looked closer, his eyes growing wide with shock.

"Good God, boy! You're a girl!"

155

Chapter 29

If I Were a Pirate

They were sailing west, the sun rising behind them and Nevis a blur on the eastern horizon. But Charlie still hadn't gotten over his surprise.

"I still don't see how I missed it, or why you didn't think you could tell me," he mused.

"I couldn't at first, or I'd never have been able to get on the ship," Chrissie said. "Afterwards, it was just easier. If I was going to be Chris instead of Chrissie, well, I had to be that way all the time for everybody."

"And I can't believe you didn't tell me," Charlie said to Jack.

"But it wasn't my secret to tell," Jack said. "Besides, what difference would it have made?"

"What difference?" he bellowed. "Holy leapin' narwhals! Me, actin' like ... well, sharin' crew quarters and ... well just generally behavin' like ... like ..."

"Like the great drunken lout you are?" Jack asked with a smile.

"If it helps any, Charlie, I never saw anything I shouldn't have," Chrissie said. "I was probably more afraid of that than I was of someone seeing me."

Charlie's face reddened as he thought about what Chris – he was still having trouble accepting that Chris was actually Chrissie – might have "seen."

"We're shipmates. You shoulda told me."

"I know, I know," Chrissie cut him off. "I know I can trust you. But I couldn't take any chances. Besides ..."

Chrissie paused, then said in a small voice, "I liked the way you treated me when you thought I was Chris. Like I was an equal. Like I belonged. I'm not saying I want to be a boy, but I liked the way everyone treated Chris. I'd hate for that to change."

"Well, your secret's safe with me," Charlie said. "Not that there's a lot of folks I could tell it to way out here. But if a mermaid swims by, you've got my word I'll not breathe your secret to her."

"You know we still haven't talked about what we're going to do when we get there." Jack said.

"I know what I'm doing," Chrissie said. "I'm going to find those pirates and rescue Pa."

"After what you just saw of those men?" Jack asked.

"All the more reason to save my father from them. What would be the point of sailing all this way, then turning around when I'm so close? Now that I know what I'm up against, I can be better prepared."

Jack threw his hands in the air in exasperation.

"There's no reasoning with you, is there?"

Chrissie nodded emphatically.

"I know why I came here, and I'm going to do it," she said.

"That's not a plan. It's a hope. I'm going to try to get some sleep."

With that he curled up in the bow and was asleep almost instantly.

They took turns manning the tiller, standing watch and catching a few hours of sleep. The sun raced them across the sky, setting in the west with a wild burst of colors against the darkening sky. And they sailed on.

The next morning, they were still alone in the middle of a vast ocean. There was little for Chrissie to do but wait, and help Nathan clean the fish his lines brought up for their breakfast.

As the day wore on, she sat in the bow, staring out at the horizon as if willing the island to appear, her excitement and frustration growing.

She pulled the tin flute from her pocket and idly began blowing a tune. The random notes began forming a pattern, and before she realized it she was playing "Eileen Aroon," the Irish ballad she had played for her father more than a year ago.

Jack sat down next to her, his thumb holding his place in the book he'd been reading.

"Nice," he said. "Have you been playing long?"

"Most of my life, I guess. I used to listen to my uncle play, then I picked it up. I'd play and Pa would sing."

"Given any more thought on what you'll do when we get there?" Jack asked.

"I have to wait to see what the situation is," she said. "How can I plan for it when I don't know?"

"Excellent point," Jack said. "Are you counting on a sudden, clever plan to help you overcome the pirates?"

"No," she shot back. "I'm counting on you boring them to death with your chatter."

"Boring?" Jack said with a grin. "I've been told I'm fascinating, a real tale spinner."

He held up his book.

"As Sir Francis here said, 'A wise man will make more opportunities than he finds,' another way of saying a wise man makes things up as he goes along," he said with a nod of his head to her. "But you'd better start looking for those opportunities, because that should be your island right there, right where Nathan said it would be."

Chrissie jumped up. Sure enough, a dark smudge had appeared on the horizon, right where the old fisherman had said they would find it.

"Don't look like much," Charlie said, scrambling to his feet.

"Oh, de Cross island, she's good sized," Nathan said, smiling happily at the tiller. "Not de biggest island, but big enough we won't sail away with papa all in a day."

Two hours later they could see details. A point of land stuck out like a finger from the eastern end, as if pointing the way back to Nevis. White sand beaches were interspersed with rocky coves, the hillsides covered with a greenish-brown growth. To the west, the hills rolled away in undulating waves of brown and green. Several higher hills in the west jutted abruptly toward the sky.

Chrissie felt a moment of dismay as she looked at the island. It was so much bigger than she had expected she wasn't sure where to begin.

"So which way do we go?" she asked.

"Anyone have a coin to flip?" Charlie asked.

"French used to have a town on de north side, and a harbor," Nathan said. "Might be some folks there."

"A harbor? Might be some pirates there," Charlie said.

"But the gentlemen we're looking for aren't the type you want to just stumble across," Jack countered. "They don't like surprises."

"Right then," Chrissie said. "The north side it is, but easy we go, and everyone keep a sharp lookout."

The sun had dipped beyond the bulk of the western hills as they rounded the eastern point and turned west to run along the island's north coast. The light had nearly faded as they passed a wide bay on their left.

"What's that?" Charlie asked, pointing to starboard.

His attention had been caught by a dark blur vaguely visible in the dying light, a smaller island off the coast. It looked to be about two miles off, and not more than a few miles wide.

"Island. So what?" Jack said.

"Nothin'," Charlie said. "But we almost missed it in this light. Maybe we oughta drop anchor and wait 'til morning so we don't miss anything."

Chrissie was disappointed but finally agreed with a sigh and a nod.

They steered the little boat into the bay and dropped anchor. Within half an hour they'd caught a few fish that Nathan cooked over a small brazier. Soon they were eating dinner while the last rays of the sun disappeared and the warm breeze blew off the sea.

"We're going to have to find fresh water soon," Jack said, glancing at the barrel. "That looks like two days at tight rations, maybe three."

"If there's folks on the island, maybe we can find something else to go with the water," Charlie said hopefully. "Hardest part of leavin' ship was giving up my nightly grog."

"Why didn't you say so?" Nathan asked, setting down his plate and crossing to the stern to rummage around in a locker. Finally he came back with a smile, holding a small black jug.

"If you're thirsty, dis may be what you're wantin'."

Charlie took the open jug and sniffed, a smile coming to his face. He took a long pull on the jug, then let out a small gasp.

"Wheeew," he breathed. "That's rum made by someone as knows a thing or two about makin' rum. Don't tell Maggie I said this, but that's the best rum I've ever had."

He held onto the jug, taking another, more carefully measured drink, before passing it to Jack.

Nathan laughed.

"Yeah, dat rum be made by a man I know down island, out Barbados way, he makes it special strong for Nathan. Got that and two more bottles left is all, but a little bit goes a long way."

Jack waved the jug under his nose and recoiled.

"I think I'll pass," he said, tilting the jug at Chrissie. "You?"

"No," she said flatly. As Jack turned the bottle back to Nathan she finished her meal quietly and stared out to sea. She chafed at the delay, but had to agree with the wisdom of waiting. The island was bigger than she'd imagined. Now that she was here, the task seemed more daunting.

As she stared, a light flared out to sea. She didn't pay attention at first, thinking it might be a passing ship. But after ten minutes of musing she realized the light had grown, and hadn't moved.

She stood and leaned out over the seaward rail, staring at the dark ocean before her. The light flickered, but it didn't move.

"That light out there, what do you think it is?" she asked.

Jack joined her at the railing.

"Looks like some kind of fire. A ship?"

"No, it's not moving. Isn't that about where that little island was?"

"Yes, yes it is," Jack answered, peering more intently.

"Think about it," she said. "A fire big enough to be seen from a couple of miles away, a small island secluded enough to be private, but right out near the shipping lanes for anything passing between Cuba and the Antilles. Does that sound like ..."

Her voice trailed off. In the dim light, Jack nodded in agreement.

"I'd say it's worth us taking a look tomorrow. That might be just the kind of place I'd stop if ..."

Charlie heard them talking and looked up.

"If what?" he asked.

"If I were a pirate," he said with a grim smile.

Chapter 30

Welcome to Pirate Island

Chrissie and Jack were in the bow, watching the small island draw closer.

The Caribbean was turning even bluer as they approached, the diamond clear water sparkling under the early morning sun. Chrissie had never seen anything like it. Schools of fish flashed deep below the boat, and below those were glimpses of coral reefs and deeper canyons.

But as fascinating as it was, the island rising in front of them held their complete attention.

They took turns with Jack's spyglass, scanning the green hillside rising up out of the emerald sea, looking for any sign of life.

"Sure looks like there's a ship there," Jack pointed out. "And that looks like a camp on the sand."

He passed the glass to Chrissie and she focused on the large dark object at the eastern edge of the little island. Through the glass she could see it was a ship, but sitting at an odd angle.

"Is it sunk or something?" she asked.

"Don't think so," Jack said, taking the glass back and staring at it again. "They've pulled her out of the water, probably careening the hull."

This made sense to Chrissie, who had often helped her Uncle Joe scrape and caulk the hull of his fishing boat. Getting rid of the tangle of kelp and sea life that accumulated on the hull made a boat faster and more maneuverable, both of which would certainly be desirable qualities in a pirate vessel.

They were now less than a mile from the island, and Jack told Nathan to steer more to the east.

"We don't want to sail right up to them," he said, "not without knowing more about them. Let's sail by at a nice safe distance and get a good look."

The beached ship was laid out with her stern pointing northeast, away from them. But Chrissie didn't need to see the name painted on the stern to recognize her. She remembered the graceful lines and the unusually long, thin bow with the carved female figurehead as it had lain alongside the pier in Hampton. No matter what the pirates decided to call her, this was *Gladys B.*

Figures were moving on the beach, and a few seemed to have noticed the approaching fishing boat and were pointing out at them. One of them was waving his arms over his head as if signaling them.

"Do we want to answer him?" Chrissie asked.

"I don't think so. Look up there." Jack pointed to the hillside above the camp. Chrissie swung the glass up.

"What?"

"Thought I saw a flash – like light on glass," he said. "Keep an eye on it."

A moment later she saw it. The sun rising behind them onto the eastern side of the island reflected off something about two thirds of the way up the hill. She concentrated on the spot and saw movement.

"What do you think that is?" she asked.

"Probably a lookout or two," Jack said. "Which tells us they're cautious about who is approaching them, and they're alert enough even this early in the morning."

"And they're a little lazy," Chrissie added.

"What makes you say that?"

"They didn't go all the way up the hill," she pointed out. "They'd have had a full view all the way around from the top, and it's not like it's that tall. Couldn't have been all that hard to climb, but they didn't want to drag themselves all the way up."

"Unless they've got a lookout on the other side," Jack pointed out.

"Maybe. But I'll bet not," Chrissie said.

"How much would you bet," Jack asked.

"Why?"

"Because if we think these are the lads you're looking for, we're going to have to land *somewhere*."

"They're coming out!" Chrissie shouted, shifting her gaze back to the beach.

A small crowd of men were dragging a longboat through the waves and tumbling in. As Chrissie watched, they began pulling at the oars, making straight towards them. One man stood in the bow, pointing at them and waving.

But the breeze blowing off the island kept the fishing boat moving fast, and it was soon clear the pirates wouldn't catch up.

On the longboat, the pirates stopped rowing, and the man who had been standing in the bow was bent over.

Then he stood again, and through the glass Chrissie could see what he was doing – aiming a musket at them! Just as she was about to shout, there was a puff of smoke.

"They're shooting at us!" she shouted.

Jack glanced to stern.

"I wouldn't worry," he said. "The odds are pretty long against them hitting us. Almost impossible."

"Almost? So if they kill one of us, it's just really bad luck?"

"Something like that."

"No worries!" Nathan said. "We're not getting caught!"

"They're turning back!" Chrissie shouted.

"So where are we going now?" Charlie asked.

"Anything else to see here, Chris?" Jack said.

She looked back at the camp. The ship's stern was now visible, cocked at a funny angle as the ship lay half over on its side. She could make out the lettering on the transom.

"It's them, all right," she said. "I can see the ship's name. Sea Devil."

"Well, that settles that," Jack said. "Now we know where they are, and with their boat on the beach it'll be at least another day or two before they're going anywhere. So the only question left is, how do we get in there?"

They kept straight on, as if sailing away to the islands they could see on the northern horizon. Once the small island had dropped out of sight, they turned back in, sailing for the western side of the islet, arriving on its northwest side with the sun setting behind them.

"Now what?" Chrissie asked.

"That's your call, isn't it?" Jacks said. "But I'd say there's only two options, over the top of the hill or around the beach. It's not a long walk either way."

Chrissie looked at the island for a long time, its beach and hill reflecting redly from the brilliant sunset behind them.

"Alright then," she said. "Who's ready to go ashore?"

Chapter 31

Finding Pa

The next morning, Chrissie and Jack set out to reconnoiter. They climbed to the top of the first hill, only to discover that they had to reach a second hill, slightly higher, to the northeast. It was that hill that overlooked the pirate camp.

They had left Charlie and Nathan on the boat, still visible offshore. From the boat those two would check the bigger island for any sign of fresh water, then poke around the pirates' islet looking for a path around to the camp to the north or south, out of sight of the camp.

From atop the island the ocean spread out around them, with no sign of any ships in any direction except directly below them, where the pirate ship was being careened. Chrissie felt lost, as if they were at the center of an empty arena where the rescue of her father was to be played out, alone and unobserved.

They crept to the top of the hill and lay prone, gazing down directly into the pirate camp. Chrissie strained her eyes impatiently as Jack thoroughly studied the situation through the glass. She could see figures moving on the beach below but couldn't make out what they were doing.

Finally, after ten minutes that felt like an hour, Jack nodded his head. They retreated back off the top of the hill slightly, to talk quietly.

"Their lookout is about a hundred feet below us, almost directly below," he said. "Looks like he's fallen asleep. Less than half the men on the beach are working on the ship. The rest are just laying in the sand, trying to stay out of the sun. Anyway, take a look and tell me what you think."

He handed Chrissie the glass and she crawled carefully back to the top and scanned the men on the beach below her.

They were a ragged looking bunch. Most were stripped to the waist and a few had only the skimpiest of rags wrapped around their hips. They were wiry looking, their muscles standing out like whipcords on their lean frames. Still, there were one or two larger figures, including a bearded giant who leaned against a palm tree watching the men work on the ship. He seemed more alert than the rest, and unlike the others she could see, he wore a cutlass at his side and seemed to have a pistol stuck in the sash around his waist.

Her eagerness to find her father defeated her, as she roamed from figure to figure too quickly to identify anyone. All the men she could see were bearded, some luxuriantly so, others with only a few weeks of growth, with uniformly tangled masses of hair hanging down their backs.

Chrissie closed her eyes for a moment, concentrating on her father's memory. Tall, broad shouldered, his blonde hair gleaming, his jaw strong and firm. She opened her eyes and looked again at the forty or so men below. At first glance, none seemed to match. She started staring at each individually, studying them.

That man was too short. The next too thin. That man hobbled about on a crutch, and his hair was lank and stringy. Another was the right height, but his hair was black.

One by one, for what felt like hours, she studied each, and each failed to match the image in her mind.

Jack nudged her and beckoned her back from the edge.

"Any sign?" he asked, offering her water from the bottles they'd carried. She was surprised to realize how thirsty she was.

"Not yet. It's hard to follow them; they keep moving around. And I can't make out the ones in the shadows under the trees. Then there are those tents; he might be in one. But he's there. I can feel it."

Jack looked as if he wanted to comment, but only nodded.

As the afternoon wore on and the shadow of the hill spread across the camp below, the men who'd slept or lazed in the shade began to stir, giving her more targets. But none matched.

She turned back to look at the men working on the boat. It made sense her father would be working. He hadn't joined the pirates willingly; he'd been taken because of his carpentry skills and they'd certainly insist he use them. Plus, he wasn't the type to idle.

A man hammering a new plank into place near the stern drew her eye. He was doing carpenter's work, but he was a short man, and his hair was a mousy brown. Still, she thought, he's hammering.

Then the man with the crutch limped over to where the first man worked. He looked bent and wizened. The man with the hammer crept down the side of the ship towards him and the two talked, the crippled man pointing to something on the boat, as if explaining the job. When he turned away Chrissie gasped.

The jawline, though covered with weeks of beard, was firm, jutting out into a prominent chin. And the man, though bent over the crutch and favoring his right leg, was tall. His hair was thin and discolored by the salt and sun, but it clearly had been blond.

It was her father!

Chapter 32

Among the Pirates

Chrissie stood to follow her father with the spyglass as he moved in toward the shore. And suddenly, she was pulled down sharply.

Jack had lain beside her in the scrub, alternately watching the camp and the lookout. Now he glared at her, releasing his grip on her blouse.

"Keep down!" he hissed. "The lookout has been awake for more than an hour. He's probably overdue to be replaced. And you gave anyone on the beach a pretty good silhouette if they looked up here, like someone about to take over lookout duty might."

"But it's him! I'm sure it's him!" she said.

"Quietl!" he whispered. He glanced over the top, then pulled back, satisfied that they hadn't been heard.

"It's him," she repeated. "Something's wrong with his leg; he has a crutch. But it's him."

"Good. Then part one is finished. Sun's heading down and the fellas are back with the boat. Let's get down the hill while there's still light."

"No, I'm going down into camp to get him."

"The hell you are," Jack snapped. He kept his voice low, but there was plenty of bite in it. "We found him. Great. Go down there now and the best you could hope to happen is you'd be captured next to him. Is that what you want?"

"No, but ..."

"And then Charlie and Nathan and I will have to go in and get you and they'll know we're here so that won't work. No, we did what we came to do. We found him."

"I didn't come to find him, I came to rescue him."

"Right. Let's get back to our boat and plan how to do that."

"You go. I'm staying here," she said.

"Wait ..."

"No, you wait," Chrissie said. "I won't be stupid, but we have to figure out what our best move is, and to do that we need to see what their patterns are. Leave me the water and that bit of dry fish and your spyglass. I'll watch them while you talk to Charlie and Nathan. I'll come down in the morning and we can figure out what comes next."

Jack looked uncomfortable with the idea, but he recognized that information about the pirates' habits would be useful, and if anyone was staying on the hill, it would be Chrissie. She just wouldn't give up.

"Alright," he said. "I'll be back up here at first light. Keep an eye on them and see if you can spot anything that'll help us. But Chrissie ..."

She looked at him.

"Be careful."

"Of course. I didn't come this far to fail now."

"Good. I'll see you in the morning. And I'll say it again. Be careful."

"Get on with ya," she said, smiling. "I'll be fine."

He looked as if he wanted to argue more, but he finally shrugged and started down the hill. She watched until he was out of sight, then turned her attention back to the pirates.

Chrissie waited for the sun to set, watching the pirates through Jack's spyglass. To haul their ship up on the sand, they had removed everything they could to lighten the load. All the ship's stores, supplies and cargo were stacked and covered on the north end of the cove. There were some crudely built lean-tos in that area, and some canvas strung up in the trees behind the beach.

Mainly she focused on the men moving back and forth on the sand. She got to where she recognized several of them right away, and began noticing several groups that seemed to stick together, as shipmates will.

They all seemed to be hard cases, but one stood out.

The bearded giant she had noticed earlier walked among the men, occasionally stopping to talk to one group or another group. It wasn't just that he was big, Chrissie saw. Through the glass she could see his face, overgrown with a thick black beard that extended a foot below his chin.

Chrissie flashed on the alley in Hampton, more than a year ago. This was one of the two men she'd seen talking with Davy Leech, the men he'd called his brothers.

Through the spyglass she tried to study his face, watching as he said something to two men, kicking at the sand in front of them as he did so, apparently snapping at them. His eyes were like two black holes burned in his ruddy, scowling face. Growing up in a waterfront town she'd seen hard cases before, some who had turned out to be generous, jovial men, and others who had lived up to the billing. This man took it to a whole new level.

Whatever he was saying, it was obviously orders. As soon as he turned away, the two men leaped to their feet and got to work. Soon a huge bonfire blazed on the sand and men were busy cooking, including two who turned a side of beef over the fire. She began to salivate and her stomach rumbled.

Chrissie reached into her bag and pulled out the few strips of dried fish Jack had left her and began chewing it, watching the activity below. The men lined up, received their portions of food and found places to sit and eat. On the beach, two barrels had been set up on the sand. The way the men made a beeline to it made it obvious it was rum.

She watched for another hour as the men – there must have been at least sixty now, she saw – lay in the red light of the bonfire. They sang and laughed, the sound carrying up the hill. Some capered in the sand in what they obviously thought was dancing. As time passed, they grew more awkward and more robust, the singing more roisterous, the behavior more obviously drunken.

In all of that, Chrissie never glimpsed her father. She hadn't seen him in the lines for dinner, the rush to the rum barrel, nor at the fire.

Where was he?

It had been two hours since the sun disappeared, and the pirates below didn't show any sign of ceasing celebration. By now she thought she could recognize pretty much any member of their crew.

She wanted a closer look. Her father had been on the beach, he must be near at hand and she had to find him. She remembered her promise to Jack, but decided she wasn't breaking it. She had said she wouldn't be stupid, not that she'd stay put.

Mindful of the lookout directly below her, Chrissie backed off the top of the hill and circled around to her left, making her way carefully until she was no more than a hundred feet above and to the left of the camp. The palm trees and brush were thicker here and the ground more uneven, so she didn't feel exposed.

Nearby the pirates broke into a new song. It was a version of one she'd sung with her father and uncle, but with different lyrics. Nearer now, she could make out the words and stopped for a moment. The song as she had sung it with her family could almost have been sung in church. These lyrics would have made souls in Hell blush, describing a trip to a "sportin' house" in Port Royal, with details that would have shocked Lucifer himself.

This wasn't just another group of sailors she was creeping up on. If they discovered her real identity, she didn't need to guess what they'd do. The song made it all too clear.

She dropped to the ground and crept forward, but stopped almost immediately. There were men right in front of her! But they were neither singing nor dancing. Apparently sleeping where they'd fallen, their snores punctuated the lewd singing. She shifted around them to the left and noticed a couple of tents under the trees about twenty paces away. If she wanted to slip around to the other side of the camp, where she could see crates and gear piled up and a couple of rude lean-tos built, she'd have to backtrack and work around them.

She lay there listening to the singing – fortunately, the men had finished their filthy song and switched to a plaintive ballad. One voice in particular, a high, clear tenor, broke out above the others. The song sounded familiar, and she realized she had heard it just a few days before in the tavern on Nevis. One of the sailors there had sung it, although his voice didn't have the clear, crystal tone of this pirate.

Thinking back to that night in the tavern, she suddenly heard a voice whispering in her memory – Maggie, the barkeep, laughing at Charlie, and at men in general. "He sees what he expects to see."

Chrissie stood up, made sure she was as disheveled as any of the men she'd seen on the beach, checked that her hair was tucked up under her wool cap and, without pausing to think if what she was doing was a good idea or not, pushed her way through the band of palm trees and into the firelight.

Reeling in the soft sand like a drunken man, she skirted the fire to the seaward side, avoiding the circle of men around it. She walked just at the edge of the light and no one said a word, no one challenged her.

The other side of the camp was near, just a dozen more staggering steps, then through the band of trees and into the area where crates and gear were stacked. She was almost there when someone came out of the darkness right in front of her.

It was the giant with the satanic look. One of the Leech brothers. He stood before her with arms akimbo. She might as well try to walk through a wall of solid stone as try to get through or around him. She stopped. He glared at her.

Chapter 33

Join the Circle

"Where do you think you're going?" the man snarled in a bass rumble.

She pointed into the trees. "Gotta take a leak," she growled back.

He bought it, but he didn't budge.

"Take it somewhere else! You know the rules. No one goes back there 'cept the captain or me without his say so," he said, taking a menacing step towards her. Her blood froze. "Drunk or not, I should take the skin off your back for comin' this way," he said.

"Sorry, my mistake. Gotta ..."

"I don't care what you gotta. Get back to the fire," he snarled, "afore I send for the cat and lay twenty on yer back. Cap'n wants a word with the crew."

With that he gave her a shove that sent her sprawling across the sand, then turned his head to the sky and shouted in a voice that would have made Mr. Connelly stand up and take notice.

"Avast thar, ye vermin! All of yiz Sea Devils front an' center. Captain wants your attention, and you'll give it to him or I'll know the reason why. Get up to the circle, you scabrous dogs!"

The men were pushed and prodded toward the ring of firelight. Chrissie held back, looking for a chance to make a break, but there wasn't any. She joined the group of pirates clustered around the fire, hanging at the back of the throng, trying to make herself invisible. She also tried to work out which would be the best direction to run if anyone noticed he had never seen her before.

"Avast!" the giant shouted again. "Cap'n Davy Leech!"

From the direction of the tent, a man broke into the circle of firelight. It was a familiar figure, one Chrissie had seen in periodic nightmares for a year. Across her memory flashed that day in Hampton, his leering gaze, probing dark eyes and air of menace.

Unlike the others, Leech was clean-shaven and dressed like a gentleman. He wore a greatcoat with a dozen brass buttons over a gold brocaded waistcoat, a pair of black leather boots over his white breeches. The only thing that marred his ensemble was the badly stitched slash in the back of the coat, and the dark bloodstain that hadn't been washed out. It was obvious how he'd acquired it.

The man turned and looked at the circle of cutthroats surrounding him, a smile on his face. This wasn't a friendly smile, or a smile of recognition. This was a smile that said he knew something the others didn't, and it delighted him. Without a word he commanded their attention. You kept an eye on him the way you'd keep an eye on a snake. You never knew when it was likely to strike, but you knew it would.

He was smart, he was cunning, and he was wicked. Not a good combination, Chrissie thought.

She eyed the circle of pirates but still didn't see her father.

The captain looked at them all as if enjoying a private joke. Then he spoke – his voice not loud, but oily and so well articulated that no one had any trouble hearing and understanding him.

"Stand easy, men, while I go over our plans."

"We'll finish careening tomorrow. Mr. Warren says he'll be finished pitching the hull, and we can put her back in the water."

Chrissie perked up at the mention of her father's name. Apparently there was some distinction between him and the pirates. That was good. She didn't know the whole situation, but she was pleased that he wasn't considered part of this mob of cutthroats.

"In three days we'll be back at sea. Seth and the boys are due back any day now – overdue, as a matter of fact – and they'll have news out of Nevis. Then we can sail down island to follow up on the sugar trade, or up to Cuba to see if the dons have provided any more ships for us. Either way a cruise of, say, a month to six weeks. Then we can circle back down to Tortuga."

"And we'll share out the booty then?" a voice from the crowd asked.

Leech shot an angry glare into the crowd, as if the point had been raised before and he was tired of answering it.

"Of course we'll share out the booty then. And why would we before then? Is there something you've found on this little island that you need gold to purchase?"

There was a light smattering of laughter at this.

"I'll say this once more. We keep the cargo together until we get to port. Don't worry, you'll all go into Port Royal with more gold in your pockets than most gentlemen can claim. And if I know you lot, you'll blow it all in two weeks and be begging me to take you back to sea," he added with a smirk, drawing even more laughter and some cheers.

"Now are there any questions?"

There were, mostly having to do with details of the planned cruise and division of labor for getting the ship back to sea.

Then a voice called out, "What about Chips?"

"Mr. Warren still declines to sign the articles. Therefore he won't have earned any of the loot we've amassed, so you won't have to share with him. He's been right useful these last weeks, but he ain't one of us; he chooses not to be. When *Sea Devil* is ready to sail we'll put it to him one more time. When he says no, we'll do what we have to do."

There was some muttering in the crowd. Chrissie was relieved to hear her father hadn't signed on yet, but also worried. There was a clock ticking on the rescue. Two more nights.

Another voice asked, "What about the navy and this talk about pardons?"

"What about it?" Leech said. "They talk about pardoning men for being free? For standing up like men and taking our rights with both hands? What are we supposed to do? Kiss the admiral's arse? 'Oh thank you sir, for pardoning us and we promise never to be men again?' Not me! Does anyone here feel like they've done anything they need a pardon for?"

There was a roar of 'No!' from the crew. Chrissie joined in so she wouldn't stand out.

"Anyone need forgiveness for being a man?"

"No!"

"Any of you want to go back to slavin' for merchants, suckin' rope on a cargo ship while the fat bankers in London and Barcelona get rich off our labor?"

A third, "No!"

"Well I didn't think so," Leech said. "Then let's hear no more talk of pardons. If the Royal bloody Navy wants to try stoppin' us, I say let 'em come! The crew of *Sea Devil* is ready!'"

The pirates roared their approval.

"I've put the plan before ye," Leech said. "Does anyone have any objection or other ideas?"

There were none.

"Then I call for a vote," he said. "All in favor, say Aye!"

The roar of ayes shook the palm trees.

"Now, before I break up this merry gathering, there's one more matter of ship's business to settle. Quince! Thomas! Stand forward for judgment."

Chapter 34

Dancing with the Devil

A hush fell over the pirate circle as two men came to the front. One walked confidently, the other edged nervously forward.

"Peter?" Leech said, and the giant stepped forward.

"Thomas," the big man said. "You have lodged a complaint against Quince here, claiming that he stole your knife and gave you the back of his hand when you called him on it. Is that right?"

The first man nodded.

"Quince? You deny that you took the knife?"

The nervous man gave a quick, nervous jerk of his head, and the giant continued in his rumbling voice. "And you deny that your behavior to Thomas was anything but respectful, as it should be among shipmates?"

Again the man nodded.

Davy Leech stepped forward.

"Has the knife been found? Was it among Quince's gear?"

"No sir, there ain't no trace of a knife such as Thomas and his friends have described, neither in Quince's swag nor Thomas's. And I didn't see it anywhere else in the camp."

"Dear me," Davy Leech said dryly. "There's no evidence. What are we to do? Thomas, given that there's no evidence, will you withdraw your complaint?"

"No, I won't," the man said firmly.

"How do you know it was Quince as took it?"

"He's had his eye on it for months, borrowed it once and didn't want to give it back."

"Quince? Have you anything to say for yourself? Will you return the property?"

"N-n-o sir."

"N-n-n-o sir," the captain mocked.

"I don't have it so how can I return it?"

"An excellent point. Do you deny you admired the knife?"

"It's a fine knife, sir. There's no arguin' that. But I didn't take it. I know my duty."

"Well, well," Davy Leech said. "It's a difficult situation. There's really only one way to settle this. You two will dance with the devil. The one who wins is telling the truth."

There was a roar of delight from the crowd of drunken sailors.

"Brother, bind them," Leech commanded. Peter Leech grabbed each man by the wrist. As he tied a rope around Thomas's wrist, the other man looked around the circle of firelight as if seeking escape, but he didn't move. Whether obedient, frightened or resigned to his fate Chrissie couldn't tell. The sailors in the ring looked away, unwilling to meet his eyes, as he searched from face to face for some way out of his predicament.

The moment when he might have tried to run was gone. The giant had grabbed him and tied the other end of the rope around his wrist. The two men stood now, blinking in the firelight, connected by about five feet of rope. Peter Leech drew a long sheath knife from his sash and plunged it into the sand between them.

"You know the rules; you've seen this before," Davy Leech said. "You've cheered with the rest of 'em. Now it's your turn to dance."

The two men looked at him, fear on their faces. He smiled.

"One of you can live. All you have to do is kill the other."

The two men were not evenly matched. Thomas was taller and broader in the shoulders, his arms heavily muscled. Quince was short and wiry, his beard grizzled, his skin turned to leather by years of sun and salty air.

Chrissie watched as the two men, silhouetted by the firelight, stared at each other. The surrounding pirates held their breath.

"One two three go," Davy Leech blurted out, and the crew's silence was broken by cheers, jeers and screams.

Thomas lunged for the knife, but Quince anticipated the move. Instead of diving forward he lunged back, using his opponent's momentum to pull him off balance, sending him flying forward to sprawl face first in the sand.

Without so much as a glance at the knife in the sand, Quince grabbed his opponent's bound wrist and leaped onto his back, twisting the man's arm behind him. His other hand grabbed Thomas's hair, jerked his head up, then thrust it sharply into the sand, leaning against the back of the man's head with all his weight.

The larger man's free hand desperately groped for his foe, but he couldn't get a grip on him. To Chrissie, watching horrified, it looked as if the fight would be over that quickly.

But the struggling man on the bottom squirmed frantically. He didn't dislodge the smaller man, but finally forced him far enough forward that he was able to roll out from under his tormenter.

The two men both found themselves on their knees, facing each other. Thomas threw a roundhouse punch at his foe, but Quince was too quick. He ducked the blow and lunged forward, his shoulder catching the bigger man in the gut. The breath went out of Thomas in a gasp.

The pirates ringing the fight were into it now, cheering the combatants. For the moment they seemed to have forgotten that both men were their shipmates, and just reveled in the barbaric spectacle.

The smaller man now was astride his opponent, a knee holding down the man's free arm while with his own he rained blows on the man's face. Thomas tried to squirm free, but Quince again used his momentum against him, flipping him onto his stomach.

As the crowd roared, Quince was on his bigger foe. Ignoring the knife, he took up the slack in the rope that linked them and looped it around the fallen man's throat, pulling it tight.

Chrissie couldn't see either man's face and she didn't want to. She did see Thomas's hands grasp at the sand, clenching and unclenching as he reached desperately for the knife just out of reach. The smaller man pulled tighter, arching the other's head back as his kicks and struggles grew more feeble and finally, after a last twitch, stopped.

Quince held on for another half minute or so, making sure, then finally released his grip. Thomas's body lay limp in the sand. The winner struggled to his feet, staggered to the knife which until that moment had been untouched, grabbed it and cut the rope binding him to the now-dead man.

"Well played, Quince," Leech said, grinning sarcastically. "I thought he had you there for a moment."

The man stared at Leech, gasping for breath, Finally he gestured toward the fallen man.

"I didn't take his knife," he repeated.

"As you've proved beyond a shadow of a doubt with your victory," Leech said. Then the captain's voice grew louder. "And let that be remembered by any particular friends of the dead man. Quince won the combat and has been proven not guilty. If anyone tries to exact revenge, he is committing mutiny against the crew and will be dealt with accordingly. Does everyone understand?"

As a roar of agreement went up, the captain's eyes darted around the circle, as if making contact with certain of Thomas's friends and warning them to put aside the idea of vengeance. For a horrifying second Chrissie felt his glance pass over her, then flick back for a moment before moving on.

"Very well, Quince, take your place at the fire. Someone get rid of this," he kicked sand toward the fallen man. Two of the pirates leaped forward and dragged the body away.

"Now drink up, lads! We'll have warm work to do in the next two days – Warren can't do it alone – and then we'll be back at sea."

The meeting broke up, men hurrying to the rum barrel. Chrissie took the opportunity to drift deeper into the shadows, then when she was past the line of trees, to turn and run farther from the camp.

She stopped behind a fallen palm tree, listening. There was no sound of pursuit. So far, so good. Part of her wanted to race back up the hill to safety, but she knew her work wasn't finished.

Carefully giving the tents a wide berth, she came across to the left side of the camp from the land. It took her more than half an hour to make it, but she was sure she'd avoided detection.

Unless her father was in one of the tents used by the captain, he had to be over on this side of the camp, she reasoned. There was no place else.

She made her way into the tangled pile of goods that had been removed from the ship to lighten it so that it could be pulled ashore.

Crouching low, she scurried between stacks of cannon balls, chests, crates, barrels, and the many items needed to keep a ship at sea.

The moon was dropping from the sky and the carousing at the campfire began to die down.

At the landward edge of the piles, Chrissie saw several tarps stretched over a pair of poles that had been driven into the sand. Approaching slowly she saw a pair of bare feet sticking out.

It might be a guard, she cautioned herself.

She tried to peer into the shelter as she drew closer, but the darkness defeated her. She put her head under the flap and let her eyes adjust slowly to the blacker darkness within. There was one man sprawled out, snoring. But it was too dark to tell who it was.

Then she saw something almost underneath her. Her heart jumped.

It was a crutch.

Very slowly, very carefully, she reached out and touched the sleeping form. There was a break in the steady, rhythmic breathing, but the man didn't stir.

She shook the man's shoulder ever so gently. There was a snort, and the man suddenly sat upright with a start. Chrissie clapped her hand over his mouth.

"Shhhhh!" she whispered. "Dan Warren?"

The man looked around wildly, and she shushed him again, pressing down more tightly on his mouth so that he wouldn't make a noise that would alert anyone.

"Dan Warren?" she asked again.

Staring into the dark at the shape over him, the man nodded his head.

Chrissie stifled a sob, then leaned closer.

"It's me, Chrissie," she whispered. "I've come to take you home."

Chapter 35

Don't Come Back

Dan Warren froze. Chrissie moved her hand away.

"Who are you?" he asked.

"Really, it's me, Chrissie," she said again in a whisper. "I've come to take you home."

"No, who...?" He peered at her. There was no light spilling into the tent so there was no way to see her face.

"On my 13th birthday, Uncle Joe gave me a tin whistle. I've brought it with me and when we get to the boat I'll play you a tune. You used to like to hear 'Eileen Aroon.'"

Silence, and finally, "Chrissie?"

"It's me, Pa."

"How did you get here? Why are you here?"

"I said if you didn't come home I'd come find you. Well, I have. I'm here to bring you home. I can explain it all once we're safe back up the hill."

"Is Joe here with you?"

"No. Look, we don't have time to talk. The sun will be up in an hour and we've got to be back up the hill. I'm here with friends and we'll get you off and away. But we've got to go now."

"Stop, Chrissie. Stop. If this plan of yours involves me walking up a hill in less than an hour, you'd best know it can't be done."

"Why not?"

"Look at this leg," he said, a trace of bitterness in his voice. "It got broke and never set proper. It's all I can do to hobble a little on the sand. You won't make a mountain climber out of me before morning."

"I can help you. Just lean on me."

"Chrissie, stop. You know I love you and I can't even guess how you got here. But you have to go. Get back up the hill, get to your friends on whatever boat you have and go back to Virginia. If Leech and his men find you here they'll kill you. These men ..."

"I know who they are. I know what they can do. They have no good in mind for you either, once they're ready to sail away."

"I'll face it when I have to."

"You'll have to now," Chrissie said, almost in tears. This was not how this was supposed to go.

"Chrissie, you've got to leave me and go home. I know it's hard."

"Hard? You mean as hard as making my way down here and finding you? Hard like that? I've traveled I don't know how many miles and been through fire and fighting, and if you think I'm just turning around and leaving you to die here while I slink back to Virginia, you don't know me at all."

The sound of someone singing drunkenly made them freeze. Dan motioned her for silence and climbed out of the flap, pulling himself up on his one good leg. She could see him scanning the area, his whole body tense.

Five minutes passed before he sank back to the sand and rolled back into the shelter. Turning back to his daughter, he spoke even more quietly and urgently.

"It's too dangerous even to try," he said. "I love you, and for the last year, thinkin' of you has been the only thing that kept me sane. But when I think of you, it's you warm and safe in Virginia with Joe and Mrs. Garrity looking after you. Knowing that you're safe is all I need to feel like I haven't wasted my life."

"Don't talk like that," Chrissie whispered. "We have to go. Now."

"No," he said. "I told you, I'll never make it up the hill, not even if we had until sunrise tomorrow. Not with this leg. But you've gotta get out of here, now. Before the camp starts stirring."

"All right. We can't make it out of here now. I'll get out and make some plans. I'll be back tomorrow and we'll ..."

"No!" he retorted. "Do not come back tomorrow. DO NOT. I'm your father and I want you to obey me on this. It's too dangerous."

"You're my father, and I'm not leaving this island without you. Like I said, my friends and I will figure out how to deal with this. But we will deal with it. I'm bringing you home."

Dan stared at her, and Chrissie realized with a start that there was now enough light for her to see his face. Time was wasting; she'd have to get out fast.

She let herself look at him once more. He looked old, tired, as if he'd been sick.

"I'll be back tonight. Be ready for me," she said. "He started to protest but she held up her hand. "Be ready. Or I'll drag you up the hill by your good leg."

He sighed and shook his head. Then with a grin, he told her, "I don't suppose there's much point in my telling you, 'Be careful,' is there?"

She shrugged and smiled at him.

The eastern sky was showing a touch of pink at the horizon. It must be nearly five, she thought. With the carousing they'd done the night before she didn't think the pirates would be up at the crack of dawn, but she had the lookout to worry about. Besides, Jack would return soon and she had to be there when he got back.

Satisfied that the coast was clear, she scuttled off into the brush, circling around to get back up the hill without being spotted.

If Pa couldn't climb, could she carry him? Could Jack or Charlie? All the way back to the boat? How early would they have to leave to make it out by morning?

Those and a dozen other questions filled her head, and she couldn't think of the answer to any of them.

The one thing she was sure of was what she'd told her father – she hadn't come all this way to say hello and go back home without him.

At the top of the hill she quickly found the spot where she'd left her few belongings. Crawling to the edge Chrissie glanced at the lookout post. Sure enough, there was a man below her, and whether he was the same guard or another, he was sound asleep.

She lay down and tipped the water jug back, draining the last of it. Then, without meaning to, she closed her eyes and fell asleep.

She awoke sometime later with a start. The sun was higher now, but she couldn't tell what time it was. She looked about nervously, but the lookout below hadn't stirred.

She watched for Jack to come over the rise to the west, but when she first spotted him, he was coming up almost due south. She waved and he signaled back. Ten minutes later he dropped to the ground beside her.

"Found a different route back last night. Didn't make sense to climb two hills," he said. "Instead I went down to the beach to the south, it's a nice easy slope all the way down, then around west on the sand to the boat. You'll see it's lot easier getting here."

She nodded, and he looked her over, with increasing scrutiny. Certainly she was even more disheveled than usual from climbing and creeping through the brush.

"I take it you didn't sleep," he observed. "Quiet night? See much?"

Chrissie hadn't thought of how she'd feel admitting to Jack what she'd done, but now was surprised to realize she felt sheepish, as if she'd let him down. She felt no guilt about her excursion, she'd learned some vital things, but she knew they'd end up arguing over her decision. And she also realized something else – she didn't have the answers herself.

So she said the four words that were as hard for her to say as any others.

"Jack. I need help."

Then she told him everything that had happened during the night, what she'd done, seen and heard. He was quiet, never raising a word of protest or concern as she talked about her father and his condition. She covered everything, gradually running down into silence.

Jack raised an eyebrow, then shook his head.

"What happened to, 'Don't be stupid?'"

"I wasn't. I had to find out and ..."

"You had to find out what it was like to walk across a pirate camp and stand with them, watching them kill each other?"

"Well, no, but once I was there, there was no way out."

"You shouldn't have been there at all."

He didn't raise his voice, didn't call her headstrong or stupid. Somehow, that was worse. His calm acceptance gave her nothing to fight back against.

"There's no point in arguing," Chrissie said sullenly.

"I'm not arguing," he said. "I'm pointing out that you led me to believe it was safe to leave you alone. I see I was misled."

"Look, I did it and it's over and now I need to come up with a plan. But I don't know what to do. He can't climb up here, and even your new route is too long for him. Can we rig a sling or something and drag him, maybe?"

Jack waved for her to be silent and looked out over the edge. He put a finger to his lips and stared down. Finally, he rolled back down the few feet to where she waited.

Very quietly, he said, "He's awake, and seems a bit confused, like maybe he heard us and can't figure out who's talking. Grab the stuff, we've got to get out of here."

"I told you," Chrissie whispered. "I'm not leaving without Pa."

"I didn't say we were. But we need to get back to the boat. If all four of us put our heads together we're bound to come up with something."

They quickly and quietly assembled their gear, trying to remove any sign that they'd been there on the off chance that the guard got curious and checked.

Chrissie then crawled back to the top and peeked over. The lookout was laying down, whether staring out to sea or asleep again, she couldn't tell.

She took Jack's spyglass and swept the pirate camp once more. She could see where the fire had been last night, where the man had died. And the tents, and the stacked goods from the ship.

Most importantly, there were the first signs of activity on the beach. By day's end the ship might be off the sand and floating again in the cove.

It would have to be tonight, Chrissie said.

She just hoped the four of them could come up with a plan.

Chapter 36

Sign or Die

She and Jack rushed downhill – he was right, his new path was much easier. They joined Charlie and Nathan on the boat and she again described everything she had seen and done.

They talked briefly, then all three men insisted that Chrissie sleep. She protested.

"The clock is ticking," she said. "We've got to go tonight."

"Aye," Jack agreed. "We've got to go tonight, and we won't be able to if we're exhausted. You can hardly see straight, let alone plan. Four hours of sleep, then we'll wake you and talk."

"Yer eyes look like two holes burned in a blanket," Charlie said. "It won't hurt for you to get a nap. We won't do anything without you."

Protesting, Chrissie settled in the stern of the boat on a pile of nets and spare canvas. Before she knew it, she was asleep.

When she awoke, the sun was halfway down the western sky. She jumped to her feet and saw the boat had been pulled in close to shore. Only Nathan was aboard.

"Why did you let me sleep so long?" she demanded.

"Not so long," Nathan reassured her. "Six hours, mebbe seven. You needed sleep."

"No, I need to figure out how I'm getting my father across this island."

"We talked a lot while you were dreaming, have some ideas. Right now we eat." He motioned to the beach, where Jack and Charlie were tending a small cook fire.

Dinner was fish – but at least it wasn't salted fish. While Chrissie slept they had caught several red snapper they were now cooking over the fire. Chrissie was ravenous, and sitting in the sand she polished off almost a whole fish by herself, along with the jelly and meat from a ripe coconut.

When she looked up from her meal she realized the men were watching her with amusement. She opened her mouth to protest and was surprised when a small belch came out. They all broke into laughter.

"What?" she asked.

"Nothin'," Charlie said. "Just never seen anyone eat so much so fast. Not even me."

"I was hungry," Chrissie said. "Now can we get to work?"

"Well, the conclusion is pretty clear," Jack said. "Like the saying goes, 'If the mountain won't come to Mohammed, Mohammed must go to the mountain."

Chrissie looked confused.

"Who's Mohammed?"

"It's Sir Francis Bacon."

"Mohammed is Sir Francis Bacon?"

"It's another saying," Jack said with a sigh, "Never mind, here's what I think we ought to do, but it's up to you. You're the one taking the risk."

Two hours later, Chrissie was back at the top of the hill as the sun set, this time accompanied by Charlie. The camp below was shadowed by the bulk of the hill. Even the lookout post was dark. With the spyglass Chrissie could see there was no one there.

In the cove, the pirate ship bobbed in the water.

"This is it," she said to Charlie, and beckoned him to follow her.

Chrissie took no chances. She circled around to the north of the hill, the side she'd climbed that morning, and scuttled across the broken terrain. Charlie was slower, crouching and stumbling down the uneven surface while trying to keep hidden.

It was fully dark when they reached the bottom, with the light of another bonfire south of them on the beach.

Creeping through the foliage to where the ship's goods were stacked, Chrissie peered through the trees. The piles of stores were already smaller, likely transferred back to the ship.

Charlie joined her at the tree line, and then Chrissie – checking to make sure her hair was under her cap and her attire suitably disheveled – slipped in among the stacks of ship's supplies, working her way toward where her father had slept.

Voices rose just ahead. She crawled closer to make out who was speaking and what he was saying.

"I've told you before and and I'll say it again, I'll not sign," her father said.

"I'm truly sorry to hear that," Davy Leech replied. "You're good at your work. Anyone can see that. You're a good man. I'd love to have you with us. But we won't make anyone sail with us that don't want to. We're a free association of gentlemen rovers ..."

"Gentlemen?" Dan snorted.

There was a pause, then a muffled sound of pain. Chrissie peeked around the barrel and almost rose to her feet. The captain's giant companion, his brother Peter, stood over Dan, his massive hand pushing the carpenter down to his knees. Standing in front of them, his back to Chrissie, not ten feet in front of her, was Davy Leech.

"See, it's that attitude that ain't going to help with the crew. We're all brothers, and equals. You ought to keep that in mind. An insult to one is an insult to all. I don't think my brother here takes kindly to your attitude and neither will the crew. Especially ..."

Davy Leech's hand stole into his coat's inner pocket and produced a long, thin object that glittered in the lamplight.

"Especially after I tell them we found this among your things." He knelt down and tucked the object into Dan's sash. "A very nice knife. I believe it belonged to Bart Thomas. Pity he died accusing the wrong man. He had several good friends in the crew who'll be eager to avenge him when they find it on you, and of course no one wants to sail with someone they think is a thief. It'll go hard on you, probably be very ugly, if they find out. This could be our little secret – if you stop being so stubborn and sign the articles."

Dan grunted.

"If they think I'm a thief? You know I didn't take that. You stole it. Why would they think I'm a thief, unless you lie to them about me?"

Leech's brother swung a heavy hand, hitting Dan in the back of the head and sending him sprawling face first into the sand. The pirate captain chuckled as he stood over the carpenter.

"Who do you think they'll believe? You? Who has spurned their company repeatedly? Or me, their captain? No, you've got a choice to make. Either sign and live, or don't sign, and die tonight on this island. It ought to be quite a show. Those are your only choices. Understand?"

Chrissie saw her father stare up at the captain without responding.

"I said do you understand me?"

Peter Leech pulled Dan to his knees, doing something hard and painful to the bones in Dan's shoulder. Chrissie saw her father grimace, then jerk his head in assent.

"Good," the captain said. He gave a nod and Pete shoved, toppling Dan Warren into the sand.

"I'm glad we understand each other," Leech said. "You'll soon be called to the circle. You've rejected our company before, but tonight you'll come to the fire and I'll put it to you. If you continue to resist, the crew will vote on your fate. You're a good carpenter, but we can find another. So I think I know what the vote will be."

"Come on," Leech said to his brother. "Let's leave Chips to think about things. Peter will be back for you. Think it over, or say your prayers."

CHRISSIE WARREN: PIRATE HUNTER

Chapter 37

Escape

Chrissie waited until the brothers retreated toward the fire. Then she gave a wave to Charlie and dashed forward to where her father lay sprawled.

"Pa," she said, her voice hushed.

"I told you not to come back," he said.

"And I told you I'm getting you out of here," she said. "This here's Charlie."

"Don't be fools. There's no way you'll get me up the hill in an hour."

"We don't have to," she said. "We're going up the beach a few hundred yards. They're bringing the boat around and it will meet us there."

"Then go to the boat. I'll be fine," he protested.

"No, you won't be fine! Look, I didn't come here to fight about this," Chrissie said. "If they come back and you're still here, I'll be standing right by your side."

"No ..."

"Only way to stop it is to come with us – right now," she said.

Charlie leaned forward.

"Charlie Stickle and pleased to meet ya, sir. Any shipmate of Chris's is a shipmate o' mine, and so forth," he said. "But the boy is right..." Dan looked puzzled at the words, but Charlie continued. "If we're gonna get out of here, now is the time."

Dan Warren sighed and nodded, putting his hand on Chrissie's shoulder.

"I'm not as spry as I was. Poor Mrs. Garrity will be so disappointed. You know how she loved my dancin'. Now help me up."

"That's what I'm here for," Charlie said. "You're a big man but I dare say I can carry ye."

"No, just fetch my crutch and keep me from toppling over. I'll make it."

Chrissie got him to his feet.

"Where's your crutch?"

"Over by the lean-to," he said.

"Anything you need to take with you?"

"From here? Nah. Now that I think about it, getting away is sounding better and better. Let's hurry."

Chrissie dashed to the lean-to, less than a dozen steps away. Dan turned to Charlie.

"Where did you meet?" he asked.

"We were crewmates on *Skipjack*," Charlie said.

"Crew ... You mean ...?"

Dan didn't get to ask his question. At that moment Chrissie hurtled through the air and fell into him, knocking them both tumbling onto the sand. Behind her loomed Peter Leech, who had thrown her.

"Good," the behemoth said, "I was hoping we wouldn't have to wait for the vote. Kinda wanted to do this meself without that rabble spoilin' my fun."

He laced his fingers together and flexed, cracking his knuckles. Then he swung his arms a few times. He reached down for Dan's shirtfront, pulling him up.

Laughter burst from the direction of the fire, where the pirate crew was gathered to carouse. A couple of voices broke into song.

Chrissie shook her head, pulling herself to her hands and knees. She caught a motion and flinched, but it wasn't the giant about to hit her, it was her father falling to the ground as Peter Leech turned to take on Charlie.

Charlie's first blow cut through the air in front of Leech, doing no harm. Leech threw his own punch, but it too sailed wide as Charlie dodged away.

Both men were broad-shouldered and stocky. The pirate was the taller by a good six inches, and his reach was longer. But Charlie was hunkered down, almost like a turtle, so most of Leech's punches bounced off the top of his head.

Charlie stepped inside and delivered a pair of blows to Leech's ribs, drawing a grunt of pain. But when he tried to pull back for a swing at Leech's jaw, the bigger man was able to block Charlie's punch, step inside and fire a right cross that hit Charlie squarely between the eyes, sending him reeling backwards where he crashed into a stack of crates that toppled over.

Chrissie pulled herself on her feet and dragged her father up. Charlie was getting back up, shaking his head to clear the cobwebs.

"Go, Chris!" Charlie said. "I'll finish this fella and be right behind ye."

This pronouncement brought an evil chuckle from Leech, a sound that sent a chill down Chrissie's spine. Even more frightening, however, was that the singing and carousing from the fireside faltered. It hadn't ceased, but there was a definite break, as if some of the pirates had heard the commotion.

Charlie put up his hands again as if to trade punches, but instead he leaped suddenly forward with a yell, wrapping his arms around Leech's chest and hurling them both to the ground. He landed a solid shot to the bigger man's jaw. But Leech rolled away as Charlie swung again and the blow went wide, leaving Charlie sprawling in the sand.

Chrissie half supported, half dragged her father to the edge of the clearing, then looked back.

Peter Leech was on his knees, his hands locked around Charlie's throat. Charlie pummeled desperately at the big man, but Leech ignored the blows.

She could hear the sound of men approaching from the fire and knew she didn't have much time. Casting about, she spied tools that had been leaning against the side of the crates. Seizing a marlinspike, she raced back over to the struggling pair, the long, metal lever in tow.

Leech's attention was firmly on his foe. An evil smile crossed his face as Charlie's resistance grew feeble. But he became aware of Chrissie's presence just as she wound up and uncorked a swing at his head. His eyes widened and he tried to duck, but he didn't make it.

The heavy instrument connected with a solid crack across the back of his skull.

He sprawled face first in the sand, not stirring. Charlie gasped for air as Chrissie pulled him to his feet and pushed him toward her father.

"Go! I'll be right there," she shouted.

The sound of men approaching grew louder. Chrissie ran to the fallen man and pulled him over. He was breathing, but barely.

"What's going on here!" shouted a voice. "Who the hell are you?"

Chrissie didn't pause. She found the gun butt and tugged it from Leech's sash, praying he was a man who never went about with an unloaded pistol. Pulling the hammer back, she grasped the butt tightly, pointed in the general direction of the oncoming voices, and squeezed the trigger.

A click, a flare, and then an explosion, all within the space of a second but seeming to take forever. The gun bucked in her hand and she had the impression of men diving for cover. Dropping the pistol, she ran back to Charlie, who now half supported, half carried her father.

Behind them the camp was in an uproar. Chrissie hoped they'd had plenty to drink.

They burst out of the fringe of trees onto the white sand beach about half a mile north of the camp. She and Charlie helped Dan hobble down the sandy strip, staying close to the water's edge. It was slow going, and Chrissie thought her lungs would burst as they trotted through the surf, all the while staring out to sea for some sign of the fishing boat.

And there it was, turning in to the shore. Leaving Dan to Charlie's care, Chrissie waded out and caught the line Jack tossed, pulling it in closer.

A cry from the beach brought her head around. Charlie was wading out, supporting Dan. A hundred feet behind them, in the sand, were the shadowy figures of running men. They'd been spotted!

Charlie heaved Dan over the side, into the waiting arms of Jack. Then, he leaped over, falling onto the deck.

Chrissie grabbed the bow of the boat and pushed it to face the sea. Scrambling to the stern, she began pushing it through the waves.

The sound of splashes told her the pirates were right behind her.

"Pistol!" she shouted to Jack.

He didn't hesitate, but tossed her his pistol. She turned, pulling back the hammer, and aimed it at the closest man.

It was Davy Leech himself. He stopped and stared at her in the moonlight as he leveled his own pistol at her.

"I don't know who you are, but there's no place on the ocean far enough for you to hide," he said. "So one of us had best get this over with."

As Chrissie aimed her pistol, the pirates who'd been following Leech scattered left and right, but he didn't give an inch, aiming his pistol at her.

They fired at the same instant. Blinded by the flare, Chrissie couldn't see what, if anything, had happened. She felt something blow by, fanning her face with the breeze of its passage, heard it slam into the stern. Then a hand grabbed her collar and she was hoisted bodily over the railing and dumped unceremoniously on deck. Another splash, and the boat began moving out past the waves. Jack had jumped overboard and pushed her out, then vaulted aboard as Chrissie and Charlie manned the oars.

A breath of wind from onshore puffed out the sail, and the little boat picked up speed. With her back to the bow, Chrissie could make out shapes on the shoreline.

"Did I hit him?" she asked, panting for breath.

"Can't say, I was busy," Jack said, pulling the sail taut to get every bit of advantage from the quickening breeze. "You got away from him; that's not a bad thing."

"Everyone falling left and right," Nathan said from the tiller. "Don't know if dey were jumping or got shot, but everyone went down."

"That was Leech, that was the captain," Chrissie said. "I hope I got him."

"I do too," her father's voice answered from the bow of the boat.

"That giant was really his brother?" Chrissie asked.

"He always said he was and I had no reason to doubt him," Dan answered.

Jack broke into the conversation.

"You must be Chris's father. I'm Jack Farmer. We can chat later. Right now let's lay onto those oars. We've got to be well clear as fast as we can."

"But we're away, we escaped!" Chrissie said, a feeling of elation rising in her.

"We're away; we haven't escaped," Jack said. "Those fellas have their own ship, remember? I dare say it's faster than this one, no offense, Nathan. It'd be very wise to be over the horizon by sun up."

"But they haven't finished restocking," Chrissie protested. "They'll need a whole day to move all that stuff back aboard their ship."

"If they decide to wait," Dan said. "They could raise anchor as soon as they get their ballast below, a few hours at most. It's seaworthy. I ought to know; I'm the one who made it so."

Chapter 38

We're Not Home Free Yet

The sun broke over the horizon to find the fishing boat sailing free under a fresh breeze, the oars shipped and the crew – now five strong – resting. Nathan was at the tiller, and all the canvas they carried was stretched on the spars, taut in the wind.

"I'd say we're making five knots, maybe a little better," Jack said. "If I'm right, we ought to make Tortola right around nightfall. That sound right, Nathan?"

The old man smiled and nodded.

Chrissie kept looking back. The small island had disappeared into the larger bulk of Holy Cross. There was no sign of pursuit.

"It's hard to believe that was so easy," Charlie said.

"Easy?" Chrissie replied incredulously. "That was easy? I'm sure glad it wasn't hard."

"All things considered, it could have gone a lot worse," he said.

"I think it's time for some stories," said her father. "How in the world did you find me? Why in the world? It's incredible, and incredibly dangerous! Reckless even."

"I knew you couldn't be lost at sea, not you. I knew you were alive and needed help, so I came for you," Chrissie said.

"I'm with your pa on this one," Charlie said with a smile that belied his words. "It's kind of amazing. But I'd like to hear the whole story too, if you don't mind."

"And I told you from the first I thought it was hopeless," Jack chimed in. "Yet here we are, the hard part done, or at least I hope so. I'll rest easier when we're out of the Caribbean."

"And Nathan always likes a good story," the fisherman grinned from the stern.

Chrissie looked around her and realized all four of her companions were focused on her. She breathed deeply and looked at her father.

"Well, these fellas know the outline – I told them my father had been captured by pirates and I'd come down here for you," she said. "And they offered to help – even insisted on it ."

"Because that's what shipmates do," Charlie said.

"Now wait," Dan protested, pushing himself up and grasping the mast to steady himself. "Are you telling me you've been disguised as a boy since you left Hampton?"

Chrissie cast her eyes down and mumbled, "Yes, sir."

Dan Warren stared at his daughter in disbelief.

"Chrissie, that was foolhardy! Anything could have happened. What about your uncle? And Mrs. Garrity? Do they have any idea what you were up to?"

"Of course not! Joe would never have allowed it, and Mrs. Garrity would have... well, she'd never have let me out of the house again."

"Where do they think you are?"

"I left them a letter that they'd find after I was gone, so they wouldn't worry about me."

Dan's eyes widened in amazement.

"You told them the girl they'd been raising had dressed as a boy and signed aboard a merchant ship, and sailed to the Caribbean to rescue her father from pirates, you told them all that so they *wouldn't* worry?"

"Well, when you put it that way, it sounds bad."

"What other way could I put it?" he demanded.

"I told them not to worry, that I'd be back in four to six months and I'd bring you with me. I didn't tell them how I was getting down here, but I said 'don't worry.'"

"Oh, so you said not to worry. That's good enough then, isn't it? Don't see why they should lose any sleep at all, if you told them not to worry."

Chrissie's felt the blood rise to her face. She stood facing her father, fists on her hips.

"And I was right, wasn't I?" she shouted. "I found you, got you out of there, and now we're on our way home. There was nothing to worry about. And who are you to talk about not worrying people? How many times have you signed on a ship and told me 'Don't worry?' How many times have I watched you sail off not knowing if you'd come back, and had only your 'don't worry' to hold onto? And I didn't worry, because you told me not to and I believed you.

"But this time you didn't come back, and what was I supposed to do? Just keep waiting? Accept it as God's will? Or go find you? I know what you would have done, so that's what I did. Seems to me like I didn't come a moment too soon."

Dan Warren stared at his daughter with a look she couldn't read. Finally he nodded.

"You're right. You're right," he told her, tears welling in his eyes. "And I'm happy to be out of there. But don't you see how it would kill me if anything had happened to you while you were looking for me?"

She threw her arms around his neck, hugging him for the first time since he'd boarded *Gladys B.* more than a year ago. Half pulling, half carrying him out of the pirate camp hadn't counted. This was a hug.

She could feel him sway, having trouble staying on his one good leg, so she shifted her weight and helped him ease back down to a sitting position on the deck.

"Don't worry Pa," she said. "I'm here, and we'll get you home and fixed up."

Dan shifted uncomfortably, then his hand stole down to the sash at his waist and pulled out the knife Leech had stuck there. He looked as if he were going to throw it overboard, then looked at it again.

The blade shone in the sun, eight inches of glittering steel, the edge honed to razor-like perfection, the spine engraved with a filigree pattern that ran from just below the point to the guard. The handle was wrapped in tooled leather that carried the filigree pattern down to the butt, in which a black stone was set.

"It's beautiful," Chrissie breathed. "No wonder Thomas ..." She stopped, remembering the pirate's hand clutching vainly in the sand as he was choked to death.

"You know about that?" Dan asked.

"I was right there in the circle. I saw it."

"I wish you hadn't," Dan said. "And now you know what really happened. Leech had it in for Bart Thomas, and he stole the knife – or more likely had his brother steal it. Then when the man accused someone else, he made them fight to the death over it. Just for fun. Watched them fight like animals because it amused him. That's the kind of man he is. Never forget it."

He jammed the knife into the ship's rail.

"As if I could," Chrissie said.

There was a cough, and she looked up. The other men had been pointedly looking away, not wanting to intrude on the family squabble. Now Jack was calling her attention to the stern, handing her his spyglass.

"Get on up the mast and see if you can see any better from up there," he said. "It's hard to be sure yet, but I think there might be a ship getting under way."

"You think it's ..."

"Oh, it almost has to be our friends from the island," Jack said. "We're not home free yet."

Chapter 39

Race to Freedom

Chrissie scurried up the short mast and wrapped her legs around the spar so she could use both hands to steady the glass.

"This could get very interesting," Jack murmured as he followed her up.

Calling down to the deck, he asked, "Mr. Warren! How fast would you say their ship is?"

"Fast," Dan replied. "I know she made eight knots in a strong wind. In a wind like this she could probably make five or six. Especially ... oh damn!"

"What" Jack shouted down.

"We just careened her," Dan said. "She'll be faster than ever. I'm afraid I'm good at my job."

"How could they raise anchor so fast?" Chrissie asked. "Most of their stores were still on the sand."

"They must have left most of their stores behind, figuring they could hunt us down, then return and pick up the rest of their things at their leisure," Jack said.

"Well, if we're lucky they didn't have time to load up the guns," Chrissie said.

"Maybe, but it's a safe bet they're still better armed than we are." Jack snapped the spyglass shut and handed it to Chrissie.

"Seems like they're headed north or a shade nor'-northwest right now, towards St. Thomas. If we're lucky we'll slide away nor'-noreast without them spotting us. Keep an eye on them."

Jack slid down the mast and began looking for any way to increase speed. It was a small boat and there wasn't much to toss overboard to lighten the load. He and Charlie tightened the mast's backstay to pull the canvas even tauter against the wind, then Charlie held Jack's legs as he leaned far overboard to make sure the hull was clean as it cut through the water.

Then the two began shifting the bundles of net and rope, draping them across the stern of the boat, careful not to foul the tiller. From atop the short mast Chrissie didn't understand their actions. It wasn't until she heard their comments that she realized they were rigging cover in case they were shot at.

And around midday it began to look as if they'd need it.

"They're coming around!" Chrissie shouted to the deck. "Looks like they're bearing nor'-nor'east, right on our track."

The pursuing ship had turned and appeared now to be on a course to intercept them. She saw more sails fly aloft until the ship was a dark smudge underneath a skyful of low canvas clouds.

"Did they see us?" Charlie asked.

"How do I know what they see?" Chrissie shouted back. "All I know is they're heading this way and crowding on the canvas!"

"Now it's just a race," Dan said.

They had drawn abreast of St. John and could see the dark mound of

Tortola ahead. Behind, the pirate ship had cut the distance between them by more than half.

Jack was peering ahead up channel.

"There's plenty of coves we can hide in, or we can make straight for Road Town," he said.

"They're not fools," Dan warned. "If they lose us in the dark, they'll shoot for town, blocking us from the harbor. Then they can work their way back to find us before dawn."

With the wind on her rear quarter the boat was going as fast as Chrissie had ever seen her. But the pirates were coming up faster.

"Even if we can't sail into the harbor, once we get ashore on Tortola I like our chances of slipping through the jungle and making it to the town on foot," Jack said.

"If we get ashore," Charlie said.

"Don't worry about dis boat," Nathan told him, clapping him on the shoulder. "She always make it, and maybe she got a little more speed in her."

Other ships were visible to the east, merchants sailing into or out of the roads – the sheltered area that gave Road Town its name. If they noticed the race between the fishing boat and the bark, they were too far distant to help even if they were so inclined. Merchant ships went out of their way to avoid pirates. They didn't go looking for them.

"I guess we know now about the guns," Dan said, staring back at the pirate ship. "They're less than a half mile off, they'd usually open fire by now."

"Even if they don't have guns, they must have brought some weapons," Jack said. "Muskets or pistols."

"Well, let's hope they were in such a rush they forgot powder and balls," Charlie said.

"Not these lads," Dan said. "These fellas are always ready for a fight, and they don't like the idea of a fair one."

Sunset was more than an hour off. The fishing boat was a mile offshore. The pirates had shifted their course slightly to the east. It cost them a little ground, but they had cut off their prey from the harbor.

"Straight in," Chrissie said.

"Doesn't look like they've left us much choice," her father agreed.

"Take her in, Nathan!" Jack shouted.

Chrissie had the spyglass and was scrutinizing what she could see of the pirate ship, now not much more than a quarter mile off their rear quarter. There was not much action amidships and the gun ports were all closed, a good sign. But men leaned over the railing, waving and shouting and brandishing muskets.

"So that's settled," Chrissie said. "They've got muskets and pistols."

"And probably swords and axes and whatnot," Charlie agreed. "But they've gotta catch us first."

Nathan smiled grimly.

"I told you! Dey not catching dis boat!" he said. "I don't know what we're gonna do when we get dere, but we're sure enough gonna get dere!"

A large peninsula jutted out from the center of the island. To the east were the roads. To the west were a series of small coves. That was where they were making, hoping to beach the boat and disappear into the forest.

The surf was breaking on the beach in front of them as they studied the shoreline for the best place to put in. Ideally, the water would be shallow enough that the pirate ship couldn't follow. That would buy a little more time, and even the odds a little to boot.

The pirate ship was now coming straight at the smaller boat. A moment later, there was a puff of smoke from the bow and Chrissie yelled, "Down!"

A "whoosh!" ripped the sky as a cannon ball flew over the boat, splashing into the waves in front of them. At the same moment there was a burst of many smaller puffs as the men lining the railings and in the rigging opened fire with small arms. Almost none hit the boat.

"Two minutes before they fire again!" Jack shouted. "Get down under the netting!"

They hunkered under the makeshift barrier, Dan keeping one hand on the tiller. More musket shots rained down, but the boat drew closer to the beach. The bow was rising and falling with the growing swell which, just a hundred yards ahead, was turning into a line of waves breaking on the sand.

Risking a look over the top, Chrissie saw another burst of smoke, and the pirates were close enough now that she could hear the boom over the roar of the surf. She dropped like a stone.

Whether the pirates had adjusted their aim, had timed the rise and fall of the boat just right, or simply gotten lucky, this volley ran true, smashing into the mast. Spars, cordage and canvas came down in a heap and the boat wallowed before another surge in the surf picked them up and drove them forward.

More musket balls slapped against the hull and cut into the makeshift protection. This time it was Jack who chanced a look back.

"They've sheered off!" he shouted. "It looks like we're in shallow enough they can't follow. They're lowering a boat!"

Jack let out a cry and reeled back under cover, blood running from his forehead.

Charlie and Chrissie cried out in alarm, but he waved them off.

"Stay down!" he ordered. "Just caught a splinter."

Indeed, a needle-thin shard of wood was embedded in his forehead, just above his left eye. Blood flowed copiously.

"Should we break out the oars?" Charlie asked.

"No! It's what they're waiting for. They'll pick us off one by one," Dan said. "Let the ocean do its work. We'll get to shore."

"So long as we get there first," Jack said.

Chrissie peeked around the side of the stern railing, keeping her head low. The approaching ship had turned away to keep from running aground, the longboat still suspended above the deck. But many hands were pushing it out, and it was lowered with a will. Before it even hit the water men clambered over the railing, racing down the side to take positions at the oars.

"Steady on the tiller," Jack called to Dan. "When we get to shore, Charlie and I will grab the line and pull her up as far as we can. Chrissie, you and Nathan help your pa over the beach and up that bluff. Then we'll all disappear into the trees."

"But what'll keep them from following us?" Dan asked.

Jack thought for a moment, then smiled.

"Nathan, do you have any of that rum left?"

The old man looked confused.

"Two bottles, but why? You wanna offer dose boys a drink, get 'em all liquored up so they can't chase. I don't see how that'll work."

"Just get ... No! Sit tight! Here we go!"

The boat rose on the crest of a wave, then hurtled toward the beach. Dan fought the tiller to keep it straight, and the fishing boat shot through the foam and up onto the beach, coming to a sudden stop in the sand as they all tumbled forward onto the deck.

Chapter 42

Run Through the Jungle

Charlie leaped over the stern, pushing the boat higher onto the sand as Jack scrambled to the locker, and came up with two black bottles of rum that were the last of Nathan's potent supply. He tucked one under his arm, grasping the other by its neck while he patted his pocket. Satisfied, he leaped off the bow onto the sand.

Chrissie didn't have time to ask why, of all the supplies on the boat, it was the rum Jack wanted. She and Nathan half led, half dragged Dan to the bow and helped him tumble over into the sand. Then they raced him towards the bluff.

The cove in which they'd been driven by the surf was like a giant bowl, half on land and half in the water. The white sandy beach ran about an eighth of a mile inland until it reached a twenty-foot tall bluff that circled the beach. The ridge reached out into the water, embracing the cove in sheer rocky arms that reached thirty feet above the water.

Charlie raced to where Chrissie and Nathan were helping Dan. The face of the bluff was steep, but not sheer, and Chrissie hastily picked a spot where the climbing didn't look too difficult. Under other circumstances she thought she could probably struggle up at any point, but with her injured father and a pursuing pack of freebooters shooting at her, this looked like the best bet.

Nathan struggled up the incline ahead of her, bracing himself in the rocks and scrub plants and turning back to give a hand up as Chrissie braced Dan underneath. With this help and the use of his one good leg and two powerful arms he was able to haul himself slowly up the bluff, but it was taking too long. The pirate's longboat was in the cove, a dozen oars biting into the water, rocketing it toward the beach. Crouching in the bow, ready to jump onto the sand as soon as it grounded, was Davy Leech. Chrissie didn't need the spyglass to see the burning look that twisted his face into a mask of hate.

Other pirates in the boat took turns standing and firing shots at the figures on the bluff. Firing from a moving boat was difficult, but as Chrissie reached for a rock to pull herself higher it exploded from a lucky shot, sending a stinging shower of rock chips into her face.

Charlie was right behind her now.

"Hang on, I'm moving past you," he shouted, and scrambled up as if the rocky climb were no more challenging than racing up the rigging of a ship.

Passing Chrissie, he got his shoulder under Dan's thighs and drove him up the face of the slope. Dan collided with Nathan and the three of them flew up the hillside in a tangle of arms and legs, Charlie's thick legs driving until all three of them tumbled onto the top of the bluff.

Chrissie gave a glance behind her to make sure Jack was coming. But he was nowhere to be seen.

"C'mon boy!" Charlie shouted, reaching down an arm.

"Where's Jack?" she shouted back.

Charlie's head turned to scan the beach. Jack should have been right

216

behind him. But he wasn't on the bluff, or at the base of it. Then Chrissie saw Charlie's face take on a look of concern and confusion. Hanging from the side of the hill she turned back and saw the source of his worry.

The spot she'd chosen to climb was to the right of where the boat came ashore. About ten feet to the left, right on the water's edge, was an outcropping of worn rock right at the shoreline. Chrissie saw a silent form laying behind it. It was Jack.

A wave of sickness almost overcame her. She started to call his name and scuttle back down the hill, but now the pirates were pulling their longboat onto the sand, Leech leading the first few in a dash toward the base of the hillside where she hung just below the top. There'd be no going down that way.

The thought was a physical pain, as if she'd been stabbed, but there was nothing she could do now except to vow that if Jack were hurt or – she almost couldn't bear thinking the word – killed, she'd see that Leech and his whole crew paid for it.

Chrissie turned and climbed towards Charlie's hand just feet in front of her. At the same time she felt a crawling sensation in the small of her back, as if anticipating the shot that would bring her down. Her hands clasped for any hold, her legs straining to give her purchase on the crumbling face of the hillside.

She could hear the pirates now directly below her, the crack of muskets and pistols, the thud as the balls drove into the hillside around her, each raising small clouds of dust to tell her just how close they were.

She lifted her knee and put her foot on a rock, pushing herself up. But the rock gave way and for a second she teetered wildly before throwing herself forward, stretching for Charlie's straining fingers. She felt them, then her hand slipped from his. But with a convulsive heave he caught her wrist and pulled. She was able to get her legs back underneath her, and a moment later, was sprawling at the top of the bluff.

At the base of the bluff a swarm of pirates gathered around a figure who had been knocked down by the rock Chrissie's foot had sent tumbling. Some of them pointed up at her, their faces twisted in fury, and she ducked back as another shot rang out.

"Get yer pa and get moving," Charlie said.

"What, where?"

"East," he said, pointing. "I'll slow 'em down here. They can't get up so easily with me at the top tossing stuff down at 'em."

"But what about Jack?"

A pained look crossed Charlie's face, but he just shook his head.

"East. Get into the jungle and we can make our way to town in the dark. Go!"

Chrissie stood and looked down to the cove. The pirate's ship had moved into deeper water and was now sailing slowly east as close to the coastline as it dared. She glanced back to the beach, and suddenly gasped, her hand pointing.

"Charlie, look!" she said.

Charlie had been looking around for stones big enough to drop on the pirates below. He had unearthed a good-sized rock, probably thirty pounds, and was hefting it in his arms. He turned to follow the direction she was pointing.

Jack was moving.

Chapter 43

Rum Punch

Chrissie couldn't see what Jack was doing, but at least he was alive. The rock outcropping hid him from the pirates, whose attention was fixed on the fugitives at the top of the bluff.

Another hail of musket balls forced Chrissie to drop her head again.

Charlie could keep them at bay until he ran out of rocks, but one way or another those pirates were going to get up the bluff eventually, and Chrissie decided it would be a good idea if they were somewhere else when it happened.

Below them, Leech was organizing his crew. Four of them gathered at the base of the bluff, muskets slung over their backs. The others, more than a dozen, had formed up in ranks and were checking their muskets.

At Leech's command the first five in line stepped back slightly and raised their muskets. Chrissie dropped to the ground, tugging at Charlie to hit the dirt as they fired a volley at the hilltop.

"Missed clean," Charlie laughed as the balls tore through the leaves.

"He's not trying to hit us. He just wants to keep our heads down while his men climb," Chrissie said.

"Well, we'll see about that," Charlie snorted. Stooping, he picked up another rock and trundled it to the edge. Another volley of shots tore through the foliage as soon as his head appeared, but he ducked back in time, then rolled the small boulder over the side, laughing as he heard the sound of curses and men falling.

"It's kinda fun," he said. "'You' should see 'em scatter. Now you and Nathan get yer pa out of here. I can handle these fellas."

Flat on her stomach she poked her head out and gave a quick glance straight down. Three of the pirates were already halfway up the bluff, flattened against the hillside as if waiting for the next missile to be hurled at them. From below she could hear Leech yelling at them, and they began reaching up for the next handholds.

She had only stuck her head out, glanced and pulled back in, exposing herself for not more than a few seconds. But as she pulled back, a shot flew directly above her, passing through the air where her face had just been.

Someone down there knew his business, she thought. She pushed herself back from the edge before rising and hazarding another look to the beach.

All of the pirates were gathered at the bottom of the bluff, looking up for a face to shoot at. None of them noticed Jack approaching from behind with the two rum bottles, flames licking from the cloth he had shoved into the bottle necks. Creeping within ten feet of the pirates, he took the bottle in his right hand and lobbed it in a long, underhand throw. Chrissie watched the bottle arc up into the sky, then descend, plummeting down just in front of the marksmen.

And land with a soft thud in the sand.

Everything stopped. Leech looked down at the bottle with the flame sputtering at the end. So did all the other pirates, leaning in to see what had just dropped down on them. They looked up, then they turned and looked back at Jack, who was standing stock still, as surprised as anyone at the failure of his gambit.

For one second, two seconds, the pirates stared at Jack and Jack stared back. Then with a yell they started swinging their weapons around. Jack looked at them, then looked at the bottle in his left hand. This time he didn't lob it at them, he hurled it straight ahead, a hard, flat throw.

It struck the side of a musket barrel of a pirate in the first row, just as he shouldered his weapon. That bottle shattered and the whole front rank of pirates was engulfed in a fireball as the volatile alcohol exploded. Between the rum, the loaded weapons and the pirates who were in the middle of pouring powder down their barrels, there were plenty of little explosions to go along with the one big one.

From atop the hill Chrissie could hear the screams and yells as the pirates flailed at their burning clothes and hair. Those who hadn't been in the front row were still spattered with flaming rum, and many of them were now dashing like human torches down the beach to throw themselves in the ocean. Few had kept the presence of mind to beat out the flames on their clothing with their hands, or roll quickly in the sand. Then those who hadn't been hobbled by the exploding gunpowder were back on their feet and really mad.

Chrissie had seen enough.

"C'mon!" she yelled at Charlie, who was calmly rolling another large rock to the edge of the hill.

"I'll be right behind you," he said. "There's one more good rock over there."

Chrissie found her father and Nathan sheltering in the foliage that ringed the hilltop, but covered with leaves and branches that had been clipped from the trees by the volleys of musket fire.

"Let's go," she said. "East, toward town."

Nathan helped Dan to his feet. As he stood, Chrissie's father brought up a long branch that had fallen from the trees above, clipped off by a musket ball. Pulling Leech's stolen knife from his sash, he quickly trimmed off the few branches and leaves. He now had a serviceable walking stick.

Then he handed the knife to Chrissie.

"You may need this yet," he told her.

Chrissie tucked it into her waistband, then turned back.

"Charlie! Time to go!" she called once more.

"Get movin'," he answered. "I'm right behind you."

The three of them set out over the uneven terrain, staying inside the trees. It slowed their progress slightly, but screened them from the beach.

They had traveled no more than fifty feet when they heard the sound of shouting, a high-pitched scream, a shot and other sounds of a fight. Chrissie allowed herself a moment to look back, just in time to see a flailing body cartwheel down the slope and crash to the bottom, where he joined another limp figure prone in the sand.

Apparently, Charlie didn't need help.

"Keep moving," she urged her companions.

Breaking out of the belt of trees, they paused to get their bearings. The sun was near the horizon. It would be dark soon, all the better for losing themselves in the jungle. To their right, the ridge they stood on swept out to sea, circling its half of the cove. To their left, denser forest dropped off sharply into a valley. Ahead, the hill descended a gentle grade down to the beach and lowlands, running towards the big point that marked the opening to the roads. Road Town was inside that bay. Even if there was no easy route over the peninsula, if they kept walking they should be at the British outpost by morning, Chrissie reasoned.

But even as she tried to decide on a path, she saw a new problem. The pirate ship had made it around the point of the cove and now stood watch over that stretch of beach, riding about a quarter mile out. With a sinking heart Chrissie saw they were lowering a second boat. Whipping out the spyglass she could see it carried another dozen men. With a gasp, she realized that the man at the tiller when the boat reached the water was Peter Leech, who wasn't nearly as dead as Chrissie had hoped.

In the distance she spotted a second set of sails, but she dismissed them. If it was a merchant ship, it would scoot out of sight the moment it heard shooting. You didn't get your cargo to port by poking your nose into other people's fights.

The pirates would be on the beach long before Chrissie, Nathan and Dan could cross the stretch of sand. They were cut off.

Going right would strand them on the point. Going left would put them on a steep slope covered thickly with trees and shrubs. They could hide there, but it was hard to imagine how they could travel through it.

As Chrissie pondered their choices, she heard footsteps approaching from behind.

"Charlie?" she asked. Then her voice died in her throat.

"Was that the big man's name?" asked Davy Leech. "I'm afraid your friend won't be able to help you."

He drew a pistol from his sash. In his other hand, he carried a cutlass. His clothes were muddy and streaked with blood.

"We have some business to settle. You," he pointed with his pistol to Nathan, "I don't know you but you're part of this. Dan Warren - you showed a great discourtesy to me and my crew, running off without even saying thanks for our hospitality. And you, boy, whoever you are, struck my brother. You took a shot at me. You ruined my good hat! I can't let such insults stand, so you'll understand that I have to kill you all now."

Chapter 42

Final Fight

Davy Leech smiled through the red light of the setting sun. He had them boxed in, with nowhere to go but down the slope to the beach, where his crew would cut them off, or back behind them, onto the ledge that ended in a cliff over the sea.

Dan hobbled a step backwards, leaning heavily on his stick, and pulled himself away from Chrissie to the right. Nathan, as if understanding without speaking, separated himself from her, moving to the left. As Leech took a step toward them, using the thumb of his cutlass-bearing hand to pull the pistol's hammer back, they each took a step backwards, fanning out a little more.

"Now please," the pirate captain said, a mocking smile on his face. "I know how this works. You spread out until I can't cover you all. You seem to forget, Dan, I've been in more fights than you'll ever know. I know how to play the odds, and I know how to even them up."

He raised the pistol and snapped off a shot. With horror, Chrissie watched Nathan spin and fall to the ground clutching his side.

Before she could move to her fallen friend, Leech tossed the empty, smoking pistol to the side and charged at Chrissie, screaming, his cutlass over his head. She threw herself backwards as he narrowly missed her with a stroke that would have split her right down to her belly if it had connected.

Before Leech could shift his balance and attack again, Dan swung his walking stick as hard as he could, catching Leech at the base of his neck and driving him to his knees.

Dan Warren swayed, fighting for balance, but Leech, stinging from the blow, rolled to his side and viciously kicked the side of Dan's knee. Chrissie scrambled to her feet, but her father crashed to the ground with a groan.

She backed away as Leech rose and advanced towards her, rolling his shoulders and swinging the cutlass loosely as if warming up before going in for the kill.

"Was it really worth your life to rescue one shipwrecked sailor?" he asked, lunging forward with a backhanded slash toward her. She ducked and the cutlass narrowly missed her face.

"He must be someone to you, boy," the pirate continued, sneering. "Your father? Your brother? He must be family. Only family is worth trading your life for."

Chrissie edged back and to the right, but Leech covered her move, slashing towards where she would have been had she not halted suddenly and thrown herself to the left, falling in the process. She rolled away from him as his next stroke clanged off the rocks.

He aimed another overhand strike at her that she evaded, but she was backing further and further out on the spur of rock. They had now moved out beyond the beach. Thirty feet below the waves splashed against the base of the cliff.

"You realize it was for nothing, don't you?" he goaded, his eyes taunting her. "You're going to die, and so is that misbegotten carpenter you tried to rescue."

He glanced back behind to where he had left Dan. Chrissie used this moment of inattention to draw back a few steps more. His eyes snapped back to her and another sword thrust slashed through the space she had just vacated, as he forced her towards the edge.

She realized he wasn't necessarily trying to hit her, he was forcing her back, step by step, toward the end of the point of rock. And she still had no idea how to stop him.

Before she could get back on her feet, Leech had stepped forward, standing over her. The sunset lit his face with a demonic light.

"No answers? No last declaration? You'll go to the grave without any last words?" He shrugged. "I'll just have to live with the disappointment."

There was nowhere for Chrissie to go. Behind her she could feel that she'd run out of real estate, there was no escape. Leech raised his cutlass.

The boom of guns stopped him – not the crack of musket fire or the single gun the pirates had been firing. This was the crash of a full broadside. Leech's face turned to the left, and his cocky smile vanished, his jaw dropping.

Chrissie didn't know what had so thoroughly distracted him, and she didn't care. Her foot lashed upward, connecting solidly with Leech right between the legs. His knees buckled, and as Chrissie rolled to her left she swept his leg out from under him, toppling him to the ground. His cutlass fell from his hand, clattering over the edge of the cliff into the surf below.

Chrissie leaped to her feet as Leech fought his way back to his knees. She didn't hesitate. As he turned to face her, she locked her hands together and put all her remaining strength into a blow that started almost from the ground and caught him on the point of the chin, snapping his head to one side and sending him sprawling on his back.

But he still barred the way to freedom. She'd have to get past him somehow.

"Since you were wondering, we've met before," she said, "Dan Warren is my pa, and I sailed down here to find him and bring him home."

Leech shook his head to clear it, one hand reaching up to his mouth, where blood dribbled from a split lip. He rose unsteadily to hands and knees.

Another explosion rocked the water and both adversaries glanced to sea. The pirate ship was burning! Chrissie gaped at the sight of a second ship, just a hundred yards off, the Union Jack fluttering from its stern and a commodore's pennant at the mainmast – a British naval sloop.

Leech pulled himself to his feet, staring at his ship as flames raced up the tarred rigging and across the deck. Pirates leaped over the railings into the water, while others already in the longboat stared and pointed, unsure what to do as the boat wallowed in the surf.

Another broadside from the naval sloop barked out, and it seemed as if the whole side of the pirate's vessel disappeared in a rain of splinters and smoke. *Sea Devil* – or as Chrissie still thought of her, *Gladys B.* – shuddered and began a slow roll as the Caribbean poured through the gaping hole in her side. The naval ship began lowering its own longboat, a file of red-coated Marines ready to move onto the beach and clean up the remaining pirates.

The sound of loose rocks shifting brought her attention back to the business at hand. Leech was on his feet, staring at her malevolently through the spreading gloom.

"They haven't got me yet, boy, and I still have time to take care of you. Then I'll go back and finish your father."

It was hand-to-hand now. Leech swung a blow that Chrissie was narrowly able to duck, then a jab with his left that caught her on the nose, sending her sprawling with blood gushing down her face. She reached for the knife tucked into her waistband. He aimed a kick at her, but she was able to catch his booted foot and twist, toppling him to the ground.

She rolled towards him, finding herself straddling his chest aiming punches at his face. One flattened his nose, sending a gusher of blood flying. Another hit his eye, another his jaw.

Then he rattled her teeth with a blow to the side of the head. Another explosion of stars rocketed through her and she collapsed. She could see him rising, see his boots in front of her, but couldn't seem to move, couldn't resist the hands that reached down and lifted her by the throat, cutting off her wind and raising her feet off the ground.

He held her at eye level, his hands squeezing her throat.

"You'll both die, first you, then him if he's not dead already," he said. The world was turning into a grey mist in front of her, but his smoldering eyes bore into hers. "Like father, like son."

And then, just as suddenly, his grip broke, his eyes confused as she tumbled to the ground, retching and gasping for breath. As if from a distance, she heard her father's voice.

"That's my daughter," he said, "and she's a better man than you'll ever be!"

Leech was on his knees in front her her, blood dribbling from a cut on his temple. Behind him stood Dan Warren, grasping the jagged end of the makeshift crutch he had broken over the pirate's head. Beside him stood Nathan, whose shirtfront was covered with blood but who stood now, supporting Dan as he tried to hobble closer.

Davy Leech looked confused, glancing with pain-filled eyes from Dan Warren to Chrissie and back as she pushed herself away from him and rose unsteadily.

"Daught ..." he croaked.

"Aye, I'm Mary Christine Warren," she managed to get out. She drew another deep, rattling breath, then said, "I beat you a year ago in Hampton, and by God, I'll beat you again."

Leech's eyes opened wide in recognition as Chrissie freed the knife from the folds of her clothing. The blade shone blood red in the sunset, the last rays of light gleaming on the filigreed steel.

Then he shook his head and leaped at Chrissie with a roar, his arms enveloping her before she could bring the blade down, lifting her off her feet, pinning her arms, crushing the breath out of her.

"Shoulda killed ya when I had the chance," Leech breathed in her ear. "Shoulda let me brother have his way with you."

His bloody face swirled in front of her as the mist closed in again and she felt as if she were drowning. The word hung in her fading consciousness – Drowning! She reared back her head and thrashed forward, butting him between the eyes with all her force.

Her head swam with an explosion of color, but the arms squeezing her relaxed – dropped her. Leech reeled backwards and Chrissie fell to the ground, twisting onto her back, her hand finding the knife.

Through the pain-filled haze she saw Leech fight for balance, recover, take a step towards her. For a moment her mind flashed on Thomas and Quince rolling in the sand, of her father, of Silas Davis. She lashed out with the knife, burying the blade in Leech's thigh and twisting it.

He screamed and lurched back, and she kicked his knee. She had the satisfaction of hearing bone crunch before he tumbled backwards and over the side of the bluff.

Chrissie scrambled to the edge just in time to see Davy Leech hit the side of the cliff about halfway down, then pinwheel out and down, splashing into the waves.

Chapter 43

Jack's Secret

"Chrissie! Are you alright?" Dan asked weakly.

"I'm fine, Pa," she said. "You?"

Dan groaned as he ran his hand down his damaged knee.

"My dancing days are done," he said.

Chrissie turned to the old fisherman, who lay on his back, his hand clutching his side.

"Nathan? You're bleeding!" Chrissie said.

"Yes, miss, I surely am," Nathan said through gritted teeth.

"You were shot!"

"Yes, and it burns like fire. But Nathan had to help."

"Let me look."

In the gloom of twilight she couldn't see much. Blood oozed from a wound on the right side of his chest. A corresponding wound on his back indicated the ball had passed through. She prayed it hadn't hit anything important.

"It doesn't look too bad," she said.

Nathan grinned weakly.

"Oh, I'm sure glad to hear you say dat," he said. "Wouldn't want to t'ink I'd been hurt."

"I mean if we can stop this bleeding I think you might be alright," she said. "You lie here. Pa, tear off a couple of pieces of your shirt."

Dan understood immediately what she needed, and tore the tail off his tattered shirt, ripping it into two pieces. Chrissie folded up the first piece and pressed it against Nathan's back, rolling him over onto it. The second piece she pressed over the front wound and placed Dan's hand over it. Nathan gasped from the pain.

"Just hold this here," she told her father. "I'll go get help."

"From who?"

"That's a British warship down there," she said. "They'll have a doctor or something like it on board."

Dan had been so engrossed in dragging himself down the ridge he'd managed to miss most of the action below.

"So that's what happened to them," he said, trying to whistle through cracked lips, but failing. "Just be careful Chrissie. Don't let them mistake you for a pirate and shoot you in the dark."

"Don't be silly, Pa," she said. "I'm a girl."

She got up and started back towards the path.

"Chrissie!" he shouted after her.

She turned back.

"I'm right proud of you."

She smiled and went looking for help.

She was almost to the spot where the ridge shot out into the sea, the spot where Leech had cornered them, when she saw two figures approaching. It wasn't soldiers and it wasn't pirates.

Charlie hobbled along with one arm around Jack's shoulder, blood running down the side of his head and caking the collar of his shirt.

"Chris!" he boomed, a smile spreading across his face. Her heart jumped in her chest.

"Lord be praised!" Jack shouted. He gently helped Charlie to the ground, then ran to where Chrissie was hobbling towards them and threw his arms around her.

"You're alright!" he said, beaming.

"I've been better, but I'm alive."

"How do you feel?"

"Suddenly, I feel very good," she said.

They both pulled back self-consciously.

"Where's Nathan and your father?" he asked.

She pointed back the way she'd come and explained briefly what had happened.

"We've got to get help," she said.

"Help? From who?"

"You didn't see it, either?" she asked. "The navy is here. They'll have a medical officer aboard, won't they? Some kind of doctor?"

"A doctor? Yes. He won't be very good, but he'll be a doctor, maybe even good enough." Jack said. He paused, and in the twilight Chrissie could see a look of concern cross his face.

"The navy," he said, almost to himself. Then he sighed. "And Nathan's been shot? Well, we've got to do what we've got to do. C'mon."

Chrissie went to Charlie, who was smiling weakly.

"What happened to you? Leech said you were dead."

"Aye, he mighta thought that, considering he's the one who dropped me. Four came up at once. I knocked the first couple off, but I couldn't get 'em all. I had one and was tossin' him back when Leech came up behind me. He didn't waste time. Hit me in the head with his cutlass and left me for dead."

"When I found him I thought he was dead for sure, there was so much blood running down his face," Jack said. "But Charlie's head is his least vulnerable spot."

Charlie just grinned. If Jack was making fun of him, it meant he probably wasn't in any real danger.

"What about you?" Chrissie asked Jack. "That business with the exploding rum bottles was terrific. At least, the one was."

"You saw that, did you?" Jack said with a sheepish look. "I'd forgotten with the first one that it wouldn't do any good if it didn't break. The second did the trick."

"It sure helped," she agreed. "But then what happened? I saw some of them chasing you down the beach, but things got hot and I lost track."

"Well, yes," Jack said, reaching for the cutlass he'd set down. "It got a little warm. I borrowed this from the first fella who caught up with me. He won't need it anymore. Then three others caught up and I was busy for a while. I was afraid by the time I found you it'd be too late."

"It almost was," Chrissie said. "But Leech is dead, and the navy should be taking care of the rest."

Jack looked as if he wanted to ask more, but Chrissie just shook her head. She wasn't ready to talk about it, wasn't sure she ever would be. Even as she thought about it, she started to shake. She gritted her teeth and shook her head.

"C'mon," she said, "We've got to get help for Nathan."

Jack stayed to look after Dan and Nathan, while Charlie and Chrissie headed down the gentle slope to where they could make out signs of military activity.

Things got tense when they appeared on the beach and the soldiers assumed they were pirates. But as bloody and beaten as they were, Chrissie was able to convince them that she and Charlie were not pirates.

A man with sergeant's insignia on his uniform and the air of command strode up.

"You men, what are you doing with these prisoners?"

"Sergeant Thorne!" Chrissie said, recognizing the bald head and beaked nose she had first seen on Nevis.

The man drew up with a start, peering into her face, trying to figure out who this was. Chrissie smiled.

"Buy you a drink, general?" she said.

"You!"

"Yes sir, thank God you're here," she said.

She had to explain all over again, but unlike the troops he commanded, the sergeant caught on quickly and didn't hesitate. Six Marines were sent up the hill with a stretcher, and the boat was sent back to the ship to report. Then he made room for Chrissie and Charlie around the soldier's fire.

Though the night was warm and the fire hot, Chrissie began to shiver. She could feel for the first time not just every ache, every pain from her fight with Leech, but every mile, every foot and inch, between her and her home in Virginia.

Charlie didn't say anything, just put his arm around her. She buried her head in his chest and began to cry softly.

The tears had run out and she'd drifted to sleep when the guards snapped to attention. The soldiers who'd been dispatched to the hilltop had returned. Two of them carried the stretcher on which Nathan lay. As they approached he tried to sit up, but couldn't muster the strength. Behind them came two more Marines supporting Dan Warren between them. And behind them came Jack, flanked by the final two Marines.

"Just as the boy said, sir," one of the Marines reported to the sergeant. "The other two were unarmed. This one had a cutlass," he displayed the weapon. "He said he took it from one of the pirates."

The sergeant gave Jack a long stare, but before he could speak a volley of gunshots rang out in the distance. He gave a grim smile.

"Sounds as if there's a few less pirates for us to worry about," he said. "I'd say you were lucky you came in on your own. My men have orders to rout this scum out."

"That's fine with us," Chrissie said.

"All's well that ends well?" the sergeant asked with a raised eyebrow. "That only applies when it's over, but it's not over for you, not yet. I have orders to send you back to the ship where the commodore will interview you. He's the one who'll decide what happens to you next."

"The commodore?" Jack asked.

"Aye, Commodore Alton of his majesty's sloop, *Lark*."

"I might have known," Jack said with a shake of his head. "Well, if we must go, then let's. Time to face the captain."

Chrissie recognized the ship's name as the one Jack fled from in Nevis, but she didn't have a chance to ask him about it. Surrounded by Marines and eight sailors who quickly rowed them to the ship, they were soon alongside the sloop.

A bos'n's chair lifted Nathan and Dan onto the deck. They offered to sling Charlie up as well, but he rebuffed them.

"The day I can't ..." Chrissie heard him mutter. Charlie climbed slowly and painfully and Jack followed. Chrissie was the last to clamber up the side.

Nathan and Dan were taken below. Charlie spurned the offer of medical attention and followed his friends as they were given a chance to wash up, then were led aft toward's the captain's quarters.

Their escort knocked on the door and they obeyed the command to enter.

"Them folks from the beach, sir," the sailor said.

"Very good. That will be all," came the curt response from the man behind the desk, and the sailor backed out and closed the door.

The commodore rose.

"If you'll please sit, I'm ..." but his voice trailed off as he got a good look at his visitors.

Chrissie and Charlie were not much to look at, but it was at Jack the officer stared.

"I'll be damned," he said at last. "I thought that might have been you in Nevis, but when you weren't on the ship the next day I decided I must have made a mistake. It's been a long time. What? Seven years?"

"Six, I think," Jack said. "How's mother?"

Chapter 46

Tales at the Captain's Table

Chrissie had been through a lot, but this was too much.

"How's mother?" she said incredulously. "HOW'S MOTHER?!? Do you mean to say ...?"

"Yes, that's what he means," the commodore said. "And mother's quite well."

Chrissie could see the resemblance – about the same build and height, the same red hair, although the officer's was streaked with grey. The same eyes. Even the same intelligent look *behind* the eyes.

Jack turned to her and said, in a voice that was almost apologetic, "Yes. I'm Jack Farmer. But I'm really John George Percival Hamilton Alton."

"Sir John, actually," the captain said.

"I'd just as soon not ..."

"Oh, have it your way. You always did," the older man interrupted. "And now, if you'll be seated and I could get your names."

Chrissie stared at Jack as he nonchalantly pulled up a chair at the commodore's desk. A thousand questions formed and reformed in

237

Chrissie's mind, but all she could hear was him saying, "I'm Jack Farmer, but I'm really..." Well, two could play that game, she decided.

She turned to the commodore.

"I'm seaman Chris Warren, but I'm really Mary Christine Warren, of Hampton."

The officer's eyebrows shot up.

"And I'm able seaman Charlie Stickle, but I'm really hungry," Charlie said.

That broke the tension.

"Of course. Where are my manners?" the commodore said. He called to his orderly, who bustled in and began setting up a dinner on a table in the small cabin.

"While he finishes, perhaps I could get some explanation of that rather extraordinary statement of yours, Miss...?

"Warren. Mary Christine Warren. Call me Chrissie."

"I'll call you Miss Warren, if you don't mind. And I'd love to hear what I'm sure is a fascinating story."

"But what about Jack?" she protested. "Are you really...?"

"This man's brother?" Jack said. "I'm afraid so."

"Now, there's no need to be like that," the officer protested.

"But how..."

"Really, Miss Warren," the commodore said. "I'm afraid as this is my cabin and my table, and my ship for that matter, we're going to do things my way. We have business to clear up before we settle into the family reunion. I've been sent out, as you've no doubt heard, as a small part of the effort to clear out this rats nest of pirates. After we outfitted in Nevis, we sailed east in search of a particular scoundrel who had been reported. We were in Road Town for two days and had just set out for Port Royal when we saw activity here that seemed to demand our attention."

"And a good thing, too," Jack said. "You were in the nick of time. I didn't think I'd be saying this, but I'm delighted to see you."

The officer's brow furrowed, then he relaxed. This was family, after all. He responded in kind.

"How nice of you to say so."

"This scoundrel you've been looking, for," Chrissie said. "His name wouldn't be Davy Leech, would it?"

"The very same!"

"You can stop looking," Chrissie said. "He's dead. Or if you want to keep looking, I can tell you where his body is likely to wash ashore."

The commodore looked at Chrissie in disbelief, and then shook his head.

"From the beginning, if you don't mind, Miss Warren, tell the story from the very beginning. How did you happen to find yourself in the Caribbean?"

"It's a long story," Chrissie said, glancing at the table where the orderly was setting out a saddle of mutton to go with the other dishes he'd arranged on the small table.

"Then perhaps you can tell it over dinner," the commodore said, rising and gesturing toward the table.

The problem with being the center of attention, Chrissie learned, was that she had to talk while the others were free to eat as they listened to her story. Even Charlie and Jack, who'd been through most of it with her, listened attentively, all the while helping themselves to the dishes at the table. Chrissie managed to snatch bites here and there, but the commodore kept drilling her, questioning and asking her to repeat bits, especially toward the end.

"So you have no doubt that this was Davy Leech you fought," he said as she neared the end of her tale.

"None."

"And you're certain he's dead."

Exhausted, she breathed a long, shuddering sigh.

"All I'm sure of is that I ... I stabbed him, and he fell off a cliff into the ocean."

"And the cliff was how high?"

"About twenty, thirty feet."

"And he hit the cliff at least once before bouncing into the surf."

Even with her eyes open, Chrissie couldn't help but seeing again the look on Leech's face as he tottered, then plummeted down, careening off the rocks.

"Yes, yes, he hit the cliff, he fell."

"Well, he's likely dead. Good work, that. We'll certainly look for a body on the beach at first light, but I'm afraid we don't know the currents here, or the sea creatures in these waters, so it's no odds on whether we find him or not."

The commodore set down his cutlery and pushed his chair back slightly.

"Really an amazing story, Miss Warren. If I may say, I'd find it impossible to believe if I didn't see you here now, and the condition you're in."

"Charlie and I can verify almost all of it," Jack said. "And you have her father below."

"Amazing. But I'm a terrible host. You are all three exhausted," the commodore said, rising to his feet. "We'll talk again in the morning. At which time, I'm afraid, I'm going to have to ask you to repeat most of this for my officers."

Chrissie couldn't imagine having to go through it all again. She also still had plenty of questions for Jack but suddenly couldn't remember any of them. Her head felt so light. Looking up, she saw the three men staring at her, and they were saying something but she couldn't quite make out their words. They seemed to be drawing away from her as well. She could still see them perfectly clearly, but somehow they seemed to be vanishing into the distance, as if she were looking at them through the wrong end of a telescope.

She started to stand, to catch up to them, and was surprised to find that she couldn't.

"Oh well," she thought to herself. "This is as good a place as any for a nap."

She didn't hear the alarmed cries from the three men at the table as her head slumped forward, making rather a mess of the plum duff the orderly had brought in for dessert.

Chapter 45

Somethin' Like You

Sunlight flooded the room as Chrissie opened her eyes. For a moment she had no idea where she was. The ceiling was only a foot above her head and she briefly wondered if she was dead and in a coffin. But when she tried to move, the pain convinced her she must still be alive. Being dead couldn't hurt this much, she thought.

Then, feeling the gentle rise and fall beneath her, she decided she must be aboard ship. If only she could remember which ship.

She realized she was in a bunk built into the side of a cabin, a sheet pulled over her.

A familiar voice called out, "Chrissie! Good morning to you – or good afternoon, actually."

It was Jack, sitting at the commodore's desk with his feet up. He sat forward, snapping shut a book he was reading.

"Two bells rang a few minutes ago, so it's just after one."

"One when?" was all she could think to say.

"One in the afternoon. You've slept round the clock."

"Where's everybody?"

"Everybody? That's a tall order," Jack said, taking his feet off the desk and snapping forward in the chair. "Let's see. Charlie's asleep in the fo'c's'le. They offered him a cabin but he said he couldn't sleep on a ship unless it was in a hammock with the regular sailors. Your father is below under the surgeon's care, as is Nathan. Both of them will pull through, although the doctor doesn't hold out much hope for your father's knee, and Nathan lost a lot of blood. You saved his life there, to hear Dan tell it and I don't doubt it's true. The commodore ..."

"Your brother."

He reddened a bit at this and glanced down at the floor. Finally he said, "Yes. My brother."

"That was your secret, right?"

"Quite right," he agreed. "Bit of a long story there."

"Tell it," she said.

"No, now first you have to eat something. The sawbones on this ship isn't bad; apparently he actually knows something about medicine. And he insists you have some eggs, bread, some beef and something to drink before you get up and start moving around."

"What about Davy Leech?" Chrissie asked.

"Not yet. At least not as far as we know. There have been quite a few bodies to look at, and as I was the only one of our merry band who was up and about, I got the honor of looking at them. The ones on land weren't so bad, I kinda felt sorry for them, especially the ones who were burnt, but under the circumstances ..."

She waited, not wanting to push his recollection.

"The ones washed ashore or still floating in the bay were not pretty to look at, and they're only going to get worse. They tend to swell up, the fish and crabs nibble on them. They're nothing you want to think about."

"And you didn't find Leech yet?"

"It's hard to say. I don't think so," Jack said. "Of course, I've only seen him briefly, and circumstances weren't such that I spent a lot of time staring at him. Plus he'd been in the water. Like I said, those bodies ..."

He trailed off.

"So what's next?"

"The Marines are making one more sweep. They've scared up a few of those fellas, who were only too happy to turn themselves in after a night in the jungle. Some of 'em are probably still running, but there's really nowhere for them to go. Once that's finished he'll sail his prisoners back to Road Town where they can expect a quick trial and ... well, you know the rest. By the way, your father will be a star witness at the trial. I don't know if they'll need any of the rest of us to testify, but he'll have to."

"How long will that take?" said Chrissie.

"Ought to take most of a day." Jack answered. "I imagine it'll all be over by Wednesday."

"Wednesday? What day is it now?" Chrissie asked, suddenly aware that she had no idea of the passage of time.

"Today's Saturday," he answered. "We'll be back in Road Town by late tonight, early tomorrow at the latest, but they won't hold a trial on the Sabbath. Ah, there's your breakfast."

Jack went to the door and answered the orderly's knock. He brought in a tray, and the aroma of food hit Chrissie so hard she nearly swooned.

She waited until the orderly left, then started to swing her legs off the bunk. It was only then that she realized she was wearing only a clean shirt many sizes too large for her.

"Uh, Jack? What happened to my clothes?"

Jack reddened.

"Oh, yes. Well, after the day we'd had, your clothes were somewhat

244

the worse for wear even before you went face first into the pudding. So my brother – who is a conventionally married man with three daughters – called the doctor in and, well he *is* a doctor, and with Charlie and I standing guard from that corner of the room, eyes averted – anyway, you were cleaned up, and popped into the captain's bunk."

Chrissie found herself blushing, something she hadn't done much of in the months since she'd run away to sea. But she hadn't come all this way to turn back into the tongue-tied girl she'd been.

"Turn your head," she commanded.

"I'm sorry?"

"No, first toss me my trousers. Then turn your head."

"I'm afraid your trousers were not in a fit state for wearing. The captain had them burned. He had these made for you." He held out a skirt and blouse sewn out of sailcloth and a slip made from some other, softer fabric. "I hope the fit is about right; the sailor who made them was working off the measurements from your sailor's slops. The captain insisted that he couldn't have a woman aboard dressed like a man. As I said, he's rather conventional. He also thinks you'll make a better witness dressed as a lady, if you're called on to testify, so he'll probably insist on outfitting you more properly once we get to town."

Chrissie looked at the garments and sighed. Finally she took them.

"These will do," she said. "Now turn your head."

She dressed quickly, then leaped from the bunk, ignoring the variety of aches that made even standing up a lesson in pain.

"I'll eat, you talk," she commanded. "Your brother?"

"Very well," said Jack, settling at the opposite side of the small table. He sighed. "I am the third and youngest son of the Earl of Alton. Not one of your more influential or rich families. We don't have much besides the title, some land that mostly isn't very productive, and tradition."

"An earl? You're an earl?"

"Nothing like that. I'm the third son of an earl. Technically I'm a commoner, although they're kind enough to give me the courtesy title 'sir' as long as my father lives. And if you ever call me that, I'll ... well, I'll thank you not to."

"So why are you here, and a common sailor? And a different name?"

"It's simple. As I said, one thing the Altons do have is tradition. And one of those traditions is that the eldest son, my brother Oliver, the most humorless fellow you'd ever want to meet, inherits the title. The next son, should there be one, always has a military career. That would be Commodore Daniel Alton, whom you've met. According to family legend, an Alton was at Henry's side at Agincourt, although if that's true I suspect he was very far to the side. Sadly, the Altons do not possess a rich martial history.

"And the third son, if there is one and that's what I am, always – without fail – pursues a life in the church."

"You mean you were supposed to ..."

"Become a minister, yes."

Chrissie let out a short clap of laughter that she stifled by shoving a slice of bread into her mouth. Jack squirmed uncomfortably in his chair.

"I actually entered Oxford and tried to study for the clergy for a full month. I knew right away it wasn't the life for me, but it took a month to decide what to do about it."

"You couldn't tell your father you were going to do something else?"

"Oh, heavens no," Jack said. "It was always made clear to me that my duty to family was the only thing that mattered. Certainly it was more important than anything I might want for myself. I would serve my family only by serving the church, no doubt as a parson at some dismal little country parish in the Midlands somewhere. If anyone thought I'd rise in the church ranks, eventually become a bishop of something or other, they didn't mention it to me. And that was that.

"But one night at school I had a long talk with God and told him I was sorry, but I was sure there were better ways I could serve him than as a clergyman. When the morning came, I was gone. I had left clues that I might flee to London to wallow in the vice of the city, a very traditional way for younger sons to rebel, but I actually went to the southwest, where I was able to sign onto a ship out of Bristol and I was on my way. That was six years ago and I've never looked back.

"So you see before you a failed cleric, a family's shame, the black sheep who turned his back on his sacred duty. But if I haven't lived up to my family's expectations, life at sea has more than lived up to mine. I'd never been alive until I took my life into my own hands and started living it."

"And what does your brother intend to do with you?" Chrissie asked. "Force you back to England and the church?"

"Of that I have no idea," Jack said. "But I've already made it clear to him that if that's his plan, it won't work. I'll be on the next ship sailing to anywhere out of the closest port. If he wants to send me back to the family he'll have to clap me in irons to do it."

After eating, she walked with Jack out on the deck. Before opening the door, Jack had warned her, "Every man on the ship knows the story, and who you are. The orderly was in and out and heard most of your tale, and it spread over the ship like wildfire. Everyone has heard it."

No one looked up, no one took undue notice, as she blinked in the sunshine. A few sailors stole glances at her as they went about their work, but that would have been true for any stranger on the ship.

"Miss Warren, good to see you up!" Commodore Alton called from the quarterdeck. "I trust you're better?"

247

Chrissie assured him she was, although her careful movements told him she was still in pain.

"Has John filled you in on our plans?"

"John? Oh, Jack," she said. "Yes, he said you'd sail back to Road Town tonight and there'll be a trial in a couple of days."

"Precisely. Your father will have to testify, but I wouldn't expect any trouble with that. I've spoken to him this morning – he's mending tolerably well, the doctor says – and we should be done with your services by the end of the week. I expect you'll be free to take your father home."

Home. Chrissie hadn't even thought about the next part of the problem. How was she going to get him back to Virginia? It might be possible for her to resume her disguise and sign on with a ship going north, but what would her father do?

Suddenly she felt a dizzying sense of the difficulties still to come. But she steeled herself. She'd been making it up step by step almost since the beginning, with only the general idea of finding her father, rescuing him, and getting him home. Fine. Two down, one to go, she told herself.

"Sir, may I ask a couple of favors?"

"If it's within my powers, you have but to name it," he said.

"I need to write a letter, and then if you could help me get it on the next ship sailing north?" she said, thinking of Joe and Mrs. Garrity waiting anxiously for word. What a relief it would be to tell them that she was fine, and so was Pa!

"That should be easy enough. There are two ships just arrived in port that will sail north in a few days, and either one can carry a letter."

"Thank you, sir. And Nathan's fishing boat on shore ..." she continued.

"Yes, my crew located it and took care that it didn't drift away. It's under guard right now. Don't want any of the pirates still alive to decide to get away on it, not that they'd get far in her, just now."

"Can we sail her into port?"

"I don't know," the commodore said. "I understand she was rather banged about, the mast is down and the rigging torn up. But if you like, we can tow it in for him."

"Please. It's all Nathan has in the world, and it wouldn't be fair for him to lose everything just because he helped me."

"I understand," he said. "But you haven't lost everything. There's a small matter of reward. Nothing extravagant, I assure you. But there will be head money for every pirate captured or killed. I daresay it will take care of the repairs needed, plus a little left over."

"Thank you," said Chrissie, surprised. She hadn't even thought about a reward. That would certainly solve the problem of getting her father home.

"Is there anything else?"

"No, I'd like to see Pa now."

The commodore nodded at Jack, who escorted Chrissie off the quarterdeck. As she stepped down to the main deck, a sailor stepped forward, his cap in his hands.

"Excuse me, miss," he said, bobbing his head and knuckling his forehead in salute.

She was surprised by the show of deference, but stopped and smiled at him.

"Yes?"

"Me and some of the fellas heard the story about you last night, how you came down and fought pirates and all to rescue your father."

She wasn't sure how to respond, so she just nodded and he continued.

"Well, I wanted to say it was a very brave thing you done. We're all

249

proud to have you aboard miss, and that's a fact. I have two daughters of me own, beautiful little things they was, last I saw 'em, which was two years ago. As a father, I couldn't hope better than that my girls grow up to be something like you."

He nodded his head again, backed away and then turned back to his work. Chrissie noticed several of the other crew members looking up at her, smiling and nodding.

She had trouble breathing for a minute, and the world seemed to swim as her eyes filled with tears. Jack took her arm.

"They won't all be like that, of course, there'll be some ready to condemn you for the disguise. But those people haven't had to make the choices you have," he said. "Sailors know. We know. I don't think there'll be a man aboard who doesn't agree with what he said."

Chrissie gulped.

"Take me below. I have to see Pa."

Chapter 46

Looking Homeward

"Well, that was about as ugly as I expected," Jack said as he came over to the tavern table where Chrissie sat with Nathan and Charlie.

He helped seat Dan Warren, whose leg was locked in a heavy brace made of leather and wood designed to keep weight off the damaged knee, then came around to the other side and sat down beside Chrissie.

"You made the right choice to stay away," Jack told Chrissie, patting her hand. A tingle ran up her arm, but she didn't withdraw it. "Honestly, I don't know why people enjoy a hanging so much. What's so entertaining about watching a group of poor doomed sods kick and jerk, with their tongues out and their faces turning purple until they're dead? I'll never understand it."

Dan Warren nodded glumly.

"I knew those men, sailed with them," he said. "Of course, I can't feel sorry for them, after what they did to me and what I saw them do to others. I'm just as glad they're dead, but I wish I hadn't watched it."

Commodore Alton had insisted that as Dan was the main witness whose testimony had condemned the seven captured pirates, it was his

251

duty to attend the execution, which took place just thirty six hours after the one-day trial.

There was a long, sad silence at the table.

Finally, Jack spoke up.

"And now it's over, or all but over. Charlie and I can get back to work, Nathan can get back to fishing, and you two can head on back to Virginia."

It was, in a way, an even sadder moment than thinking about the corpses dangling from the gallows at the waterfront. They'd come so far together, and now, just like that, it was over.

"At least we don't have to worry about how we're getting home," Dan said. "Our share of the reward will pay for two berths on any merchantman going north, with a little left over for putting things to rights when we get there."

Another long silence.

Commodore Alton had stretched a point in authorizing the reward, but it had solved Chrissie's main worry. The pirate's ship had been sunk, so there was no claim to be made on the ship's salvage. But their share of the head count on the captured or slain pirates would be enough to get them back to Virginia. And there had been a special reward for Davy Leech, so they'd have something left over to start life again.

Chrissie stirred uncomfortably. At the commodore's insistence, she had dressed like "a young lady" since arriving in Road Town, and was still wearing the skirt, blouse and shawl she had worn to the trial. Commodore Alton had purchased the fabric as soon as they arrived in town and one of his sailors had whipped it together during Sunday's "make and mend" day. She had to admit he'd done a good job, but it didn't feel natural to her anymore.

She also noticed how people looked at her differently when she dressed as a girl, treated her differently. She'd even noticed Jack looking at her differently, and it made her feel different about herself in a way she didn't fully understand. Charlie, Nathan and even her father all acted differently towards her as well. More polite. More respectful.

She'd have to get used to it, she thought glumly. She'd have to go back to Hampton and pick up the threads of her old life. The life that had Mrs. Wharton telling her how to behave, and Mrs. Garrity trying to turn her into a lady and Arne Wharton and his oafish friends staring at her. A life that didn't have Charlie in it, or Nathan.

Or Jack.

"Your brother isn't sending you back to England?" she asked him.

"No, I have to give him credit. He thinks I'm making a mistake, and letting down the family. But there's no legal reason to send me home in chains on the next packet for England. And he was decent enough not to press me into the service, so there's no problem on that score. I'm free, as he said, to be a disgrace to the family and a poor, overworked seaman just as long as I want to be. Of course, when my father finds out, he'll likely send someone out for me. I'm going to need to keep moving, and perhaps find a new name."

Another long, solemn silence. Finally Charlie stirred.

"You know, the pirates' ship sank."

Everyone looked at him, surprised. Was he just now realizing that?

"Yes Charlie, the pirate's ship sank," Jack said. "What of it?"

"Well, at the trial, Dan said the pirates chased us after we'd whisked him away, right? But he never mentioned that they didn't have time to reload all their gear before they followed us."

"True," Dan said. "They didn't ask about the details."

"And the last of the survivors just got strung up, so they won't be doing any talking, will they?"

"Nathan don't see how," said the black man, who was out of the sick bay for the first time since being shot. "The dead men, they usually pretty quiet as far as I ever see."

"Well then," said Charlie, "it seems to me that there are only five people in the world who know that back on that little island there's a whole stack o'cargo just sittin' there. And those five people are all sitting at this table."

The other four traded looks, small grins creeping onto their faces as Charlie continued.

"Even if all it is are ship's stores, cord and canvas, the rest of their guns, tools and whatnot, that's a pretty decent pile of swag laying out there in the jungle."

"That's not all," Dan said. He looked around the tavern, making sure that no one was paying attention to their conversation.

"Leech and his crew had done quite well for themselves. It's not stowed with the rest of the goods, but I know for a fact that there was plenty of plunder from three Spanish ships, a couple of Dutch freighters and an English merchant. Silks, gold, some small chests of jewels."

"But surely they wouldn't have left that behind. Would they?" Jack asked.

"Can't say," Dan said. "But when we got to the island the first thing the Leeches did was take the most valuable parts of the booty and hide it ashore where no one else would find it. At least three big chests. And they left in a mighty big hurry. So maybe ..."

His voice trailed off. There was another long silence, but this one wasn't solemn or sad. During the minutes that followed, each of them was contemplating what came next.

Finally, Jack broke the quiet.

"So when do we leave?"

Everyone looked around the table, smiles breaking out on their faces.

"We've got to get some supplies," Jack said. "And we don't want to look too eager to be off."

"Maybe we should get back to Nathan's boat to do any more planning," Dan said. "But I can't see why we couldn't be on our way in a day or two. A week at most."

Charlie was looking thoughtful.

"There's an awful lot of gear out there," he observed. "I'm just thinking, before this is through we're going to need a bigger boat."

Dan lowered his voice even more, and leaned in towards the others. Even then, he avoided using the word "treasure," because that one word would draw the attention of every man in the harbor town.

"The ... the things we're most interested in won't take too much space. If we can find them, we can probably take them in Nathan's boat. That is, if Nathan is willing to come with us."

Nathan beamed.

"Oh yes. You know, Nathan has had a happy life as a fisherman," he said. Then he lowered his own voice to match Dan's. "But Nathan wouldn't mind seeing what it's like to be very rich. Just to see."

"Then we're settled?" Jack asked.

Five heads nodded.

"Good," he said. "Let's get going. Delay is folly when there's money on the line."

They all turned to him with expectant looks.

"What?" he said.

"Who said that? Who are you quoting."

"Quoting? I'm not quoting anyone. I said that. Me. Just now. So shall we go? Anyone have anything else to say?"

Chrissie raised a hand for attention. They all looked at her.

"Before we go anywhere I want to get back into some good honest trousers, if that's all right with everyone," she said. "These skirts are impossible."

There were nods all around.

Charlie beamed, slapped her on the shoulder and said, "Welcome back, boy!"

The End

Acknowledgements

Thanks and Ever Thanks

There are so many people to thank for making this book a reality.

Starting with my wife, Tori, the perfect partner. In so many ways, this book is hers. She encouraged it. She had me reading it to her class every Thursday, chapter by chapter as I wrote the first draft. She helped me talk through problems, challenged me to get out of my comfort zone, and edited over and over again. If there are any mistakes still in there, and I assume there are, it's my fault, not hers. I can commit more typos (typoes?) than anyone can possibly catch.

Tori – every day has a dance time. Thank you.

My kids (now not kids at all, but always an amazing family) – Jack, Alex, Ben, Kate, Millie and Max. They are the greatest creation I've ever been involved with, and they put up with so much as their dad flailed away trying to be a writer. Alex, we still miss you every day.

(And in case this comes up, Millie has first dibs on playing Chrissie in any movie version of the story. Ever.)

Big thanks to my agent, Eddie Schneider of JABerwocky Literary Management. His notes and insights – not to mention his enthusiasm for the story – were essential in shaping the book. That it didn't find a publisher after his 18 months of pitching it attests to their lack of foresight rather than any drawback on his part. But then, don't all writers have a "They just don't get it" story?

And about Tori's fifth grade class at the Good Hope School on St. Croix (the Island of the Holy Cross) in the U.S. Virgin Islands – huge thanks to:

Braxton Lansiquot, Josie Furnell, Shania Moore, Ryan Hunter, Christopher Ashley, Jonathan Thomas, Mason Trask, Adriel Sanes, Gabriella Trout, Sophie Leklou, Deandra Erysthee, Amanda George and Antonio Gomez. You guys meant so much to me and the creation of this book. And not just because you always said "Awww!" when I finished the day's reading. I particularly liked it when you *didn't* like something and could tell me why. I'll never forget, as long as I live, Gabriella saying, "That was kind of boring" after I'd finished a chapter. Thank you for the honesty. You guys kept me on my toes. I'll also never forget, when I was reading the first pirate attack, watching Chris moving his hands in the air, one to represent *Skipjack* and the other the pirate ship, to follow the maneuvers. That made me feel like, "Yeah, this can work."

And Shania, who wanted me to add vampires but was satisfied with just a hint of potential romance. You convinced me that even though it's not something I'm comfortable writing, it was an important part of creating a full character. Or Mason, who when asked to write a journal entry about whether I should talk about the problems of a girl "on the verge of becoming a woman" disguising herself as a boy, replied with three pages of "No, no, no, no, no, no, no ..." I trust now that you're a few years older, you'll agree that it helps the story.

The book is very different than when I read it to you – even the title is different. It wasn't until a year later that I realized the name of the book is "Chrissie Warren: Pirate Hunter." When I read it to the kids, it was called, "*The Wreck of the Glady B.*" I hope you like what I've done with our story.

I also owe so much to all my friends in the pirate community – Yes, there is such a thing as the pirate community, men, women and children who "trade the mundane for the old Spanish Main" and, at least on weekends, live the dream of the Golden Age freebooters. Far too many to name, but here's a sampling –

First, to Mark "Capn' Slappy" Summers, my first partner in piracy. One day we went to the YMCA to play racquetball, and together came up with the idea for Talk Like a Pirate Day (celebrated every Sept. 19!) and then rode that wave together on a journey neither one of us could have imagined. He's been my writing partner on several books, my stage partner performing our filibuster tomfoolery all over the U.S., and just generally a better friend than I deserve.

Alongside him is another longtime friend, Pat "Jezebel" Kight, the "Webwench," who keeps our website, talklikeapirate.com, running through the onslaught each September. She has a lot of patience and a wicked sense of humor.

Among the many others "on the account," there's Robert "Cockroach Blair" Ramstead, Clay "Talderoy" Clement, The MacKay, Butch Thompson, Tom Mason and the Blue Buccaneers, Kevin and Loren (once of Cap'n Bog and Salty, now performing on "Jake and the Neverland Pirates,") Christine "Jamaica Rose" Lampe, Mike "Captain Kily" Belcheff, Clapeye and all the gang at the Seafair Pirates in Seattle, Tom Smith (who wrote the quintessential "Talk Like a Pirate Day" song,) Charles Duffy and the Krewe of Pirates in New Orleans, Foxmorton, Michael "Captain McLeod" Lampe, and ...

Well, you see the problem. There literally are thousands I need to thank. Everyone of you have given me so much. Thanks mateys!

Thanks to our friend George Lauris and all the folks at Albany Civic Theater, who taught me how to harness my imagination; Brian Rhodes, the "fifth Beatle" of Talk Like a Pirate Day; and Dave Barry, for providing the launch pad that allowed us to rocket from obscurity into semi-obscurity. And his research staff, Judy.

Finally, to my parents:

Ed and Mary Ellen Baur didn't live to see the whole pirate thing explode, let alone see this book. But I learned so much from them. Dad was the best storyteller I've ever known. Both of them taught us to read, pushed books into our hands, read us stories almost nightly, and made weekly library trips part of the family schedule. They raised eight kids and all of us went to college and none of us went to jail (yet,) and managed to do it with the kind of love and devotion that you read about but so rarely see. It's almost a cliche, but it's true – I never heard a cross word between them. Never. They were the "most married couple" I've ever known.

Everything I am, they gave me.

About the Author

John Baur was a fairly normal guy – a family man and a reporter/editor for newspapers and magazines. Then, in 1995, he and his friend, Mark Summers, invented International Talk Like a Pirate Day and his life took a whole different turn. They became well-known figures in the pirate community, wrote several books of pirate-based humor, performed on stages from Philadelphia to Los Angeles, New Orleans to Seattle, and have been featured on television, radio and newspapers all around the world. John, his wife Tori and their kids moved to the the Caribbean, where they lived four years while he wrote the first draft of what became this book. They now live in New Orleans, but when son Max graduates from high school, who knows where John and wife Tori are likely to get off to.